Winston Groom

Forrest Gump

Winston Groom is the author of sixteen books, including *Forrest Gump*, *Gump and Co.*, *Patriotic Fire*, *Shrouds of Glory*, and *Conversations with the Enemy* (with Duncan Spencer), a finalist for the Pulitzer Prize. He lives with his wife and daughter in Point Clear, Alabama.

www.winstongroom.com

Forrest Gump

A Novel

Winston Groom

Vintage Books
A Division of Random House, Inc.
New York

FIRST VINTAGE BOOKS EDITION, FEBRUARY 2012

The Cataloging-in-Publication is on file at the Library of Congress.

Vintage ISBN: 978-0-307-94739-0

www.vintagebooks.com

Printed in the United States of America
20 19 18

For Jimbo Meador and George Radcliff —

who have always made a point of being
kind to Forrest and his friends.

There is a pleasure sure in being mad which none but madmen know.

—DRYDEN

Forrest Gump

1

Let me say this: bein a idiot is no box of chocolates. People laugh, lose patience, treat you shabby. Now they says folks sposed to be kind to the afflicted, but let me tell you—it ain't always that way. Even so, I got no complaints, cause I reckon I done live a pretty interestin life, so to speak.

I been a idiot since I was born. My IQ is near 70, which qualifies me, so they say. Probly, tho, I'm closer to bein a imbecile or maybe even a moron, but personally, I'd rather think of mysef as like a *halfwit,* or somethin—an not no idiot —cause when people think of a idiot, more'n likely they be thinkin of one of them *Mongolian idiots*—the ones with they eyes too close together what look like Chinamen an drool a lot an play with theyselfs.

Now I'm slow—I'll grant you that, but I'm probly a lot brighter than folks think, cause what goes on in my mind is a sight different than what folks see. For instance, I can *think* things pretty good, but when I got to try sayin or writin them, it kinda come out like jello or somethin. I'll show you what I mean.

The other day, I'm walkin down the street an this man was out workin in his yard. He'd got hissef a bunch of shrubs to plant an he say to me, "Forrest, you wanna earn some money?" an I says, "Uh-huh," an so he sets me to movin dirt. Damn near ten or twelve wheelbarrows of dirt, in the heat of the day, truckin it all over creation. When I'm thru he reach in his pocket for a dollar. What I shoulda done was raised Cain about the low wages, but instead, I took the damn dollar an all I could say was "thanks" or somethin dumb-soundin like that, an I went on down the street, waddin an unwaddin that dollar in my hand, feelin like a idiot.

You see what I mean?

Now I *know* somethin bout idiots. Probly the only thing I do know bout, but I done read up on em—all the way from that Doy-chee-eveskie guy's idiot, to King Lear's fool, an Faulkner's idiot, Benjie, an even ole Boo Radley in *To Kill a Mockingbird*—now he was a *serious* idiot. The one I like best tho is ole Lennie in *Of Mice an Men.* Mos of them writer fellers got it straight—cause their idiots always smarter than people give em credit for. Hell, I'd agree with that. Any idiot would. Hee Hee.

When I was born, my mama name me Forrest, cause of General Nathan Bedford Forrest who fought in the Civil War. Mama always said we was kin to General Forrest's fambly someways. An he was a great man, she say, cept'n he started up the Ku Klux Klan after the war was over an even my grandmama say they's a bunch of no-goods. Which I would tend to agree with, cause down here, the Grand Exalted Pishposh, or whatever he calls hissef, he operate a gun store in town an once, when I was maybe twelve year ole, I were walkin by there and lookin in the winder an he got a big hangman's noose strung up inside. When he seen me watchin, he done thowed it around his own neck an jerk it up like he was hanged an let his tongue stick out an all so's to scare me. I done run off and hid in a parkin lot behin some cars til somebody call the police an they come an take me home to my mama. So whatever else ole General Forrest done, startin up that Klan thing was not a good idea—any idiot could tell you that. Nonetheless, that's how I got my name.

My mama is a real fine person. Everbody says that. My daddy, he got kilt just after I's born, so I never known him. He worked down to the docks as a longshoreman an one day a crane was takin a big net load of bananas off one of them United Fruit Company boats an somethin broke an the bananas fell down on my daddy an squashed him flat as a pancake. One time I heard some men talkin bout the accident— say it was a helluva mess, half ton of all them bananas an my daddy squished underneath. I don't care for bananas much myself, cept for banana puddin. I like that all right.

My mama got a little pension from the United Fruit people an she took in boarders at our house, so we got by okay. When I was little, she kep me inside a lot, so as the other kids wouldn't bother me. In the summer afternoons, when it was real hot, she used to put me down in the parlor an pull the shades so it was dark an cool an fix me a pitcher of limeade. Then she'd set there an talk to me, jus talk on an on bout nothin in particular, like a person'll talk to a dog or cat, but I got used to it an liked it cause her voice made me feel real safe an nice.

At first, when I's growin up, she'd let me go out an play with everbody, but then she foun out they's teasing me an all, an one day a boy hit me in the back with a stick wile they was chasin me an it raised some fearsome welt. After that, she tole me not to play with them boys anymore. I started tryin to play with the girls but that weren't much better, cause they all run away from me.

Mama thought it would be good for me to go to the public school cause maybe it would hep me to be like everbody else, but after I been there a little wile they come an told Mama I ought'n to be in there with everbody else. They let me finish out first grade tho. Sometimes I'd set there wile the teacher was talkin an I don't know what was going on in my mind, but I'd start lookin out the winder at the birds an squirrels an things that was climbin an settin in a big ole oak tree outside, an then the teacher'd come over an fuss at me. Sometimes, I'd just get this real strange thing come over me an start shoutin an all, an then she'd make me go out an set on a bench in the hall. An the other kids, they'd never play with me or nothin, cept'n to chase me or get me to start hollerin so's they could laugh at me—all cept Jenny Curran, who at least didn't run away from me an sometimes she'd let me walk nex to her goin home after class.

But the next year, they put me in another sort of school, an let me tell you, it was wierd. It was like they'd gone aroun collectin all the funny fellers they coud find an put em all together, rangin from my age an younger to big ole boys bout sixteen or seventeen. They was retards of all kinds an spasmos an kids that couldn't even eat or go to the toilet by theyselfs. I was probly the best of the lot.

They was one big fat boy, musta been fourteen or so, an he was afflicted with some kinda thing made him shake like he's in the electric chair or somethin. Miss Margaret, our teacher, made me go in the bathroom with him when he had to go, so's he wouldn't do nothin wierd. He done it anyway, tho. I didn't know no way of stoppin him, so I'd just lock mysef in one of the stalls and stay there till he's thru, an walk him back to the class.

I stayed in that school for about five or six years. It wadn't all bad tho. They'd let us paint with our fingers an make little things, but mostly, it jus teachin us how to do stuff like tie up our shoes an not slobber food or get wild an yell an holler an thow shit aroun. They wadn't no book learnin to speak of—cept to show us how to read street signs an things like the difference between the Men's an the Ladies' rooms. With all them serious nuts in there, it woulda been impossible to conduct anythin more'n that anyway. Also, I think it was for the purpose of keepin us out of everbody else's hair. Who the hell wants a bunch of retards runnin aroun loose? Even I could understand that.

When I got to be thirteen, some pretty unusual things begun to happen. First off, I started to grow. I grew six inches in six months, an my mama was all the time havin to let out my pants. Also, I commenced to grow *out*. By the time I was sixteen I was six foot six an weighed two hundrit forty-two pounds. I know that cause they took me in an weighed me. Said they jus couldn't believe it.

What happen nex caused a real change in my life. One day I'm strollin down the street on the way home from nut school, an a car stop longside of me. This guy call me over an axed my name. I tole him, an then he axed what school I go to, an how come he ain't seen me aroun. When I tell him bout the nut school, he axed if I'd ever played football. I shook my head. I guess I mighta tole him I'd seen kids playin it, but they'd never let me play. But like I said, I ain't too good at long conversation, an so I jus shook my head. That was about two weeks after school begun again.

Three days or so later, they come an got me outta the nut school. My mama was there, an so was the guy in the car an two other people what look like goons—who I guess was present in case I was to start somethin. They took all the stuff outta my desk an put it in a brown paper bag an tole me to say goodbye to Miss Margaret, an alls of a sudden she commence to start cryin an give me a big ole hug. Then I got to say goodbye to all the other nuts, an they was droolin an spasmoin an beatin on the desks with they fists. An then I was gone.

Mama rode up in the front seat with the guy an I set in back in between them goons, jus like police done in them ole movies when they took you "downtown." Cept we didn't go downtown. We went to the new highschool they had built. When we got there they took me inside to the principal's office an Mama an me an the guy went in wile the two goons waited in the hall. The principal was an ole gray-haired man with a stain on his tie an baggy pants who look like he coulda come outta the nut school hissef. We all sat down an he begun splainin things an axein me questions, an I just nodded my head, but what they wanted was for me to play football. That much I figgered out on my own.

Turns out the guy in the car was the football coach, name of Fellers. An that day I didn't go to no class or nothin, but Coach Fellers, he took me back to the locker room an one of the goons rounded me up a football suit with all them pads and stuff an a real nice plastic helmet with a thing in front to keep my face from gettin squished in. The only thing was, they couldn't find no shoes to fit me, so's I had to use my sneakers till they could order the shoes.

Coach Fellers an the goons got me dressed up in the football suit, an then they made me undress again, an then do it all over again, ten or twenty times, till I could do it by mysef. One thing I had trouble with for a wile was that jockstrap thing—cause I couldn't see no real good reason for wearing it. Well, they tried splainin it to me, an then one of the goons says to the other that I'm a "dummy" or somethin like that, an I guess he thought I wouldn't understand him, but I did, on account of I pay special attention to that kind of shit. Not that it hurt my feelins. Hell, I been called a sight worse than that. But I took notice of it, nonetheless.

After a wile a bunch of kids started comin into the locker room an takin out they football stuff and gettin into it. Then we all went outside an Coach Fellers got everybody together an he stood me up in front of them an introduced me. He was sayin a bunch of shit that I wadn't followin real close cause I was haf scared to death, on account of nobody had ever introduced me before to a bunch of strangers. But afterward some of the others come up an shook my hand an say they is glad I am here an all. Then Coach Fellers blowed a whistle, what like to make me leap outta my skin an everbody started jumpin around to get exercise.

It's a kind of long story what all happened nex, but anyway, I begun to play football. Coach Fellers an one of the goons hepped me out special since I didn't know how to play. We had this thing where you sposed to block people an they were tryin to splain it all, but when we tried it a bunch of times everbody seemed to be gettin disgusted cause I couldn't remember what I was sposed to do.

Then they tried this other thing they call the *defense*, where they put three guys in front of me an I am sposed to get thru them an grap the guy with the football. The first part was easier, cause I could just shove the other guys' heads down, but they were unhappy with the way I grapped the guy with the ball, an finally they made me go an tackle a big oak tree about fifteen or twenty times—to get the feel of it, I spose. But after a wile, when they figgered I had learnt somethin from the oak tree, they put me back with the three guys an the ball carrier an then got mad I didn't jump on him real vicious-like after I moved the others out of the way. I took a lot of abuse that afternoon, but when we quit practicin I went in to see Coach Fellers an tole him I didn't want to jump on the ball guy cause I was afraid of hurtin him. Coach, he say that it wouldn't hurt him, cause he was in his football suit an was protected. The truth is, I wasn't so much afraid of hurtin him as I was that he'd get mad at me an they'd start chasin me again if I wadn't real nice to everbody. To make a long story short, it took me a wile to get the hang of it all.

Meantime I got to go to class. In the nut school, we really

didn't have that much to do, but here they was far more serious about things. Somehow, they had worked it out so's I had three homeroom classes where you jus set there an did whatever you wanted, an then three other classes where there was a lady who was teachin me how to read. Jus the two of us. She was real nice an pretty and more'n once or twice I had nasty thoughts about her. Miss Henderson was her name.

About the only class I liked was lunch, but I guess you couldn't call that a class. At the nut school, my mama would fix me a sambwich an a cookie an a piece of fruit—cept no bananas—an I'd take it to school with me. But in this school they was a cafeteria with nine or ten different things to eat an I'd have trouble makin up my mind what I wanted. I think somebody must of said somethin, cause after a week or so Coach Fellers come up to me an say to just go ahead an eat all I wanted cause it been "taken care of." Hot damn!

Guess who should be in my homeroom class but Jenny Curran. She come up to me in the hall an say she remember me from first grade. She was all growed up now, with pretty black hair an she was long-legged an had a beautiful face, an they was other things too, I dare not mention.

The football was not goin exactly to the likin of Coach Fellers. He seemed displeased a lot an was always shoutin at people. He shouted at me too. They tried to figger out some way for me to just stay put an keep other folks from grappin our guy carryin the ball, but that didn't work cept when they ran the ball right up the middle of the line. Coach was not too happy with my tacklin neither, an let me tell you, I spent a lot of time at that oak tree. But I just couldn't get to where I would thow mysef at the ball guy like they wanted me to do. Somethin kep me from it.

Then one day a event happen that changed all that too. In the cafeteria I had started gettin my food and goin over to set nex to Jenny Curran. I wouldn't say nothin, but she was jus bout the only person in the school I knew halfways, an it felt good setting there with her. Most of the time she didn't pay me no attention, an talked with other people. At first I'd been settin with some of the football players, but they acted like I was invisible or somethin. At least Jenny Curran acted like I was there. But after a wile of this, I started to notice this other guy was there a lot too, an he starts makin wisecracks bout me. Sayin shit like "How's Dumbo?" an all. And this gone on for a week or two, an I was sayin nothin, but finally I says—I can't hardly believe I said it even now—but I says, "I ain't no Dumbo," an the guy jus looked at me an starts laughin. An Jenny Curran, she say to the guy to keep quiet, but he takes a carton of milk an pours it in my lap an I jump up an run out cause it scares me.

A day or so later, that guy come up to me in the hall an says he's gonna "get" me. All day I was afraid terribly, an later that afternoon, when I was leaving to go to the gym, there he is, with a bunch of his friends. I tried to go the other way, but he come up to me an start pushin me on the shoulders. An he's sayin all kinds of bad things, callin me a "stupo" an all, an then he hit me in the stomach. It didn't hurt so much, but I was startin to cry and I turned an begun to run, an heard him behind me an the others was runnin after me too. I jus run as fast as I could toward the gym, across the practice football field an suddenly I seen Coach Fellers, settin up in the bleachers watchin me. The guys who was chasin me stop and go away, an Coach Fellers, he has got this real peculiar look on his face, an tell me to get suited up right away. A wile later, he come in the locker room with these plays drawn on a piece of paper—three of them—an say for me to memorize them best I can.

That afternoon at the football practice, he line everybody up in two teams an suddenly the quarterback give *me* the ball an I'm sposed to run outside the right end of the line to the goalpost. When they all start chasin me, I run fast as I can—it was seven or eight of them before they could drag me down. Coach Fellers is mighty happy; jumpin up and down an yellin an slappin everbody on the back. We'd run a lot of races before, to see how fast we could run, but I get a lot faster when I'm bein chased, I guess. What idiot wouldn't?

Anyway, I become a lot more popular after that, an the other guys on the team started bein nicer to me. We had our first game an I was scared to death, but they give me the ball an I run over the goal line two or three times an people never been kinder to me after that. That highschool certainly begun to change things in my life. It even got to where I *liked* to run with the football, cept it was mostly that they made me run aroun the sides cause I still couldn't get to where I liked to just run over people like you do in the middle. One of the goons comments that I am the largest highschool *halfback* in the entire world. I do not think he mean it as a compliment.

Otherwise, I was learnin to read a lot better with Miss Henderson. She give me *Tom Sawyer* an two other books I can't remember, an I took them home an read em all, but then she give me a test where I don't do so hot. But I sure enjoyed them books.

After a wile, I went back to settin nex to Jenny Curran in the cafeteria, an there weren't no more trouble for a long time, but then one day in the springtime I was walkin home from school and who should appear but the boy that poured that milk in my lap an chased me that day. He got hissef a stick an start callin me things like "moron" and "stupo."

Some other people was watchin an then along comes Jenny Curran, an I'm bout to take off again—but then, for no reason I know, I jus didn't do it. That feller take his stick an poke me in the stomach with it, an I says to mysef, the hell with this, an I grapped a holt to his arm an with my other hand I knock him upside the head an that was the end of that, more or less.

That night my mama get a phone call from the boy's parents, say if I lay a han on their son again they is goin to call the authorities an have me "put away." I tried to splain it to my mama an she say she understand, but I could tell she was worried. She tell me that since I am so huge now, I got to watch mysef, cause I might hurt somebody. An I nodded an promised her I wouldn't hurt nobody else. That night when I lyin in bed I heard her cryin to hersef in her room.

But what that did for me, knockin that boy upside the head, put a definate new light on my football playin. Next day, I axed Coach Fellers to let me run the ball straight on and he say okay, an I run over maybe four or five guys till I'm in the clear an they all had to start chasin me again. That year I made the All State Football team. I couldn't hardly believe it. My mama give me two pair of socks an a new shirt on my birthday. An she done saved up an bought me a new suit that I wore to get the All State Football award. First suit I ever had. Mama tied my tie for me an off I went.

2

The All State Football banquet was to be helt in a little town called Flomaton, what Coach Fellers described as a "switch up the railroad tracks." We was put on a bus—they was five or six of us from this area who won the prize—an we was trucked up there. It was a hour or two before we arrived, an the bus didn't have no toilet, an I had drank two slurpees fore we lef, so when we get to Flomaton, I really got to go bad.

The thing was helt at the Flomaton Highschool auditorium, an when we git inside, me and some of the others find the toilet. Somehow, tho, when I go to unzip my pants, the zipper is stuck in my shirttail an won't come down. After a bit of this, a nice little guy from a rival school goes out and finds Coach Fellers an he come in with the two goons an they be tryin to get my pants open. One of the goons say the only way to git it down is jus rip it apart. At this, Coach Fellers put his hans on his hips an say, "I spose you expect me to send this boy out there with his fly unzipped an his thing hangin out—now what kind of a impression do you think that would make?" Then he turn to me an say, "Forrest, you jus got to keep a lid on it till this thing's over, an then we get it open for you—okay?" An I nod, cause I don't know what else to do, but I figgerin I be in for a long evenin.

When we get out to the auditorium there's a million people all settin there at tables, smilin an clappin as we come out. We is put up at a big long table on the stage in front of everbody an my worst fears was realized about the long evenin. Seem like ever soul in the room got up to make a speech—even the waiters an janitor. I wished my mama coulda been there, cause she'd of hepped me, but she back at home in bed with the grippe. Finally it come time to get handed our prizes, which was little gold-colored footballs, an when our names was called we was sposed to go up to the microphone an take the prize an say "thank you," an they also tole us if anybody has anythin else he wants to say, to keep it short on account of we want to be gettin out of there before the turn of the century.

Most everbody had got they prize an said "thank you," an then it come my turn. Somebody on the microphone call out "Forrest Gump," which, if I hadn't tole you before, is my last name, an I stand up an go over an they han me the prize. I lean over to the mike an say, "Thank you," an everbody starts to cheer an clap an stand up in they seats. I spose somebody tole them aforehan I'm some kind of idiot, an they makin a special effort to be nice. But I'm so surprised by all this, I don't know what to do, so I jus kep standin there. Then everbody hush up, an the man at the mike he lean over and axe me if I got anythin else I want to say. So I says, "I got to pee."

Everbody in the audience didn't say nothin for a few moments, an jus started lookin funny at each other, an then they begun a sort of low mumblin, an Coach Fellers come up an grap me by the arm and haul me back to my seat. Rest of the night he be glarin at me, but after the banquet is over, Coach an the goons done take me back to the bathroom an rip open my pants an I done peed a bucket!

"Gump," Coach say after I am finished, "you sure got a way with words."

Now nex year wadn't too eventful, cept somebody put out the word that a idiot got hissef on the All State Football team an a bunch of letters start comin in from all round the country. Mama collect them all and start keepin a scrapbook. One day a package come from New Yawk City that contain a official baseball signed by the entire New Yawk Yankees baseball team. It was the best thing ever happen to me! I treasure that ball like a goldbrick, till one day when I was tossin it aroun in the yard, a big ole dog come up an grap it outta the air an chewed it up. Things like that always happenin to me.

One day Coach Fellers call me in an take me into the principal's office. They was a man there from up to the University who shook my han an axe me whether I ever thought bout playin football in college. He say they been "watchin" me. I shook my head, cause I hadn't.

Everbody seemed to be in awe of this man, bowin an scrapin an callin him "Mister Bryant." But he say for me to call him "Bear," which I thought was a funny name, cept he do look similar to a bear in some respects. Coach Fellers point out that I am not the brightest person, but the Bear, he say that is plenty true of most of his players, an that he figgers to get me special hep in my studies. A week later they give me a test with all sorts of screwy questions the like of which I am not familiar with. After a wile I get bored and stop takin the test.

Two days afterward, the Bear come back again and I get hauled into the principal's office by Coach Fellers. Bear lookin distressed, but he still bein nice; he axe me have I done tried my best on that test. I nod my head, but the principal be rollin his eyes, an the Bear say, "Well, this is unfortunate then, cause the score appears to indicate that this boy is a idiot."

The principal be noddin his head now, an Coach Fellers is standin there with his hands in his pockets lookin sour. It seem to be the end of my college football prospects.

The fact that I were too dumb to play college football did not seem to impress the United States Army none. It were my last year at highschool an in the springtime everybody else graduated. They let me set up on the stage tho, an even give me a black robe to put on, an when it come time, the principal announce they was gonna give me a "special" diploma. I got up to go to the microphone an the two goons stan up an go with me—I spose so's I don't make no remarks like I did at the All State Football thing. My mama is down in the front row cryin and wringin her hans an I really feel good, like I actually done accomplish somethin.

But when we git back home, I finally realize why she bawlin an carryin on—they was a letter come from the Army say I got to report to the local daft board or somesuch. I didn't know what the deal was, but my mama did—it was 1968 an they was all sorts of shit fixin to hoppen.

Mama give me a letter from the school principal to han to the daft-board people, but somehow I lost it on the way there. It was a loony scene. They was a big colored guy in a Army suit yellin at people an dividin them up into bunches. We was all standin there and he come up an shout, "All right, I want half of you to go over there an half of you to go over here, an the other half of you to stay put!" Everybody millin aroun an lookin bewildered an even *I* could figger out this guy's a moron.

They took me in a room and line us up an tell us to remove our clothes. I ain't much for that, but everybody else done it an so I did too. They lookin at us everplace—eyes, noses, mouths, ears—even our private parts. At one point they tell me, "Bend over," an when I do, somebody jam his finger up my ass.

That's it!

I turn an grapped that bastid an knock him upside the head. They was suddenly a big commotion an a bunch of people run up an jump on top of me. However, I am used to that treatment. I thowed them off an run out the door. When I get home an tell my mama what happen, she all upset, but she say, "Don't worry, Forrest—everthin gonna be okay."

It ain't. Next week, a van pull up at our house and a number of men in Army suits an shiny black helmets come up to the door be axin for me. I'm hidin up in my room, but Mama come up an say they jus wanta give me a ride back down to the daft board. All the way there, they be watchin me real close, like I'm some kinda maniac.

They was a door that lead to a big office where there's a older man all dressed up in a shiny uniform an he eyein me pretty careful too. They set me down an shove another test in front of me, an wile it's one hell of a lot easier than the college football test, it still ain't no piece of cake.

When I'm done, they take me to another room where they's four or five guys settin at a long table what start axin me questions an passin around what looked like the test I took. Then they all git into a huddle and when they finish one of em sign a paper an han it to me. When I take it home, Mama read it an begin pullin at her hair an weepin an praisin the Lord, cause it say I am "Temporarily Deferred," on account of I am a numbnuts.

Somethin else occurred durin that week that was a major event in my life. There was this lady boarder livin with us that worked down to the telephone company as a operator. Miss French was her name. She was a real nice lady, what kep mostly to hersef, but one night when it was terribily hot, an they was thunderstorms, she stuck her head out the door to her room as I was walkin by an say, "Forrest, I just got a box of nice divinity this afternoon—would you like a piece?"

An I say "yes," an she bring me into her room an there on the dresser is the divinity. She give me a piece of it, then she axe if I want another, an she points for me to set down on the bed. I must of ate ten or fifteen pieces of the divinity an lightnin was flashin outside an thunder an the curtains was blowin an Miss French kinda pushes me an makes me lie back on the bed. She commences to start strokin me in a personal way. "Jus keep your eyes closed," she say, "an everthing will be all right." Nex thing you know there is somethin happenin that had not happen before. I cannot say what it was, because I was keepin my eyes closed, an also because my mama woulda kilt me, but let me tell you this—it give me an entirely new outlook on things for the future.

The problem was that wile Miss French was a nice kind lady, the things that she done to me that night was the kinds of things I'd have preferred to have done to me by Jenny Curran. An yet, there was no way I could see to even begin gettin that accomplished cause what with the way I am, it is not so easy to ask anyone for a date. That is to put it mildly.

But on account of my new experience, I got up the courage to axe my mama what to do about Jenny, tho I certainly didn't say nothin bout me an Miss French. Mama said she'll take care of it for me, an she call up Jenny Curran's mama an splain the situation to her, an the nex evenin, lo an behole, who should appear at our door but Jenny Curran herself!

She is all dressed up in a white dress an a pink flower in her hair an she look like nothin I have ever dreamt of. She come inside an Mama took her to the parlor an give her a ice-cream float an call for me to come down from my room, where I had run to as soon as I seen Jenny Curran comin up the walk. I'd of rather had five thousand people chasin me than to come out of my room jus then, but Mama come up an take me by the han an lead me down an give me a ice-cream float too. That made it better.

Mama said we can go to the movies an she give Jenny three dollars as we walk out of the house. Jenny ain't never been nicer, talkin an laughin an I am noddin an grinnin like a idiot. The movie was jus four or five blocks from our house, an Jenny went up an got some tickets an we went in an set down. She axed me if I want some popcorn an when she come back from gettin it, the picture done started.

It is a movie about two people, a man an a lady called Bonnie an Clyde that robbed banks an they was some interestin other people in it also. But it was a lot of killin an shootin an shit like that, too. It seemed to me funny that folks would be shootin an killin one another that way, so's I laughed a lot when that went on, an whenever I did, Jenny Curran seemed to squnch down in her seat a lot. Halfway thru the movie, she was almost squnched down to the floor. I suddenly saw this an figgered she had somehow felled out of her seat, so I reached over an grapped her by the shoulder to lif her up again.

As I did this, I heard somethin tear, an I look down an Jenny Curran's dress is ripped completely open an everthing is hangin out. I took my other han to try to cover her up, but she start makin noises an flail about wild-like, an me, I'm tryin to hole onto her so's she don't fall down again or come undone an there's people around us lookin back tryin to see what all the commotion is about. Suddenly a fellow come down the aisle an shine a bright light right on Jenny an me, but bein exposed an all, she commenced to shriek an wail an then she jump up an run out of the show.

Nex thing I know, two men come an tell me to get up an I follow them to a office. A few minutes later, four policemen arrive an axe me to come with them. They show me to a police car an two get in front an two get in back with me, jus like it was with Coach Fellers' goons, cept'n this time we *do* go "downtown," an they escort me to a room an jab my fingers onto a pad an I get my picture taken an they thowed me in jail. It was a horrible experience. I was worried all the time bout Jenny, but after a bit my mama showed up an come in wipin her eyes with a handkerchief an twistin her fingers an I knowed I'm in the doghouse again.

There was some kind of ceremony a few days later down to the courthouse. My mama dressed me in my suit an took me there, an we met a nice man with a moustache carrying a big purse who tole the judge a bunch of things an then some other people, includin my mama, say some other shit an finally it was my turn.

The man with the moustache took me by the arm so's I'd stand up, an the judge axed me how all this done happen? I couldn't figger out what to say, so I jus shrugged my shoulders an then he axes if there's anything else I want to add, an so I says, "I got to pee," cause we'd been settin there almost haf a day an I'm about to bust! The judge, he lean forward from behind his big ole desk an peer at me like I am a Marsman or somethin. Then the feller with the moustache speaks up and followin this the judge tells him to take me to the toilet, which he does. I look back as we leavin the room an see po ole Mama holdin her head an daubin at her eyes with the handkerchief.

Anyhow, when I get back, the judge be scratchin his chin an he say the whole deal is "very peculiar," but that he think I ought to go in the Army or somethin which might hep straighten me out. My mama inform him that the United States Army won't have me, account of I am a idiot, but that this very mornin a letter done come from up to the University sayin that if I will play football for them, I can go to school there scot free.

The judge say that sounds kinda peculiar too, but it's okay with him so long as I get my big ass out of town.

The nex mornin I am all packed up an Mama, she take me

3

When we git up to the University, Coach Bryant he come out to the gym where we all settin in our shorts and sweatshirts an begin makin a speech. It bout the same kind of speech Coach Fellers would make, cept even a simpleton like mysef could tell this man mean bidness! His speech short an sweet, an conclude with the statement that the last man on the bus to the practice field will get a ride there not on the bus, but on Coach Bryant's shoe instead. Yessiree. We do not doubt his word, an stack ourselfs into the bus like flapjacks.

All this was durin the month of August, which in the state of Alabama is somewhat hotter than it is elsewhere. That is to say, that if you put a egg on top of your football helmet it would be fried sunnyside up in about ten seconds. Of course nobody ever try that on account of it might get Coach Bryant angry. That was the one thing nobody wish to do, because life was almost intolerable as it was.

Coach Bryant have his own goons to show me around. They take me to where I is gonna stay, which is a nice brick building on the campus that somebody says is called the "Ape Dorm." Them goons escort me over there in a car an lead me upstairs to my room. Unfortunately, what might of looked nice from the outside was not true for the inside. At first, it appear that nobody had lived in this building for a long time, they was so much dirt an shit aroun, an most of the doors had been torn off they hinges an bashed in, an most of the winders are busted out too.

A few of the fellers is lyin on they cots inside, wearin very little cause it about 110 degrees hot in there, an flies an things be hummin an buzzin. In the hall they is a big stack of newspapers, which at first I afraid they gonna make us read, it being college an all, but soon I learn they are for puttin down on the floor so's you don't have to step on all the dirt an shit when you walk aroun.

The goons take me to my room an say they be hopin to find my roomate there, whose name is Curtis somebody, but he nowhere to be foun. So they get my stuff unpacked an show me where the bathroom is, which look worse than what you might expect to find at a one-pump gasoline station, an they be on they way. But before they go, one of the goons say Curtis an me should get on fine cause both of us have about as much brains as a eggplant. I look real hard at the goon what said that, cause I be tired of hearin all that shit, but he tell me to drop down and give him fifty pushups. After that, I just be doin what I'm tole.

I went to sleep on my cot after spreadin a sheet over it to cover up the dirt, an was havin a dream bout settin down in the parlor with my mama like we use to do when it was hot, an she'd fix me a limeade an talk to me hour after hour—an then suddenly the door of the room done crashed in flat an scare me haf to death! A feller be standin there in the doorway with a wild look on his face, eyes all bugged out, no teeth in front, nose look like a yeller squash an his hair standin straight up like he done stuck his thing in a light-socket. I figger this be Curtis.

He come inside the room like he expectin somebody to pounce on him, lookin from side to side, an walk right over the door that he just caved in. Curtis ain't very tall, but he look like an icebox otherwise. First thing he axe me is where I'm from. When I say Mobile, he say that is a "candyass" town, an informs me he's from Opp, where they make peanut butter, an if I don't like it, he gonna open up a jar hissef an butter my butt with it! That were the extent of our conversation for a day or so.

That afternoon at football practice it be about ten thousan degrees hot on the field, an all Coach Bryant's goons runnin roun scowlin an yellin at us an makin us exercise. My tongue hangin down like it was a necktie or somethin, but I tryin to do the right thing. Finally they divides up everbody an puts me with backs an we start to run pass patterns.

Now before I come up to the University, they done sent me a package which contain about a million different football plays, an I done axed Coach Fellers what I'm spose to do with it an he jus shake his head sadly an say not to try to do nothin —jus to wait till I get to the University an let them figger somethin out.

I wish I had not taken Coach Fellers' advice now, cause when I run out for my first pass I done turned the wrong way an the head goon come rushin up hollerin an shoutin at me an when he stop shoutin he axed me don't I study the plays they send me? When I says, "Uh, uh," he commence to jump up an down an flail his arms like hornets is upon him, an when he calm down he tell me to go run five laps aroun the field wile he consult with Coach Bryant bout me.

Coach Bryant be settin up in a great big tower lookin down on us like the Great Gawd Bud, I'm runnin the laps and watchin the goon clime up there, an when he get to the top an say his piece, Coach Bryant crane his neck forward an I feel his eyes burnin hot on my big stupid ass. Suddenly a voice come over a megaphone for everbody to hear, say, "Forrest Gump, report to the coachin tower," an I seen Coach Bryant an the goon climin down. All the time I be runnin over there I am wishin I were runnin backwards instead.

But imagine my suprise when I see Coach Bryant smilin. He motion me over to some bleachers an we set down an he axed me again if I'd not learnt them plays they send me. I begin to splain what Coach Fellers had tole me, but Coach Bryant he stop me an say for me to git back in the line an start catchin passes, an then I tole him somethin else I guess he didn't want to hear, which was that I had never even caught a pass at highschool, cause they figgered it hard enough to get me to remember where our own goaline is, let alone runnin aroun tryin to grap the ball outta the air too.

At this news, Coach Bryant get a real odd squint in his eyes, an he look off in the distance, as if he was lookin all the way to the moon or somethin. Then he tell the goon to go fetch a football an when the football come, Coach Bryant hissef tell me to run out a little ways an turn aroun. When I do, he thowed the football at me. I see it comin almost like slow-motion but it bounce off my fingers an fall on the ground. Coach Bryant be noddin his head up an down like he should of figgered this out earlier, but somehow I get the idea he is not pleased.

From the time I'm little, ever time I do somethin wrong, my mama, she'd say, "Forrest, you got to be careful, cause they gonna put you away." I was so scairt of bein put in this "away" place I'd always try to be better, but I'm damned if there's a worst place they could of sent me than this Ape Dorm thing I'm livin in.

People be doin shit they wouldn't of tolerated even in the nut school—rippin out the toilets, for instance, so's you'd go to the bathroom an wouldn't fine nothin but a hole in the floor to shit in, an they'd have heaved the toilet out the winder onto the top of somebody's car drivin past. One night some big ole goofball what played in the line got out a rifle an commence to shoot out all the winders in somebody's fraternity house across the street. The campus cops come rushin over, but the feller drop a big outboard motor he found someplace out the winder onto the top of the cop car. Coach Bryant make him run a bunch of extra laps for doing that.

Curtis an me ain't gettin along so hot, an I never been so lonely. I miss my mama, an wanta go back home. Trouble with Curtis is, I don't understand him. Everthing he say got so many cusswords in it, time I get to figgerin out what they are, I miss his point. Most of the time, I gather his point is that he ain't happy bout somethin.

Curtis had a car an he used to give me a ride to practice, but one day I go to meet him an he cussin an growlin an bent over a big drain grate in the street. Seems he's got a flat tire an when he go to change it he put the lug nuts in his hubcap and accidentally knock em down into the drain. We fixin to be late to practice which was not real good to do, so's I say to Curtis, "Why don't you take one lug nut off each of them three other tires an that way you will have three nuts on each tire, which ought to be enough to get us to practice?"

Curtis stop cussin for a moment an look up at me an say, "You supposed to be a *idiot,* how you figure that out?" An I say, "Maybe I am a idiot, but at least I ain't *stupid,*" an at this, Curtis jump up an commence chasin me with the tire tool, callin me ever terrible thing he can think up, an that pretty much ruin our relationship.

After that, I decide I got to find another place to stay, so when we git off from practice I gone down into the basement of the Ape Dorm an spen the rest of the night there. It wadn't no dirtier than the upstairs rooms an there was an electric lightbulb. Nex day I moved my cot down there an from then on, it was where I lived.

Meantime, school is done started an they got to figger out what to do with me. They was a guy with the atheletic department that seemed to do nothin but figger out how to get dummos to where they could pass a class. Some of the classes was sposed to be easy, such as Physical Education, an they enroll me in that. But also I have got to take one English course an one science or math, an there is no gettin aroun that. What I learnt later was that there was certain teachers that would give a football player a sort of break, meanin that they'd appreciate he is consumed with playin football an cannot spend much of his time on school. They was one of these teachers in the science department, but unfortunately, the only class he taught was somethin called "Intermediate Light," which was apparently for graduate physics majors or something. But they put me in there anyhow, even though I didn't know physics from phys-ed.

I was not so lucky in English. They apparently did not have no sympathetic people over in that department, so's they tole me just to go ahead an take the class an fail it, an they'd figger out somethin else later.

In Intermediate Light, they provide me with a textbook that weigh five pounds an look like a Chinaman wrote it. But ever night I take it down to the basement an set on my cot under the lightbulb, an after a wile, for some peculiar reason, it begun to make sense. What did *not* make sense was why we was sposed to be doin it in the first place, but figgerin out them equations was easy as pie. Professor Hooks was my teacher's name, an after the first test, he axed me to come to his office after class. He say, "Forrest, I want you to tell me the truth, did somebody provide you the answers to these questions?" An I shake my head, an then he han me a sheet of paper with a problem written on it and says for me to set down an figger it out. When I'm thru, Professor Hooks look at what I done an shake his head an say, "Greatgodamighty."

English class was another deal entirely. The teacher is a Mister Boone, an he a very stern person who talk a lot. At the end of the first day, he say for us to set down that night an write a short autobiography of ourselfs for him. It's jus bout the most difficult thing I ever try to do, but I stay up most of the night, thinkin an writin, an I just say whatever come to mine on account of they tole me to fail the class anyhow.

A few days later, Mister Boone start handin back our papers an he criticisin an makin fun of everbody's autobiography. Then he come to what I done, an I figger I'm in the doghouse for sure. But he hold up my paper an start readin it out loud to everbody an he commences laughin an everbody else is too. I had tole bout bein in the nut school, an playin football for Coach Fellers an goin to the All State Football banquet, an about the daft board, an Jenny Curran an the movie an all. When he's thru, Mr. Boone, he say, "Now here is *originality!* Here is what I *want,* an everbody turn an look at me, an he says, "Mister Gump, you ought to think about gettin into the creative writing department—how did you think this up?" An I says, "I got to pee."

Mister Boone kinda jump back for a secont, an then he bust out laughin an so does everbody else, an he says, "Mister Gump, you are a very amusing feller."

An so I am surprised again.

The first football game was on a Saturday a few weeks later. Most of the time practice had been pretty bad, till Coach Bryant figgered out what to do with me, which was bout what Coach Fellers had done at highschool. They jus give me the ball an let me run. I run good that day, an score four touchdowns, an we whip the University of Georgia 35 to 3 an everbody slappin me on the back till it hurt. After I get cleaned up I phoned my mama an she done listened to the game over the radio an is so happy she can bust! That night, everbody goin to parties an shit, but nobody axed me to any, so I go on down to the basement. I'm there a wile when I hear this kind of music comin from someplace upstairs and it's real pretty-like, an, I don't know why, but I went on up there to find out what it was.

There was this guy, Bubba, settin in his room playin a mouth organ. He'd broke his foot in practice an couldn't play an didn't have nowhere to go either. He let me set on a cot an listen to him, we didn't talk or nothing, he jus settin on one cot an me on the other, an he's playing his harmonica. An after bout a hour I axed him if I could try it an he says, "Okay." Little did I know that it would change my life forever.

After I'd played aroun on the thing for a wile, I got to where's I could play pretty good, an Bubba was goin crazy, sayin he's never heard such good shit. After it got late, Bubba says for me to take the harmonica with me, an I did, an played it a long time, till I got sleepy and went to bed.

Next day, Sunday, I went to take the harmonica back to Bubba but he say for me to keep it, cause he got another one, an I was real happy, an went for a walk an set down under a tree an played all day long, till I run out of things to play.

It was late in the afternoon, an the sun was almost gone when I begun to walk back to the Ape Dorm. I was goin across the Quadrangle when suddenly I hear this girl's voice shout out, "Forrest!"

I turn aroun an who should be behin me but Jenny Curran.

She has a big smile on her face and she come up and took me by the han, an says she saw me play football yesterday and how good I was an all. It turns out she ain't mad or anythin bout what happen in the movie, an says it ain't my fault, it was jus one of them things. She axe if I want to have a Co'Cola with her.

It was too nice to believe, settin there with Jenny Curran,

an she say she takin classes in music an drama an that she plannin on bein a actress or a singer. She also playin in a little band that do folk music stuff, an tells me they gonna be at the Student Union buildin tomorrow night an for me to come by. Let me tell you, I can hardly wait.

4

Now there is a secret thing that Coach Bryant an them done figgered out, an nobody sposed to mention it, even to our-selfs. They been teachin me how to catch a football pass. Ever day after practice I been workin with two goons an a quarter-back, runnin out an catchin passes, runnin out an catchin passes, till I'm so exhausted my tongue hangin down to my navel. But I gettin to where I can catch em, an Coach Bryant, he say this gonna be our "secret weapon"—like a "Adam Bomb," or somethin, cause after a wile them other teams gonna figger out they ain't thowin me the ball an will not be watchin for it.

"Then," Coach Bryant say, "we is gonna turn your big ass loose—six foot six, two hundrit forty pounds—an run the hundrit yards in 9.5 seconds flat. It is gonna be a sight!"

Bubba an me is real good friends by now, an he heped me learn some new songs on the harmonica. Sometimes he come down to the basement and we set aroun an play along to-gether, but Bubba say I am far better than he ever will be. I got to tell you, that if it weren't for that harmonica music, I might of jus packed up an gone home, but it made me feel so good, I can hardly describe it. Sort of like my whole body is the harmonica an the music give me goosebumps when I play it. Mostly the trick is in the tongue, lips, fingers and how you move your neck. I think perhaps runnin after all them passes has caused my tongue to hang out longer, which is a hell of a note, so to speak.

Nex Friday, I git all slicked up an Bubba lend me some hair tonic an shavin lotion an I go on over to the Student Union building. They is a big crowd there an sure enough, Jenny Curran an three or four other people is up on stage. Jenny is wearin a long dress an playin the guitar, an somebody else has a banjo an there is a guy with a bull fiddle, pluckin it with his fingers.

They sound real good, an Jenny seen me back in the crowd, an smiles an points with her eyes for me to come up an set in the front. It is just beautiful, settin there on the floor listenin an watchin Jenny Curran. I was kinda thinkin that later, I would buy some divinity an see if she wanted some too.

They had played for an hour or so, an everbody seemed happy an feelin good. They was playin Joan Baez music, an Bob Dylan an Peter, Paul an Mary. I was lying back with my eyes closed, listenin, an all of a sudden, I ain't sure what happen, but I had pulled out my harmonica an was jus playin along with them.

It was the strangest thing. Jenny was singin "Blowin in the Wind" an when I begun to play, she stopped for a secont, an the banjo player, he stopped too, an they get this very suprised looks on they faces, an then Jenny give a big grin an she commence to pick up the song again, an the banjo player, he stop an give me a chance to ride my harmonica for a wile, an everbody in the crowd begun to clap an cheer when I was done.

Jenny come down from the stage after that an the band take a break an she say, "Forrest, what in the world? Where you learn to play that thing?" Anyhow, after that, Jenny got me to play with their band. It was ever Friday, an when there wasn't an out of town game, I made twenty-five bucks a night. It were jus like heaven till I foun out Jenny Curran been screwin the banjo player.

Unfortunately, it was not goin so good in English class. Mister Boone had called me in bout a week or so after he read my autobiography to the class and he say, "Mister Gump, I believe it is time for you to stop tryin to be amusin and start gettin serious." He han me back an assignment I had writ on the poet Wordsworth.

"The Romantic Period," he say, "did not follow a bunch of 'classic bullshit'. Nor were the poets Pope and Dryden a couple of 'turds.'"

He tell me to do the thing over again, an I'm beginnin to realize Mister Boone don't understand I'm a idiot, but he was bout to find out.

Meantime, somebody must of said somethin to somebody, cause one day my guidance counselor at the atheletic department call me in an tells me I'm excused from other classes an to report the next mornin to a Doctor Mills at the University Medical Center. Bright an early I go over there an Doctor Mills got a big stack of papers in front of him, lookin through them, an he tell me to sit down and start axin me questions. When he finished, he tell me to take off my clothes—all but my undershorts, which I breathed easier after hearin cause of what happen the last time with the Army doctors—an he commenced to studyin me real hard, lookin in my eyes an all, an bongin me on the kneecaps with a little rubber hammer.

Afterward, Doctor Mills axed if I would mine comin back that afternoon an axed if I would bring my harmonica with me, cause he had heard bout it, an would I mine playin a tune for one of his medical classes? I said I would, although it seemed peculiar, even to somebody dumb as me.

They was about a hundrit people in the medical class all wearin green aprons an takin notes. Doctor Mills put me up on the stage in a chair with a pitcher an a glass of water in front of me.

He's sayin a whole bunch of crap I don't follow, but after a wile I get the feelin he's talkin bout *me*.

"Idiot savant," he say loudly, an everbody be starin my way.

"A person who cannot tie a necktie, who can barely lace up his shoes, who has the mental capacity of perhaps a six- to ten-year-old, and—in this case—the body of, well, an *Adonis."* Doctor Mills be smilin at me in a way I don't like, but I'm stuck, I guess.

"But the mind," he says, "the mind of the idiot savant has rare pockets of brilliance, so that Forrest here can solve advanced mathematical equations that would stump any of you, and he can pick up complex musical themes with the ease of Liszt or Beethoven. Idiot *savant,"* he says again, sweepin his han in my direction.

I ain't sure what I'm sposed to do, but he had said for me to play somethin, so I pull out the harmonica an start playin "Puff, the Magic Dragon." Everbody settin there watchin me like I'm a bug or somethin, an when the song's over they still jus settin there lookin at me—don't even clap or nothin. I figgered they don't like it, so I stood up an said, "Thanks," an I lef. Shit on them people.

They is only two more things the rest of that school term that was even halfway important. The first was when we won the National College Football Championship an went to the Orange Bowl, an the second was when I found out Jenny Curran was screwin the banjo player.

It was the night we was sposed to play at a fraternity house party at the University. We had had a terribily hard practice that afternoon, an I was so thirsty I coulda drank out of the toilet like a dog. But they was this little stow five or six blocks from the Ape Dorm an after practice I walked on up there fixin to git me some limes and some sugar an fix me a limeade like my mama used to make for me. They is a ole cross-eyed woman behin the counter an she look at me like I'm a holdup man or somethin. I'm lookin for the limes an after a wile she says, "Kin I hep you?" an I says, "I want some limes," an she tells me they ain't got no limes. So I axed her if they got any lemons, cause I's thinkin a lemonade would do, but they ain't got none of them either, or oranges or nothin. It ain't that kind of stow. I musta look aroun maybe an hour or mo, an the woman be gettin nervous, an finally she say, "Ain't you gonna buy nothin?" so I get a can of peaches off the shef, an some sugar, thinkin if I can't have anythin else I can maybe make me a *peachade*—or somethin, I bout dyin of thirst. When I git back to my basement I open the can with a knife an squash the peaches up inside one of my socks an strain it into a jar. Then I put in some water an sugar an get it stirred up, but I'll tell you what—it don't taste nothin like a limeade —matter of fact, it taste more than anythin else like hot socks.

Anyhow, I sposed to be at the fraternity house at seven o'clock an when I get there some of the fellers is settin up the stuff an all, but Jenny and the banjo guy are nowhere to be found. I assed aroun for a wile, an then I went out to get mysef some fresh air in the parkin lot. I saw Jenny's car, an thought maybe she just get here.

All the winders in the car is steamed up, so's you can't see inside. Well, all of a sudden I think maybe she's in there an can't git out, an maybe gettin that exhaust poison or some- thin, so I open the door an look in. When I do, the light come on.

There she is, lying on the back seat, the top of her dress pulled down an the bottom pulled up. Banjo player there too, on top of her. Jenny seen me an start screamin an flailin jus like she done in the pitcher show, an it suddenly occur to me that maybe she bein *molested,* so's I grapped the banjo player by his shirt, which was all he's got on anyhow, an snatched his ass off her.

Well, it did not take no idiot to figger out that I gone an done the wrong thing again. Jesus Christ, you can't imagine such carryin on. He cussin me, she cussin me an tryin to git her dress pulled up an down, an finally Jenny say, "Oh Forrest—how *could* you!" an walk off. Banjo player pick up his banjo an leave too.

Anyhow, after that, it were apparent I was not welcome to play in the little band no more, an I went on back to the basement. I still couldn't understan exactly what had been goin on, but later that night Bubba seen my light on an he stop down an when I tell him bout the thing, he say, "Good grief, Forrest, them people was makin love!" Well, I reckon I might have figgered that out mysef, but to be honest, it was not somethin I wanted to know. Sometimes, however, a man got to look at the facts.

It is probly a good thing I was kep busy playin football, cause it was such a awful feelin, realizin Jenny was doin that with the banjo player, an that she probly hadn't even a thought bout me in that regard. But by this time we was undefeated the entire season an was goin to play for the National Championship at the Orange Bowl against them corn shuckers from Nebraska. It was always a big thing when we played a team from up North cause for sure they would have colored on their side, an that be a reason for a lot of consternation from some of the guys—like my ex-roomate Curtis, for example—altho I never worried bout it mysef, on account of most of the colored I ever met be nicer to me than white people.

Anyhow, we gone on down to the Orange Bowl in Miami, an come game time, we is some kind of stirred up. Coach

Bryant come in the locker room an don't say much, cept that if we want to win, we got to play hard, or somesuch, an then we be out on the field an they kicked off to us. The ball come directly to me an I grap it outta the air an run straight into a pile of Nebraska corn shucker niggers an big ole white boys that weigh about 500 pounds apiece.

It were that way the whole afternoon. At halftime, they was ahead 28 to 7 an we was a forelorn an sorry lot of guys. Coach Bryant come into the dressing room an he be shakin his head like he expected all along that we was goin to let him down. Then he start drawin on the chalk board and talkin to Snake, the quarterback, an some of the others, an then he call out my name an axe me to come with him into the hallway.

"Forrest," he says, "this shit has got to stop." His face right up against mine, an I feel his breath hot on my cheeks. "Forrest," he say, "all year long we been runnin them pass patterns to you in secret, an you been doin great. Now we is gonna do it against them Nebraska corn jackoffs this second half, an they will be so faked out, they jockstraps gonna be danglin roun they ankles. But it is up to you, boy—so go out there an run like a wild animal is after you."

I nod my head, an then it be time to get back on the field. Everbody be hollerin an cheerin, but I sort of feel they is a unfair burden on my shoulders. What the hell, tho—that's jus the way it is sometimes.

First play when we git the ball, Snake, the quarterback, say in the huddle, "Okay, we gonna run the *Forrest Series* now," an he says to me, "You jus run out twenty yards an look back, an the ball be there." An damn if it wadn't! Score is 28 to 14 all of a sudden.

We play real good after that, cept them Nebraska corn jerkoff niggers an big ole dumb white boys, they ain't jus settin there observin the scene. They has got some tricks of they own—mainly like runnin all over us as if we was made of cardboard or somethin.

But they is still somewhat suprised that I can catch the ball, an after I catch it four or five more times, an the score is 28 to 21, they begin to put two fellers to chasin after me. However, that leave Gwinn, the end, with nobody much to chase him aroun, an he catch Snake's pass an put us on the fifteen yard line. Weasel, the place kicker, get a field goal an the score now be 28 to 24.

On the sideline, Coach Bryant come up to me an say, "Forrest, you may be a shit-for-brains, but you has got to pull this thing out for us. I will personally see that you are made President of the United States or whatever else you want, if you can jus haul that football over the goal line one more time." He pat me on the head then, like I was a dog, an back in the game I go.

The Snake, he get caught behin the line right at the first play, an the clock is runnin out fast. On the second play, he try to fake em out by handin me the ball, sted of thowin it, but bout two tons of Nebraska corn jackoff beef, black an white, fall on top of me right away. I lying there, flat on my back, thinkin what it must of been like when that netload of bananas fall on my daddy, an then I gone back in the huddle again.

"Forrest," Snake says, "I gonna fake a pass to Gwinn, but I am gonna thow the ball to you, so I want you to run down there to the cornerback an then turn right an the ball be right there." Snake's eyes are wild as a tiger's. I nod my head, an do as I am tole.

Sure enough, Snake heaves the ball into my hans an I be tearin toward the middle of the field with the goalposts straight ahead. But all of a sudden a giant man come flyin into me and slow me down, an then all the Nebraska corn jerkoff niggers an big ole dumb white boys in the world start grappin an gougin an stompin on me an I fall down. Damn! We ain't got but a few yards to go fore winnin the game. When I git off my back, I see Snake got everbody line up already for the last play, on accounta we got no more time-outs. Soon as I git to my place, he calls for the snap an I run out, but he suddenly thowed the ball bout 20 feet over my head, outta bounds on purpose—to stop the clock I guess, which only has 2 or 3 seconts lef on it.

Unfortunately tho, Snake done got confused about things, I spose he's thinkin it third down an we got one more play lef, but in fact it were *forth* down, an so we lose the ball an also, of course, we lose the game. It sound like somethin I woulda done.

Anyhow, it was extra sad for me, cause I kinda figgered Jenny Curran was probly watchin the game an maybe if I done got the ball and win the game, she try to forgive me for doin what I done to her. But that were not to be. Coach Bryant were mighty unhappy over what happen, but he suck it up an say, "Well, boys, there's always nex year."

Cept for me, that is. That was not to be either.

5

After the Orange Bowl, the atheletic department get my grades for the first term, an it ain't long before Coach Bryant send for me to come to his office. When I get there, he lookin bleak.

"Forrest," he say, "I can understan how you flunked remedial English, but it will mystify me to the end of my days how you managed to get an *A* in something called Intermediate Light, an then an *F* in phys-ed class—when you is jus been named the Most Valuable College Back in the Southeastern Conference!"

It was a long story that I did not want to bore Coach Bryant with, but why in hell do I need to know the distance between goalposts on a soccer field anyway? Well, Coach Bryant lookin at me with a terrible sad expression on his face. "Forrest," he say, "I regret awfully havin to tell you this, but you is done flunked out of school, an there is nothin I can do."

I jus stood there, twistin my hands, till it suddenly come to me what he is sayin—I ain't gonna get to play no more foot-ball. I got to leave the University. Maybe I never see any of the other guys no more. Maybe I never see Jenny Curran no more either. I got to move outta my basement, an I won't get to take Advanced Light nex term, like Professor Hooks have said I would. I didn't realize it, but tears begun comin to my eyes. I ain't sayin nothin. I jus standin there, head hangin down.

Then Coach, he stand up hissef, an come over to me an he put his arm aroun me.

He say, "Forrest, it okay, son. When you first come here, I expect somethin like this would happen. But I tole em then, I said, just give me that boy for one season—that is all I ask. Well, Forrest, we has had ourselfs one hell of a season. That is for sure. An it certainly weren't your fault that Snake thowed the ball out of bounds on forth down. . . ."

I look up then, an they is little tears in Coach's eyes, too, an he is lookin at me real hard.

"Forrest," he say, "there has never been nobody like you ever played ball at this school, an there won't be never again. You was very fine."

Then Coach go over an stand lookin out the winder, an he say, "Good luck, boy—now git your big dumb ass outta here."

An so I had to leave the University.

I gone back an pack up my shit in the basement. Bubba come down an he done brought two beers an give one to me. I ain't never drank a beer, but I can see how a feller could acquire a taste for it.

Bubba walk with me outside the Ape Dorm, an lo an behole, who should be standin there but the entire football team.

They is very quiet, an Snake, he come up an shake my han an say, "Forrest, I am very sorry about that pass, okay?" An I says, "Sure Snake, okay." An then they all come up, one by one, an shake my han, even ole Curtis, who is wearin a body brace from his neck down on accounta bashin down one door too many in the Ape Dorm.

Bubba say he'd hep me carry my shit down to the bus depot, but I say I'd rather go alone. "Keep in touch," he say. Anyhow, on the way to the bus station, I pass by the Student Union store, but it ain't Friday night, an Jenny Curran's band is not playin, so I say, the hell with it, an catch the bus on home.

It was late at night when the bus got to Mobile. I had not tole my mama what had happened, cause I knew she'd be upset, so I walk on home, but they is a light on up in her room an when I get inside, they she is, crying and bawling jus like I remember. What had happen, she tell me, is that the United States Army has already heard bout me not makin my grades, an that very day a notice done come for me to report to the U.S. Army Induction Center. If I had known then what I know now, I would never had done it.

My mama take me down there a few days later. She has packed me a box lunch in case I get hungry on the way to wherever we is going. They is about a hundrit guys standin aroun an four or five busses waiting. A big ole sergeant be hollerin an yellin at everbody, an Mama goes up to him an says, "I don't see how you can take my boy—cause he's a *idiot,*" but the sergeant jus look back at her an say, "Well, lady, what do you think all these other people is? Einsteins?" an he gone on back to hollerin an yellin. Pretty soon he yell at me, too, an I git on the bus an away we went.

Ever since I lef the nut school people been shoutin at me— Coach Fellers, Coach Bryant an the goons, an now the people in the Army. But let me say this: them people in the Army yell longer an louder an nastier than anybody else. They is *never* happy. An furthermore, they do not complain that you is dumb or stupid like coaches do—they is more interested in your private parts or bowel movements, an so always precede they yellin with somethin like "dickhead" or "asshole." Sometimes I wonder if Curtis had been in the Army before he went to play football.

Anyhow, after about a hundrit hours on the bus we get to Fort Benning, Georgia, an all I'm thinkin is 35 to 3, the score when we whupped them Georgia Dogs. The conditions in the barracks is actually a little better than they was in the Ape Dorm, but the food is not—it is terrible, altho there is a lot of it.

Other than that, it was just doin what they tole us an gettin yelled at in the months to come. They taught us to shoot guns, thow hand grenades an crawl aroun on our bellies. When we wadn't doin that we was either runnin someplace or cleanin toilets an things. The one thing I remember from Fort Benning is that they didn't seem to be nobody much smarter than I was, which was certainly a relief.

Not too long after I arrive, I get put on KP, on account of I have accidentally shot a hole in the water tower when we was down at the rifle range. When I get to the kitchen, it seems the cook is took sick or somethin, an somebody point to me an say, "Gump, you is gonna be the cook today."

"What I'm gonna cook?" I axed. "I ain't never cooked before."

"Who cares," somebody say, "This ain't the Sans Souci, y'know."

"Why don't you make a stew?" Somebody else say. "It's easier."

"What of?" I axed.

"Look in the icebox an the pantry," the feller say, "Just thow in everthin you see an boil it up."

"What if it don't taste good?" I axed.

"Who gives a shit. You ever eat anythin around here that did?"

In this, he is correct.

Well, I commenced to get everthin I could from the ice-boxes an the pantry. They was cans of tomatos an beans an peaches an bacon an rice an bags of flour an sacks of potatoes an I don't know what all else. I gathered it all together an say to one of the guys, "What I'm gonna cook it in?"

"They is some pots in the closet," he say, but when I looked in the closet, they is jus small pots, an certainly not large enough to cook a stew for two hundrit men in the company.

"Why don't you axe the lieutenant?" somebody say.

"He's out in the field on maneuvers," come the reply.

"I don't know," say one feller, "but when them guys get back here today, they gonna be damn hungry, so you better think of somethin."

"What about this?" I axed. They was an enormous iron thing bout six feet high an five feet aroun settin in the corner.

"That? That's the goddamn steam boiler. You can't cook nothin in there."

"How come," I say.

"Well, I dunno. I jus wouldn do it if I was you."

"It's hot. It's got water in it." I says.

"Do what you want," somebody say, "we got other shit to do."

An so I used the steam boiler. I opened all the cans an peeled all the potatoes an thowed in whatever meat I could find an onions an carrots an poured in ten or twenty bottles of catsup an mustard an all. After bout a hour, you could begin to smell the stew cookin.

"How's the dinner comin?" somebody axed after a wile.

"I'll go taste it," I say.

I unfastened the lid to the boiler an there it was, you could see all the shit bubblin an boilin up, an ever so often a onion or a potato woud come to the top an float aroun.

"Let me taste it," a feller axed. He took a tin cup an dip out some stew.

"Say, this shit ain't near done yet," he says. "You better turn up the heat. Them fellers'll be here any minute."

So I turned up the heat on the boiler an sure enough, the company begun comin in from the field. You coud hear them in the barracks takin showers an gettin dressed for the evenin meal, an it weren't long afterward that they begun arrivin in the mess hall.

But the stew still wadnt ready. I tasted it again an some things was still raw. Out in the mess hall they begun a kind of disgruntled mumblin that soon turned to chantin an so I turned the boiler up again.

After a haf hour or so, they was beatin on the tables with they knives an forks like in a prison riot, an I knowed I had to do somethin fast, so I turned the boiler up high as it could go.

I'm settin there watchin it, so nervous I didn't know what to do, when all of a sudden the first sergeant come bustin thru the door.

"What in hell is goin on here?" he axed. "Where is these men's food?"

"It is almost ready, Sergeant," I say, an jus about then, the boiler commenced to rumble an shake. Steam begun to come out of the sides an one of the legs on the boiler tore loose from the floor.

"What is that?" the sergeant axed. "Is you cookin somethin in that *boiler!*"

"That is the supper," I says, an the sergeant got this real amazed look on his face, an a secont later, he got a real frightened look, like you might get jus before an automobile wreck, an then the boiler blew up.

I am not exactly sure what happened nex. I do remember that it blowed the roof off the mess hall an blowed all the winders out an the doors too.

It blowed the dishwasher guy right thru a wall, an the guy

what was stackin plates jus took off up in the air, sort of like Rocket Man.

Sergeant an me, we is miraculously spared somehow, like they say will happen when you are so close to a han grenade that you aren't hurt by it. But somehow it blowed both our clothes off, cept for the big chef's hat I was wearin at the time. An it blowed stew all over us, so's we looked like—well, I don't know what we looked like—but man, it was strange.

Incredibly, it didn't do nothin to all them guys settin out there in the mess hall neither. Jus lef em settin at they tables, covered with stew, actin kinda shell-shocked or somethin—but it sure did shut their asses up about when they food is gonna be ready.

Suddenly the company commander come runnin into the buildin.

"What was that!" he shouted. "What happen?" He look at the two of us, an then holler, "Sergeant Kranz, is that you?"

"Gump—Boiler—Stew!" the sergeant say, an then he kind of git holt of hissef an grapped a meat cleaver off the wall.

"Gump—Boiler—Stew!" he scream, an come after me with the cleaver. I done run out the door, an he be chasin me all over the parade grounds, an even thru the Officer's Club an the Motorpool. I outrunned him tho, cause that is my specialty, but let me say this: they ain't no question in my mind that I am up the creek for sure.

One night, the next fall, the phone rung in the barracks an it was Bubba. He say they done dropped his atheletic scholarship cause his foot broke worst than they thought, an so he's leavin school too. But he axed if I can git off to come up to Birmingham to watch the University play them geeks from Mississippi. But I am confined to quarters that Saturday, as I have been ever weekend since the stew blowed up and that's nearly a year. Anyway, I cannot do it, so I listen to the game on the radio while I'm scrubbin out the latrine.

The score is very close at the end of the third quarter, an Snake is having hissef a big day. It is 38 to 37 our way, but the geeks from Mississippi score a touchdown with only one minute to go. Suddenly, its forth down an no more time-outs for us. I prayin silently that Snake don't do what he done at the Orange Bowl, which is to thow the ball out of bounds on fourth down an lose the game again, but that is *exactly* what he done.

My heart sunk low, but suddenly they is all sorts of cheering so's you can't hear the radio announcer an when it is all quieted down, what happened was this: the Snake done *faked* an out of bounds pass on fourth down to stop the clock, but he *actually* give the ball to Curtis who run it in for the winning touchdown. That will give you some idea of jus how crafty Coach Bryant is. He done already figgered them geeks from Mississippi is so dumb they will assume *we* is stupid enough to make the same mistake twice.

I'm real happy bout the game, but I'm wonderin if Jenny Curran is watchin, an if she is thinkin of me.

As it turned out, it don't matter anyhow, cause a month later we is shipped out. For nearly a year we has been trained like robots an are going to somewhere 10,000 miles away, an that is no exaggeration. We is going to Vietnam, but they says it is not nearly as bad as what we has gone thru this past year. As it turn out, tho, that *is* an exaggeration.

We got there in February an was trucked on cattle cars from Qui Nhon on the South China Sea coast up to Pleiku in the highlands. It wadnt a bad ride an the scenery was nice an interestin, with banana trees an palms an rice paddies with little gooks plowin in them. Everbody on our side is real friendly, too, wavin at us an all.

We could see Pleiku almost haf a day away on account of a

humongus cloud of red dust that hovered over it. On its outskirts was sad little shanties that is worst than anythin I seen back in Alabama, with folks huddled neath cloth lean-to's an they ain't got no teeth an they children ain't got no clothes an basically, they is beggars. When we get to the Brigade Headquarters an Firebase, it don't look real bad either, cept for all that red dust. Ain't nothin much going on that we can see, an the place is all neat an clean with tents stretched far as you can see in rows an the dirt an sand aroun them raked up nice an tidy. Don't hardly look like a war going on at all. We might as well of been back at Fort Benning.

Anyhow, they says it is real quiet cause it is the beginning of the gook new years—Tet, or somesuch—an they is a truce goin on. All of us is tremendously relieved, because we is frightened enough as it is. The peace and quiet, however, did not last very long.

After we get squared away in our area, they tell us to go down to Brigade Showers an clean ourselfs. Brigade Showers is just a shallow pit in the groun where they has put three or four big water tank trucks an we tole to fold our uniforms up on the edge of the pit an then get down in there an they will squirt us with water.

Even so, it ain't haf bad, account of we been for nearly a week without a bath, an was beginnin to smell pretty ripe. We is assin aroun in the pit, gettin hosed down an all, an it is jus bout gettin dark, an all of a sudden there is this funny soun in the air an some jackoff who is squirting us with the hose holler, *"Incomin,"* and everbody on the edge of the pit vanish into thin air. We standin there butt neckid, lookin at each other, an then they is a big explosion close by an then another one, an everbody start shoutin and cussin an tryin to get to they clothes. Them incomin explosions fallin all aroun us, an somebody shoutin, "Hit the dirt!" which was kind of rediculous since we was all press so flat in the bottom of the pit by now we resemble worms rather than people.

One of them explosions send a bunch of shit flyin into our pit an them boys on the far side get hit with it an start screamin an yellin an bleedin an grappin at theyselfs. It were all too apparent that the pit was not a safe place to be hidin. Sergeant Kranz suddenly appear over the edge of the pit, an he holler for all us to get the hell out of there an follow him. There is a little break between explosions an we haul ass out of the pit. I come over the top an look down an godamighty! Lyin there is four or five of the fellers who was squirtin the hose on us. They is hardly recognizable as people—all mangled up like they has been stuffed thru a cotton baler or somethin. I ain't never seen nobody dead, an it is the most horrible and scary thing ever happen to me, afore or since!

Sergeant Kranz motion for us to crawl after him, which we do. If you could of looked down on it from above, we must of made a sight! A hundrit fifty or so fellers all butt neckid squirmin along the groun in a long line.

They was a bunch of foxholes dug in a row an Sergeant Kranz put three or four of us in each hole. But soon as we get in em, I realize I'd of almost rather stayed back in the pit. Them foxholes was filled waist stinkin deep with slimy ole water from the rain, an they was all sorts of frawgs an snakes and bugs crawlin an leapin an squirmin aroun in them.

It went on the entire night, an we had to stay in them foxholes an didn't get no supper. Jus afore dawn, the shellin eased up, an we was tole to haul our asses outta the foxholes an get our clothes an weapons an prepare for the attack.

Since we was relatively new, they was really not much we could do—they didn't even know where to put us, so they tole us to go guard the south perimeter, which is where the officers' latrine was located. But it were nearly worse than the foxholes, account of one of the bombs has hit the latrine an blowed up about five hundrit pounds of officer shit all over the area.

We had to stay there all that day, no breakfast, no lunch; an then at sundown they commenced shellin us again so we had to lie there in all that shit. My, my, it were repulsive.

Finally somebody remember we might be gettin hungry, an had a bunch of c-ration cases brought over. I got the cold ham an eggs that was dated 1951 on the can. They was all kinds of rumors goin on. Somebody said the gooks was runnin over the town of Pleiku. Somebody else says the gooks got a atomic bomb an is just shellin us with mortars to soften us up. Somebody else says it ain't the gooks shellin us at all, but Austrailians, or maybe the Dutch or the Norwegians. I figger it don't matter who it is. Shit on rumors.

Anyhow, after the first day, we begun tryin to make ourselfs a livable place on the south perimeter. We dug us foxholes an used the boards an tin from the officers' latrine to make us little hooches. The attack never come tho, an we never saw no gooks to shoot at. I figger maybe they smart enough not to attack a shithouse anyway. Ever night for about three or four days they shellin us tho, an finally one mornin when the shellin stops, Major Balls, the battalion executive officer, come crawlin up to our company commander an say we has got to go up north to help out another brigade that is catchin hell in the jungle.

After a wile, Lieutenant Hooper say for us to "saddle up," an everbody stuffin as many c-rations an han grenades in his pockets as he can—which actually present sort of a dilemma, since you can't eat a han grenade but you might nevertheless come to need it. Anyway, they load us on the heliocopters an off we flew.

You could see the shit Third Brigade had stepped into even fore the heliocopters landed. They was all sorts of smoke an stuff risin up outta the jungle an huge chunks had been blown outta the groun. We had not even got to earth afore they commenced shootin at us. They blowed up one of our heliocopters in the air, an it was a dreadful sight, people set on fire an all, an nothin we could do.

I am the machine gun ammo bearer, cause they figger I can carry a lot of shit on account of my size. Before we lef, a couple of other fellers axed if I would mind carryin some of their han grenades so's they could carry more c-rations, an I agreed. It didn't hurt me none. Also, Sergeant Kranz made me carry a ten-gallon water can that weighed about fifty pounds. Then jus fore we lef, Daniels, who carries the tri-pod for the machine gun, he gets the runs an he can't go, so's I got to tote the tri-pod too. When it all added up, I might as well of been toting aroun one a them Nebraska corn shucker jackoffs as well. But this ain't no football game.

It is gettin to be dusk an we is tole to go up to a ridge an relieve Charlie Company which is either pinned down by the gooks or has got the gooks pinned down, dependin on whether you get your news from the *Stars an Stripes* or by just lookin aroun at what the hell is goin on.

In any event, when we get up there, all sorts of crap is flyin aroun an they is about a dozen fellers badly hurt an moanin and cryin an they is so much noise from all quarters that nobody can hardly hear nothin. I be crouchin down real low an tryin to get all that ammo an the water can an the tri-pod plus all my own shit up to where Charlie Company is, an I'm strugglin past a slit trench when this guy down in it pipe up an say to the other, "Lookit that big Bozo—he look like the Frankenstein Monster or somethin," and I'm bout to say somethin back, cause things seem bad enough already without nobody pokin fun at you—but then, I'll be damned! The other guy in the slit trench suddenly jump up an cry out, "Forrest—Forrest Gump!"

Lo an behole, it were Bubba.

Briefly, what had happen was that even if Bubba's foot was

hurt too bad to play football, it were not bad enough to keep from gettin him sent halfway roun the earth on behalf of the United States Army. Anyhow, I drag my sorry butt an everthin else up to where I sposed to be, an after a wile Bubba come up there an in between the shellin (which stop ever time our airplanes appear) Bubba an me caught up with each other.

He tells me he hear Jenny Curran done quit school an gone off with a bunch of war protesters or somethin. He also say that Curtis done beat up a campus policeman one day for givin him a parkin ticket, an was in the process of drop-kickin his official ass aroun the campus when the authorities show up an thowed a big net over Curtis an drug him off. Bubba say Coach Bryant make Curtis run fifty extra laps after practice as punishment.

Good ole Curtis.

That night was long an uncomfortable. We couldn't fly our airplanes, so's they got to shell us most of the evenin for free. They was a little saddle between two ridges, an they was on one ridge an we on the other, an down in the saddle was where the dispute were takin place—tho what anybody would want with that piece of mud an dirt, I do not know. However, Sergeant Kranz have said to us time an again that we was not brought over here to understand what is goin on, only to do what we is tole.

Pretty soon, Sergeant Kranz come up an start tellin us what to do. He says we has got to move the machine gun about fifty meters aroun to the lef of a big ole tree stickin up in the middle of the saddle, an fine a good safe place to put it so's we is not all blowed away. From what I can see an hear, anyplace, includin where we presently are, is not safe, but to go down in that saddle is goddamn absurd. However, I am tryin to do the right thing.

Me an Bones, the machine gunner, an Doyle, another

ammo bearer, an two other guys crawl out of our holes an start to moving down the little slope. Halfway down, the gooks see us an commence to shootin with they own machine gun. Fore anything bad happens, tho, we has scrambled down the slope an into the jungle. I cannot remember how far a meter is exactly, but it almost the same as a yard, so when we get near the big tree, I say to Doyle, "Maybe we better move lef," an he look at me real hard-like, an growl, "Shut you ass, Forrest, they is gooks here." Sure nuf, they was six or eight gooks squattin under the big ole tree, havin they lunch. Doyle take a han grenade an pull the pin an sort of lob it into the air toward the tree. It blowed up fore it hit the groun an they is all sorts of wild chatterin from where the gooks is— then Bones open up with the machine gun an me an the two other guys heave in a couple more han grenades for good measure. All of that gone down in just a minute or so, an when it come quiet again, we be on our way.

We foun a place to put the gun an stayed there till it got dark—an all night long, too, but nothin happen. We could hear all sorts of shit goin on everplace else, but we be lef to ourselfs. Sunup come, an we hungry an tired, but there we is. Then a runner come from Sergeant Kranz who say Charlie Company is goin to start movin into the saddle soon as our airplanes have totally wiped out the gooks there, which is to be in a few minutes. Sure enough, the planes come an drop they shit an everthin get exploded an wipe out all the gooks.

We can see Charlie Company movin off the ridge line, comin down into the saddle, but no sooner does they get over the edge of the ridge an start strugglin along the slope, than all the weapons in the world commence to shootin at Charlie Company an droppin mortars an all, an it is terrible confusion. From where we is, we cannot see any gooks, on account of the jungle is thick as bonfire brush, but *somebody* sure be in there shootin at Charlie Company. Maybe it the Dutch—or even the Norwegians—who knows?

Bones, the machine gunner, lookin extremely nervous durin all this, on accounta he's already figgered out that the shootin is comin from in *front* of us, meanin that the gooks is in between us an our own position. In other words, we is out here alone. Sooner or later, he says, if the gooks do not overrun Charlie Company, they will come back this way, an if they find us here, they will not like it one bit. Point is, we got to move our asses.

We get our shit together an begin to work back towards the ridge, but as we do, Doyle suddenly look down off our right to the bottom of the saddle an he see an entire busload of new gooks, armed to the teeth, movin up the hill towards Charlie Company. Best thing we coulda done then was to try an make friends with em an forget all this other shit, but that were not in the cards. So we jus hunkered down in some big ole shrubs an waited till they got to the top of the hill. Then Bones let loose with the machine gun and he must of kilt ten or fifteen of them gooks right off. Doyle an me an the other two guys is thowin grenades, an things is goin our way until Bones runs out of ammo an need a fresh belt. I feed one in for him, but just as he bout to sqeeze the trigger, a gook bullet hit him square in the head an blowed it inside out. He lyin on the ground, han still holdin to the gun for dear life, which he does not have any more of now.

Oh God, it were awful—an gettin worst. No tellin what them gooks would of done if they caught us. I call out to Doyle to come here, but they is no answer. I jerk the machine gun from po ole Bones' fingers an squirm over to Doyle, but he an the two other guys layin there shot. They dead, but Doyle still breathin, so's I grap him up an thow him over my shoulder like a flour sack an start runnin thru the brush towards Charlie Company, cause I scared outta my wits. I runnin for maybe twenty yards an bullets wizzin all aroun me from behin, an I figger I be shot in the ass for sure.

But then I crash thru a canebreak an come upon a area with low grass an to my suprise it is filled with gooks, lyin down, lookin the other way, an shootin at Charlie Company—I guess.

Now what do I do? I got gooks behin me, gooks in front of me an gooks right under my feet. I don't know what else to do, so I charge up full speed an start to bellowin an howlin an all. I sort of lose my head, I guess, cause I don't remember what happen nex cept I still be bellowin an hollerin loud as I can an runnin for dear life. Everthin were completely confused, an then all of a sudden I am in the middle of Charlie Company an everbody be slappin me on the back jus like I made a touchdown.

It seem like I done frightened off the gooks an they hightail it back to wherever they live. I put down Doyle on the groun an the medics come an start fixin him up, an pretty soon the Charlie Company commander come up to me an start pumpin my han an tellin me what a good fellow I am. Then he say, "How in hell did you do that, Gump?" He be waitin for a answer, but I don't know how I done it mysef, so I says, "I got to pee"—which I did. The company commander look at me real strange, an then look at Sergeant Kranz, who had also come up, an Sergeant Kranz say, "Oh, for Chrissakes Gump, come with me," an he take me behin a tree.

That night Bubba an me meet up an share a foxhole an eat our C-rations for supper. Afterward, I get out my harmonica Bubba had gave me an we play a few tunes. It sound real eerie, there in the jungle, playin "Oh Suzanna" an "Home on the Range." Bubba got a little box of candy his mama have sent him—pralines an divinity—an we both ate some. An let me tell you this—that divinity sure brung back some memories.

Later on, Sergeant Kranz come over an axe me where is the ten-gallon can of drinkin water. I tole him I done lef it out in the jungle when I was tryin to carry in Doyle an the machine gun. For a minute I think he gonna make me go back out there an get it, but he don't. He jus nod, an say that since Doyle is hurt an Bones is kilt, now I got to be the machine gunner. I axe him who gonna carry the tri-pod an the ammo an all, an he say I got to do that too, cause nobody else lef to do it. Then Bubba say he'll do it, if he can get transferred to our company. Sergeant Kranz think bout that for a minute, an then he say it can probly be arranged, since there is not enough lef of Charlie Company to clean a latrine anyway. An so it was, Bubba an me is together again.

The weeks go by so slow I almost think time passin backwards. Up one hill, down the other. Sometimes they be gooks on the hills, sometimes not. Sergeant Kranz say everthing okay tho, cause actually we be marchin back to the United States. He say we gonna march outta Vietnam, thru Laos an then up across China an Russia, up to the North Pole an across the ice to Alaska where our mamas can come pick us up. Bubba says don't pay no attention to him cause he's a idiot.

Things is very primitive in the jungle—no place to shit, sleep on the groun like a animal, eat outta cans, no place to take a bath or nothin, clothes is all rottin off too. I get a letter once a week from my mama. She say everthing fine at home, but that the highschool ain't won no more championships since I done lef. I write her back too, when I can, but what I'm gonna tell her that won't start her to bawlin again? So I jus say we is havin a nice time an everbody treatin us fine. One thing I done tho, was I wrote a letter to Jenny Curran in care of my mama an axe if she can get Jenny's folks to send it to her—wherever she is. But I ain't heard nothin back.

Meantime, Bubba an me, we has got us a plan for when we get outta the Army. We gonna go back home an get us a srimp boat an get in the srimpin bidness. Bubba come from

Bayou La Batre, an work on srimp boats all his life. He say maybe we can get us a loan an we can take turns bein captain an all, an we can live on the boat an will have somethin to do. Bubba's got it all figgered out. So many pounds of srimp to pay off the loan on the boat, so much to pay for gas, so much for what we eat an such, an all the rest is left for us to ass aroun with. I be picherin it in my head, standin at the wheel of the srimp boat—or even better, settin there on the back of the boat eatin srimp! But when I tell Bubba bout that, he say, "Goddamn, Forrest, your big ass'll eat us outta house an home. We don't be eatin none of the srimp afore we start makin a profit." Okay, that make sense—it all right with me.

It commenced rainin one day an did not stop for two months. We went thru ever different kind of rain they is, cep'n maybe sleet or hail. It was little tiny stingin rain sometimes, an big ole fat rain at others. It came sidewise an straight down an sometimes even seem to come up from the groun. Nevertheless, we was expected to do our shit, which was mainly walkin up an down the hills an stuff lookin for gooks.

One day we foun them. They must of been holdin a gook convention or somethin, cause it seem like the same sort of deal as when you step on a anthill and they all come swarmin aroun. We cannot fly our planes in this kind of stuff either, so in about two minutes or so, we is back in trouble again.

This time they has caught us with our pants down. We is crossin this rice paddy an all of a sudden from everwhere they start thowin shit at us. People is shoutin and screamin an gettin shot an somebody says, "Fall back!" Well, I pick up my machine gun an start running alongside everbody else for some palm trees which at least look like they might keep the rain offen us. We has formed a perimeter of sorts an is gettin ready to start preparin for another long night when I look-aroun for Bubba an he ain't there.

Somebody say Bubba was out in the rice paddy an he is

hurt, an I say, "Goddamn," an Sergeant Kranz, he hear me, an say, "Gump, you can't go out there." But shit on that—I leave the machine gun behind cause it jus be extra weight, an start pumpin hard for where I last seen Bubba. But halfway out I nearly step on a feller from 2nd platoon who is mighty hurt, an he look up at me with his han out, an so I think, shit, what can I do? so I grap him up an run back with him fast as I can. Bullets an stuff be flyin all over. It is somethin I simply cannot understand—why in hell is we doin all this, anyway? Playin football is one thing. But this, I do not know why. Goddamn.

I brung that boy back an run out again an damn if I don't come across somebody else. So I reach down to pick him up an bring him back, too, but when I do, his brains fall out on the paddy groun, cause the back of his head blowed off. Shit.

So I drop his ass an kep on goin an sure enough, there is Bubba, who is been hit twice in the chest, an I say, "Bubba, it gonna be okay, you hear, cause we gotta get that srimp boat an all," an I carry him back to where we is set up an layed him on the groun. When I catch my breath, I look down an my shirt all covered with blood an bluish yeller goo from where Bubba is hurt, an Bubba is lookin up at me, an he say, "Fuck it, Forrest, why this happen?" Well, what in hell am I gonna say?

Then Bubba axe me, "Forrest, you play me a song on the harmonica?" So I get it out, an start playin somethin—I don't even know what, an then Bubba say, "Forrest, would you please play "Way Down Upon the Swanee River?" an I say, "Sure, Bubba." I have to wipe off the mouthpiece, an then I start to play an there is still a terrible lot of shootin goin on, an I know I ought to be with my machine gun, but what the hell, I played that song.

I hadn't noticed it, but it had quit rainin an the sky done turned a awful pinkish color. It made everbody's face look like death itsef, an for some reason, the gooks done quit shootin for a wile, an so had we. I played "Way Down Upon the Swanee River" over an over again, kneelin nex to Bubba wile the medic give him a shot an tend to him best he could. Bubba done grapped a holt to my leg an his eyes got all cloudy an that terrible pink sky seem to drain all the color in his face.

He was tryin to say somethin, an so I bent over real close to hear what it was. But I never coud make it out. So I axed the medic, "You hear what he say?"

An the medic say, "Home. He said, *home.*"

Bubba, he died, an that's all I got to say bout that.

The rest of the night was the worst I have ever known. They was no way they could get any hep to us, since it begun stormin again. Them gooks was so close we could hear them talkin with each other, an at one point it was han to han fightin in the 1st platoon. At dawn, they call in a napalm airplane, but it drop the shit damn near right on top of *us*. Our own fellers be all singed an burnt up—come runnin out into the open, eyes big as biscuits, everbody cussin an sweatin an scared, woods set on fire, damn near put the rain out!

Somewhere in all this, I got mysef shot, an, as luck would have it, I was hit in the ass. I can't even remember it. We was all in awful shape. I don't know what happened. Everthing all fouled up. I jus left the machine gun. I didn't give a shit no more. I went to a place back of a tree an jus curl up an start cryin. Bubba gone, srimp boat gone; an he the only friend I ever had—cept maybe Jenny Curran, an I done mess that up too. Wadn't for my mama, I might as well of jus died right there—of ole age or somethin, whatever—it didn't matter.

After a wile, they start landin some relief in heliocopters, and I guess the napalm bomb have frightened away the gooks. They must of figgered that if we was willing to do that to ourselfs, then what the hell would we of done to *them?*

They takin the wounded outta there, when along come

Sergeant Kranz, hair all singed off, clothes burnt up, looking like he jus got shot out of a cannon. He say, "Gump, you done real good yesterday, boy," an then he axe me if I want a cigarette.

I say I don't smoke, an he nod. "Gump," he says, "you are not the smartest feller I have ever had, but you is one hell of a soldier. I wish I had a hundrit like you."

He axe me if it hurt, an I say no, but that ain't the truth. "Gump," he say, "you is goin home, I guess you know that."

I axe him where is Bubba, an Sergeant Kranz look at me kind of funny. "He be along directly," he says. I axed if I can ride on the same heliocopter with Bubba, an Sergeant Kranz say, no, Bubba got to go out last, cause he got kilt.

They had stuck me with a big needle full of some kind of shit that made me feel better, but I remember, I reached up an grapped Sergeant Kranz by the arm, an I say, "I ain't never axed no favors afore, but would you put Bubba on the heliocopter yoursef, an make sure he get there okay?"

"Sure, Gump," he say. "What the hell—we will even get him accommodations in first class."

7

I was at the hospital at Danang for most of two months. So far as a hospital went, it were not much, but we slep on cots with mosquito nets, an they was wooden plank floors that was swep clean twice a day, which was more than you can say for the kind of livin I'd got used to.

They was some people hurt far worst than I was in that hospital, let me tell you. Po ole boys with arms an legs an feet an hans an who knows what else missin. Boys what had been shot in they stomachs an chests an faces. At night the place sound like a torture chamber—them fellers be howlin and cryin an callin for they mamas.

They was a guy nex to my cot name of Dan, who had been blowed up inside a tank. He was all burnt an had tubes goin in an out of him everplace, but I never heard him holler. He talk real low an quiet, an after a day or so, him an me got to be friends. Dan come from the state of Connecticut, an he were a teacher of history when they grapped him up an thowed him into the Army. But cause he was smart, they sent

him to officer school an made him a lieutenant. Most of the
lieutenants I knowed was bout as simple-minded as me, but
Dan were different. He have his own philosophy bout why
we was there, which was that we was doin maybe the wrong
thing for the right reasons, or visa-versa, but whatever it is,
we ain't doin it right. Him bein a tank officer an all, he say it
rediculous for us to be wagin a war in a place where we can't
hardly use our tanks on account of the land is mostly swamp
or mountains. I tole him bout Bubba an all, an he nod his
head very sadly an say they will be a lot more Bubbas to die
afore this thing is over.

After bout a week or so, they move me to another part of
the hospital where everbody be put so's they can get well,
but ever day I gone back to the tensive care ward an set for a
wile with Dan. Sometimes I played him a tune on my harmonica, which he like very much. My mama had sent me a
package of Hershey bars which finally catch up to me at the
hospital an I wanted to share them with Dan, cept he can't eat
nothin but what goin into him thru the tubes.

I think that settin there talkin to Dan was a thing that had a
great impression on my life. I know that bein a idiot an all, I
ain't sposed to have no philosophy of my own, but maybe it's
just because nobody never took the time to talk to me bout it.
It were Dan's philosophy that everythin that happen to us, or
for that matter, to anythin anywhere, is controlled by natural
laws that govern the universe. His views on the subject was
extremely complicated, but the gist of what he say begun to
change my whole outlook on things.

All my own life, I ain't understood shit about what was
goin on. A thing jus happen, then somethin else happen, then
somethin else, an so on, an haf the time nothin makin any
sense. But Dan say it is all part of a scheme of some sort, an
the best way we can get along is figger out how we fits into
the scheme, an then try to stick to our place. Somehow
knowin this, things get a good bit clearer for me.

Anyhow, I's gettin much better in the next weeks, an my ass heal up real nice. Doctor say I got a hide like a "rhinoceros" or somethin. They got a rec room at the hospital an since they wadn't much else to do, I wandered over there one day an they was a couple of guys playin ping-pong. After a wile, I axed if I could play, an they let me. I lost the first couple of points, but after a wile, I beat both them fellers. "You shore is quick for such a big guy," one of them say. I jus nod. I tried to play some ever day an got quite good, believe it or not.

In the afternoons I'd go see Dan, but in the mornins I was on my own. They let me leave the hospital if I wanted, an they was a bus what took fellers like me into the town so's we could walk aroun an buy some of the shit they sold in the gook shops in Danang. But I don't need any of that, so I jus walk aroun, takin in the sights.

They is a little market down by the waterfront where folks sells fish an srimp an stuff, an one day I went down there an bought me some srimp an one of the cooks at the hospital boil em for me an they sure was good. I wished ole Dan could of ate some. He say maybe if I squash em up they could put em down his tube. He say he gonna axe the nurse about it, but I know he jus kiddin.

That night I be lyin on my cot thinkin of Bubba an how much he might of liked them srimp too, an about our srimp boat an all. Po ole Bubba. So the next day I axed Dan how is it that Bubba can get kilt, an what kind of haf-assed nature law would allow that. He think bout it for a wile, an say, "Well, I'll tell you, Forrest, all of these laws are not specially pleasing to us. But they is laws nonetheless. Like when a tiger pounce on a monkey in the jungle—bad for the monkey, but good for the tiger. That is jus the way it is."

Couple of days later I gone on back to the fish market an they is a little gook sellin a big bag of srimp there. I axed him where he got them srimp, an he start jabberin away at me, count of he don't understan English. Anyway, I make sign language like a Indian or somethin, an after a wile he catch on, an motion for me to follow him. I be kind of leary at first, but he smilin an all, an so's I do.

We must of walked a mile or so, past all the boats on the beach an everthin, but he don't take me to a boat. It is a little place in a swamp by the water, kind of a pond or somethin, an he got wire nets laid down where the water from the China Sea come in at high tide. That sumbitch be *growin* srimp in there! He took a little net an scoop up some water an sure enough, ten or twelve srimp in it. He give me some in a little bag, an I give him a Hershey bar. He so happy he could shit.

That night they is a movie outdoors near Field Force Headquarters an I go on over there, cep'n some fellers in the front row start a great big fight over somethin an somebody get hissef heaved through the screen an that be the end of the movie. So afterwards, I be layin on my cot, thinkin, an suddenly it come to me. I know what I gotta do when they let me out of the Army! I goin home an find me a little pond near the Gulf an raise me some srimp! So maybe I can't get me a srimp boat now that Bubba is gone, but I sure can go up in one of them marshes an get me some wire nets an that's what I'll do. Bubba would of like that.

Ever day for the next few weeks I go down in the mornin to the place where the little gook is growin his srimp. Mister Chi is his name. I jus set there an watched him an after a wile he showed me how he was doin it. He'd catched some baby srimps aroun the marshes in a little han net, an dump them in his pond. Then when the tide come in he thowed all sorts of shit in there—scraps and stuff, which cause little teensey slimy things to grow an the srimps eat them an get big an fat. It was so simple even a imbecile could do it.

A few days later some muckity-mucks from Field Force Headquarters come over to the hospital all excited an say,

"Private Gump, you is been awarded the Congressional Medal of Honor for extreme heroism, an is bein flown back to the U.S.A. day after tomorrow to be decorated by the President of the United States." Now that was early in the mornin an I had jus been lyin there, thinkin about going to the bathroom, but here they are, expectin me to say somethin, I guess, an I'm bout to bust my britches. But this time I jus say, "Thanks," an keep my big mouth shut. Perhaps it be in the natural scheme of things.

Anyhow, after they is gone, I go on over to the tensive care ward to see Dan, but when I git there, his cot is empty, an the mattress all folded up an he is gone. I am so scarit somethin has happen to him, an I run to fine the orderly, but he ain't there either. I seen a nurse down the hall an I axed her, "What happen to Dan," an she say he "gone." An I say, "Gone where?" an she say, "I don't know, it didn't happen on my shif." I foun the head nurse an axe her, an she say Dan been flown back to America on account of they can take better care of him there. I axed her if he is okay, an she say, "Yeah, if you can call two punctured lungs, a severed intestin, spinal separation, a missing foot, a truncated leg, an third degree burns over haf the body *okay*, then he is jus fine." I thanked her, an went on my way.

I didn't play no ping-pong that afternoon, cause I was so worried bout Dan. It come to me that maybe he went an died, an nobody want to say so, cause of that bidness bout notifying nex of kin first, or somethin. Who knows? But I am down in the dumps, an go wanderin aroun by mysef, kickin rocks an tin cans an shit.

When I finally get back to my ward, there is some mail lef on my bed for me that finally catch up with me here. My mama have sent a letter sayin that our house done caught on fire, an is totally burnt up, an there is no insurance or nothin an she is gonna have to go to the po house. She say the fire begun when Miss French had washed her cat an was dryin it with a hair dryer, an either the cat or the hair dryer caught afire, an that was that. From now on, she say, I am to send my letters to her in care of the "Little Sisters of the Po." I figger there will be many tears in the years to come.

They is another letter addressed to me which say, "Dear Mister Gump: You has been chosen to win a bran new Pontiac GTO, if only you will send back the enclosed card promising to buy a set of these wonderful encyclopedias an a updated yearbook every year for the rest of your life at a $75 per year." I thowed that letter in the trash. What the hell would a idiot like me want with encyclopedias anyway, an besides, I can't drive.

But the third letter is personally writ to me an on the back of the envelope it say, "J. Curran, General Delivery, Cambridge, Mass." My hans is shakin so bad, I can hardly open it.

"Dear Forrest," it say, "My mama has forwarded your letter to me that your mama gave to her, and I am so sorry to hear that you have to fight in that terrible immoral war." She say she know how horrible it must be, with all the killin an maimin goin on an all. "It must tax your conscience to be involved, although I know you are being made to do it against your will." She write that it must of been awful not to have no clean clothes an no fresh food, an all, but that she do not understand what I mean when I wrote about "havin to lie face-down in officer shit for two days."

"It is hard to believe," she say, "that even *they* would make you do such a vulgar thing as that." I think I could of explained that part a little better.

Anyhow, Jenny say that "We are organizing large demonstrations against the fascist pigs in order to stop the terrible immoral war and let the people be heard." She go on bout that for a page or so, an it all soundin sort of the same. But I read it very carefully anyway, for jus to see her hanwritin is enough to make my stomach turn flip-flops.

"At least," she say at the end, "you have met up with Bubba, and I know you are glad to have a friend in your misery." She say to give Bubba her best, an add in a p.s. that she is earnin a little money by playin in a little musical band a couple of nights a week at a coffeehouse near the Harvard University, an if ever I get up that way to look her up. The group, she say, is called The Cracked Eggs. From then on, I be lookin for some excuse to get to Harvard University.

That night I am packin up my shit to go back home to get my Medal of Honor an meet the President of the United States. However, I do not have nothin to pack cept my pajaymas an the toothbrush an razor they have gave me at the hospital, cause everthin else I own is back at the firebase at Pleiku. But there is this nice lieutenant colonel that has been sent over from Field Force, an he say, "Forgit all that shit, Gump—we is gonna have a bran new tailor-made uniform sewn up for you this very night by two dozen gooks in Saigon, on account of you cannot meet the President wearin your pajaymas." The colonel say he is gonna accompany me all the way to Washington, an see to it that I have got a place to stay an food to eat an a ride to wherever we is going an also will tell me how to behave an all.

Colonel Gooch is his name.

That night I get into one last ping-pong match with a feller from the headquarters company of Field Force, who is sposed to be the best ping-pong player in the Army or somesuch as that. He is a little wiry feller who refuse to look me in the eye, an also, he bring his own paddle in a leather case. When I be whippin his ass he stop an say the ping-pong balls ain't no good cause the humidity done ruint them. Then he pack up his paddle an go on home, which be okay with me, cause he lef the ping-pong balls he brung, an they could really use them at the hospital rec room.

The morning I was to leave, a nurse come in an lef a envelope with my name written on it. I open it up, an it was a note from Dan, who is okay after all, an had this to say:

Dear Forrest,

I am sorry there was no time for us to see each other before I left. The doctors made their decision quickly, and before I knew it, I was being taken away, but I asked if I could stop long enough to write you this note, because you have been so kind to me while I was here.

I sense, Forrest, that you are on the verge of something very significant in your life, some change, or event that will move you in a different direction, and you must seize the moment, and not let it pass. When I think back on it now, there is something in your eyes, some tiny flash of fire that comes now and then, mostly when you smile, and, on those infrequent occasions, I believe what I saw was almost a Genesis of our ability as humans to think, to create, to *be*.

This war is not for you, old pal—nor me—and I am well out of it as I'm sure you will be in time. The crucial question is, what will you do? I don't think you're an idiot at all. Perhaps by the measure of tests or the judgment of fools, you might fall into some category or other, but deep down, Forrest, I have seen that glowing sparkle of curiosity burning deep in your mind. Take the tide, my friend, and as you are carried along, make it work for you, fight the shallows and the snags and never give in, never give up. You are a good fellow, Forrest, and you have a big heart.

Your Pal,
DAN

I read over Dan's letter ten or twenty times, an there is things in it I do not understand. I mean, I *think* I see what he is gettin at, but there is sentences an words that I cannot figger out. Next morning Colonel Gooch come in an say we got to go now, first to Saigon to get me the new uniform that done been sewn up by the twenty gooks last night, then right off to the United States an all that. I shown him Dan's letter an axed him to tell me what exactly it means, an Colonel Gooch look it over an han it back an say, "Well, Gump, it is pretty plain to me he means that you had better the hell not fuck up when the President pins the medal on you."

We be flyin high over the Pacific Ocean, an Colonel Gooch is tellin me what a great hero I am going to be when we get back to the United States. He say people will turn out for parades an shit an I will not be able to buy mysef a drink or a meal on account of everbody else will be wantin to do it for me. He also say that the Army is gonna want me to go on a tour to drum up new enlistments an sell bonds an crap like that, an that I will be given the "royal treatment." In this, he is correct.

When we land at the airport at San Francisco, a big crowd is waiting for us to get off the plane. They is carryin signs an banners and all. Colonel Gooch look out the winder of the plane an say he is suprised not to see a brass band there to greet us. As it turn out, the people in the crowd is quite enough.

First thing that happen when we come off the plane is the people in the crowd commence to chantin at us, an then somebody thowed a big tomato that hit Colonel Gooch in the face. After that, all hell break loose. They is some cops there, but the crowd busted thru an come runnin towards us shoutin an hollerin all kinds of nasty things, an they is about two thousan of them, wearing beards an shit, an it was the mos frightenin thing I have seen since we was back at the rice paddy where Bubba was kilt.

Colonel Gooch is tryin to clean the tomato off his face an act dignified, but I figger, the hell with that, cause we is outnumbered a thousan to one, an ain't got no weapons to boot. So I took off runnin.

That crowd was sure as hell lookin for somethin to chase too, cause ever one of them start chasin me jus like they used to do when I was little, hollerin and shoutin and wavin they signs. I run damn near all over the airport runway, an back again an into the terminal, an it was even scarier than when them Nebraska corn shucker jackoffs was chasin me aroun the Orange Bowl. Finally, I done run into the toilet an hid up on the seat with the door shut until I figger they have give up an gone on home. I must of been there an hour or so.

When I come out I walked down to the lobby an there is Colonel Gooch surrounded by a platoon of M.P.'s an cops, an he is lookin very distressed till he seen me. "C'mon, Gump!" he say. "They is holdin a plane for us to get to Washington."

When we get on the plane to Washington they is a bunch of civilians on it too, an Colonel Gooch an me set in a seat up front. We has not even took off yet, before all the people aroun us get up an go set somewhere else in the back of the plane. I axed Colonel Gooch why that was, an he say it probly cause we smell funny or somethin. He say not to worry about it. He say things be better in Washington. I hope so, cause even a moron like me can figger out that so far, it is not like the colonel say it would be.

When the plane get to Washington I am so excited I can bust! We can see the Washington Monument an the Capitol an all from out the winder an I have only saw picures of them things, but there they are, real as rain. The Army have sent a car to pick us up an we is taken to a real nice hotel, with elevators an stuff an people to lug your shit aroun for you. I have never been in a elevator before.

After we get squared away in our rooms, Colonel Gooch come over an say we is goin out for a drink to this little bar he remembers where they is a lot of pretty girls, an he say it is a lot different here than in California on account of people in the East are civilized an shit. He is wrong again.

We set down at a table an Colonel Gooch order me a beer an somethin for hissef an he begin tellin me how I got to act at the ceremony tomorrow when the President pin the medal on me.

Bout halfway through his talk, a pretty girl come up to the table an Colonel Gooch look up an axe her to git us two more drinks cause I guess he think she is the waitress. But she look down an say, "I wouldn get you a glass of warm spit, you filthy cocksucker." Then she turn to me an say, "How many babies have you kilt today, you big ape?"

Well, we gone on back to the hotel after that, an ordered some beer from room service, an Colonel Gooch get to finish tellin me how to act tomorrow.

Nex morning we up bright an early an walk on over to the White House where the President live. It is a real pretty house with a big lawn an all that look almost as big as city hall back in Mobile. A lot of Army people be there pumpin my han an tellin me what a fine feller I am, an then it is time to get the medal.

The President is a great big ole guy who talk like he is from Texas or somethin an they has assembled a whole bunch of people some of which look like maids an cleanin men an such, but they is all out in this nice rose garden in the bright sunshine.

A Army guy commence to readin some kind of bullshit an everbody be listenin up keen, cept for me, on account of I is starvin since we has not had our breakfast yet. Finally the Army guy is thru an then the President come up to me an take the medal out of a box an pin it on my chest. Then he shake my han an all these people start takin pichers an clappin an such as that.

I figger it is over then, an we can get the hell out of there, but the President, he still standin there, lookin at me kind of funny. Finally he say, "Boy, is that your stomach that is growlin like that?"

I glance over at Colonel Gooch but he jus roll his eyes up, an so I nod, an say, "Uh, huh," an the President say, "Well, c'mon boy, lets go an git us somethin to eat!"

I foller him inside an we go into a little roun room an the President tell a guy who is dressed up like a waiter to bring me some breakfast. It jus the two of us in there, an wile we is waitin for the breakfast he start axin me questions, such as do I know why we is fightin the gooks an all, an is they treatin us right in the Army. I jus nod my head an after a wile he stop axin me questions an they is this kind of silence an then he say, "Do you want to watch some television wile we is waitin for your food?"

I nod my head again, an the President turn on a tv set behin his desk an we watch "The Beverly Hillbillies." The President is most amused an say he watches it ever day an that I sort of remin him of Jethro. After breakfast, the President axe me if I want him to show me aroun the house, an I say, "Yeah," an off we go. When we get outside, all them photographer fellers are followin us aroun an then the President decide to set down on a little bench an he say to me, "Boy, you was wounded, wasn't you?" an I nod, an then he say, "Well, look at this," an he pull up his shirt an show me a big ole scar on his stomach where he has had an operation of some kind, an he axe, "Where was you wounded?" an so I pull down my pants an show him. Well, all them photographer fellers rush up an start to take pichers, an several folks come runnin over an I am hustled away to where Colonel Gooch is waitin.

That afternoon back at our hotel, Colonel Gooch suddenly come bustin into my room with a hanful of newspapers an boy is he mad. He begun hollerin an cussin at me an flung the papers down on my bed an there I am, on the front page, showin my big ass an the President is showin his scar. One of the papers has drawn a little black mask over my eyes so they can't recognize me, like they do with dirty pitchers.

The caption say, "President Johnson and War Hero Relaxing in the Rose Garden."

"Gump, you idiot!" Colonel Gooch say. "How could you do this to me? I am ruint. My career is probly finished!"

"I dunno," I says, "but I am tryin to do the right thing."

Anyhow, after that I be in the doghouse again, but they has not give up on me yet. The Army have decided that I will go on the recruitment tour to try to get fellers to sign up for the war, an Colonel Gooch has gotten somebody to write up a speech that they expect me to make. It is a long speech, an filled with such things as "In time of crisis, nothin is more honorable an patriotic than to serve your country in the Armed Forces," an a whole bunch of shit like that. Trouble was, I could not never get the speech learnt. Oh, I could see all the words in my head okay, but when it come time to say it, everthin get all muddled up.

Colonel Gooch is beside hissef. He make me stay up till almost midnight ever day, tryin to get the speech right, but finally he thowed up his hans an say, "I can see this is not gonna work."

Then he come up with a idea. "Gump," he say, "here's what we is gonna do. I am gonna cut this speech shorter, an so all you will have to do is say a few things. Let us try that."

Well, he cut it shorter an shorter an shorter, till he is finally satisfied that I can remember the speech an not look like a idiot. In the end, all I have got to say is "Join the Army an fight for your freedom."

Our first stop on the tour is a little college an they have got some reporters and photographers there, an we is in a big auditorium up on the stage. Colonel Gooch get up an he begin givin the speech I done sposed to have made. When he is thru, he say, "An now, we will have a few remarks from the latest Congressional Medal of Honor winner, P.F.C. Forrest Gump," an he motion for me to come forward. Some people are clappin, an when they stop, I lean forward an say, "Join the Army an fight for your freedom."

I reckon they be expectin somethin more, but that's all I been tole to say, so I jus stand there, everbody lookin at me, me lookin back at them. Then all of a sudden somebody in the front shout out, "What do you think of the war?" an I say the first thing that come into my mind, which is, "It is a bunch of shit."

Colonel Gooch come an grapped the microphone away from me an set me back down, but all the reporters be scribblin in they notebooks an the photographers be takin pichers, an everbody in the audience goin wild, jumpin up an down an cheerin. Colonel Gooch get me out of there pronto, an we be in the car drivin fast out of town, an the colonel ain't sayin nothin to me, but he is talkin to hissef an laughin this weird, nutty little laugh.

Next mornin we is in a hotel ready to give our second speech on the tour when the phone ring. It is for Colonel Gooch. Whoever on the other end of the line seem to be doin all the talkin, an the colonel is doin the listenin an sayin "Yessir" a whole lot, an ever so often he is glarin over at me. When he finally put the phone down, he be starin at his shoes an he say, "Well, Gump, now you has done it. The tour is canceled, I have been reassigned to a weather station in Iceland, an I do not know or care what is to become of your sorry ass." I axed Colonel Gooch if we could get ourselfs a Co'Cola now, an he jus look at me for a minute, then start that talkin to hissef again an laughin that weird, nutty laugh.

They sent me to Fort Dix after that, an assign me to the Steam Heat Company. All day an haf the night I be shovelin coal into the boilers that keep the barracks warm. The company commander is a kind of ole guy who don't seem to give much of a damn bout nothin, an he say when I get there I has just got two more years left in the Army before I am discharged, an to keep my nose clean an everthin will be okay. An that is what I am tryin to do. I be thinkin a lot about my mama an bout Bubba an the little srimp bidness an Jenny Curran up at Harvard, an I am playin a little ping-pong on the side.

One day next spring there is a notice that they is gonna have a post ping-pong tournament an the winner will get to go to Washington to play for the All Army championship. I signed mysef up an it was pretty easy to win on account of the only other guy that was any good had got his fingers blowed off in the war an kep droppin his paddle.

Next week I am sent to Washington an the tournament is bein helt at Walter Reed Hospital, where all the wounded fellers can set an watch us play. I won pretty easy the first roun, an the secont too, but in the third, I have drawn a little bitty feller who puts all sorts of spin on the ball an I am havin a terrible time with him, an gettin my ass whipped. He is leadin me four games to two an it look like I am gonna lose, when all of a sudden I look over in the crowd an who should be settin there in a wheelchair but Lieutenant Dan from the hospital back at Danang!

We have a little break between games an I go over to Dan an look down at him an he ain't got no legs no more.

"They had to take them off, Forrest," he say, "but other than that, I am jus fine."

They have also taken off the bandages from his face, an he is terrible scarred an burnt from where his tank caught fire. Also, he still have a tube runnin into him from a bottle hooked onto a pole on his wheelchair.

"They say they gonna leave that like it is," Dan say. "They think it looks good on me."

Anyhow, he lean forward an look me in the eye, an say, "Forrest, I believe that you can do any damn thing you want to. I have been watchin you play, an you can beat this little guy because you play a hell of a game of ping-pong an it is your destiny to be the best."

I nod an it is time to go on back out there, an after that, I did not lose a single point, an I go on to the finals an win the whole tournament.

I was there for about three days, an Dan an me got to spend some time together. I would roll him aroun in his wheelchair, sometimes out in the garden where he could get some sun, an at night I would play my harmonica for him like I did for Bubba. Mostly, he liked to talk bout things—all sorts of things—such as history and philosophy, an one day he is talkin bout Einstein's theory of relativity, an what it mean in terms of the universe. Well, I got me a piece of paper an I drawed it out for him, the whole formula, cause it was somethin we had to do in the Intermediate Light class back at the University. He look at what I have done, an he say, "Forrest, you never cease to amaze me."

One day when I was back at Fort Dix shovelin coal in the Steam Heat Company, a feller from the Pentagon showed up with a chest full of medals an a big smile on his face, an he say, "P.F.C. Gump, it is my pleasure to inform you that you is been chosen as a member of the United States Ping-Pong Team to go to Red China an play the Chinese in ping-pong.

This is a special honor, because for the first time in nearly twenty-five years our country is having anything to do with the Chinamen, an it is an event far more important than any damn ping-pong game. It is diplomacy, and the future of the human race might be at stake. Do you understand what I am saying?"

I shrug my shoulders an nod my head, but somethin down in me sinkin fast. I am jus a po ole idiot, an now I have got the whole human race to look after.

Here I am, halfway roun the world again, this time in Peking, China.

The other people that play on the ping-pong team are real nice fellers what come from ever walk of life, an they is specially nice to me. The Chinamen is nice, too, an they is very different sorts of gooks from what I seen in Vietnam. First off, they is neat an clean an very polite. Second, they is not tryin to murder me.

The American State Department have sent a feller with us who is there to tell us how to behave aroun the Chinamen, an of all I have met, he is the only one not so nice. In fact, he is a turd. Mister Wilkins is his name, an he have a little thin moustache and always carry a briefcase an worry about whether or not his shoes is shined an his pants is pressed or his shirt is clean. I bet in the mornin he get up an spit-shines his asshole.

Mister Wilkins is always on my case. "Gump," he say, "when a Chinaman bow to you, you gotta bow back. Gump, you gotta quit adjustin yoursef in public. Gump, what are them stains on your trousers? Gump, you have got the table manners of a hog."

In that last, maybe he is right. Them Chinamen eat with two little sticks an it is almost impossible to shovel any food in your mouth with em, an so a lot of it wind up on my clothes. No wonder you do not see a lot of fat Chinamen aroun. You would think they would of learnt to use a fork by now.

Anyway, we is playin a whole lot of matches against the Chinamen an they has got some very good players. But we is holdin our own. At night they has almost always got somethin for us to do, such as go out for supper someplace, or listen to a concert. One night, we is all sposed to go out to a restaurant called the Peking Duck, an when I get down to the lobby of the hotel, Mister Wilkins say, "Gump, you has got to go back to your room an change that shirt. It look like you has been in a food fight or somethin." He take me over to the hotel desk an get a Chinaman who speak English to write a little note for me, saying in Chinese that I am goin to the Peking Duck restaurant, an tell me to give it to the cab driver.

"We are going ahead," Mister Wilkins say. "You give the driver the note an he will take you there." So I gone on back to my room an put on a new shirt.

Anyhow, I find a cab in front of the hotel an get in, an he drive away. I be searchin for the note to give him, but by the time I figger out I must of lef it in my dirty shirt, we is long gone in the middle of town. The driver keep jabberin back at me, I reckon he's axin me where I want to go, an I keep sayin, "Peking Duck, Peking Duck," but he be thowin up his hans an givin me a tour of the city.

All this go on for bout a hour, an let me tell you, I have seed some sights. Finally I tap him on the shoulder an when he turn aroun, I say, "Peking Duck," an start to flap my arms like they is ducks' wings. All of a sudden, the driver get a big ole smile, an he start noddin an drive off. Ever once in a wile he look back at me, an I start flappin my wings again. Bout a hour later, he stop an I look out the winder an damn if he ain't took me to the airport!

Well, by this time, it is gettin late, an I ain't had no dinner or nothin, an I'm gettin bout starved, so we pass this restaurant an I tole the driver to let me out. I han him a wad of this gook money they give us, an he han me some back an away he go.

I went in the restaurant an set down an I might as well of been on the moon. This lady come over an look at me real funny, an han me a menu, but it is in Chinese, so after a wile, I jus point to four or five different things an figger one of them has to be eatable. Actually, they was all pretty good. When I am thru, I paid up an went on out on the street an try to fine my way back to the hotel, but I be walkin for hours I guess, when they pick me up.

Next thing I knowed, I has been thown in jail. They is a big ole Chinaman what speak English, an he is axin me all sorts of questions an offerin me cigarettes, jus like they did in them old movies. It were the nex afternoon before they finally got me out; Mister Wilkins come down to the jail an he is talkin for bout a hour, an they let me go.

Mister Wilkins is hoppin mad. "Do you realize, Gump, that they think you are a spy?" he say. "Do you know what this can do to this whole effort? Are you crazy?"

I started to tell him, "No, I is jus a idiot," but I let it go. Anyhow, after that, Mister Wilkins buy a big balloon from a street vender an tied it on my shirt button, so he can tell where I is "at all times." Also, from then on, he pinned a note on my lapel, sayin who I was an where I am stayin. It made me feel like a fool.

One day they load us up in a bus an take us way out of town to a big river an they is a lot of Chinamen standin aroun lookin official an all, an the reason, we find out soon enough, is that the head Chinaman of them all, Chairman Mao, is there.

Chairman Mao is a big ole fat Budda-lookin guy, an he has taken off his pajaymas an is in his swimming trunks an they says Chairman Mao at the age of eighty is gonna swim this river by hissef an they want us to watch him do it.

Well, the Chairman, he wade on in an start swimming an folks is takin pichers an all them other Chinamen be chatterin away an lookin pleased. He is bout halfway cross the river, when he stop an raise his han an wave at us. Everbody wave back.

Bout a minute later, he wave again, an everbody wave back.

Not too long after that, Chairman Mao wave for a third time, an suddenly it begun to dawn on everbody that he is not waving, he is drownin!

Well, the shit done hit the fan, an I finally understan what a "Chinese Fire Drill" is. People is jumpin in the water an boats is racin out from the other side of the river an everbody on shore is cryin an leapin up an down an smackin they palms against the side of they heads. I say, the hell with this, cause I saw where he went under, an I thowed off my shoes an into the river I went. I past all the Chinamen who was swimming out there an got to the place where Chairman Mao had gone under. The boat be circlin, an people lookin over the sides like they is gonna see somethin, which was kind of silly since the river is bout the same color as sewer water back home.

Anyhow, I dived down three or four times an sure enough, I bumped into the ole bastid floatin aroun underwater. I haul him up an some Chinamen grapped him an thowed him in the boat an took off. Didn't even bother to take me along, an so's I have got to swim all the way back by mysef.

When I get to the bank, all the people there be jumpin up an down an cryin an slappin me on the back, an they pick me up an carry me on they shoulders to the bus. But when we is on the road again, Mister Wilkins come up to me an be shakin his head. "You big dumb goof," he say, "do you not realize that the best thing that could of happened for the United States was to let that sumbitch drown! You, Gump, is lost us the opportunity of a lifetime."

So I guess I done screwed up again. I dunno. I am still jus tryin to do the right thing.

We is about thru with the ping-pong games, an I have lost count of who is winnin or losin. But what has happen in the meanwhile is that on account of my pullin ole Chairman Mao out of the river, I has become sort of a national hero to the Chinamen.

"Gump," Mister Wilkins say, "your stupidity seems to have turned into an advantage. I have received a report that the Chinese envoy would like to start discussions bout the possibility of reopening foreign relations with us. Furthermore, the Chinese wish to thow you a big parade thru downtown Peking, an so I expect you to be on your good behavior."

They helt the parade two days later, an it were a sight to see. They was bout a billion Chinamen along the streets, an they was wavin an bowin an all when I went by. The thing was sposed to wind up at the Kumingtang, which is like the capitol of China, an I am sposed to get thanked by Chairman Mao personally.

When we get there, the Chairman is all dried out an glad to see me. They has put on a big spread for lunch an I get to sit nex to the Chairman hissef. In the middle of the lunch, he lean over to me an say, "I have heard you was in Vietnam. May I ask what you think of the war?" An interpreter translate that for me, an I think about it for a moment or two, but then I figger, what the hell, if he didn't want to know, he wouldn't of axed, an so I say, "I think it's a bunch of shit."

The interpreter translate that back to him, an Chairman Mao get a odd expression on his face, an look at me funny, but then his eyes light up an he break out with a big smile, an start shakin my han an noddin his head like one of them little dolls with a spring for a neck. People took pitchers of that, an afterward they was in the American newspapers. But I ain't never tole nobody till now what I said to make him smile that way.

The day we lef, we is goin out of the hotel an they is a big crowd watchin us leave an cheerin an clappin. I look over an they is this Chinese mama with a little boy on her shoulders, an I can see he is a real Mongolian idiot—eyes all crossed, tongue hangin out, droolin an babbling like them kinds of idiots do. Well, I can't hep mysef. Mister Wilkins have ordered us not to never go up to any Chinamen without first gettin his permission, but I went on over there an I got me a couple of ping-pong balls in my pocket an I take one of em out an get a pen an put my X on it an give it to the little boy. Firs thing he does is put it in his mouth, but then, when that all straightened out, he reach out an grap my fingers with his han. An then he start to smile—great big ole grin—an all of a sudden I seen tears in his mama's eyes, an she start chatterin, an our interpreter say to me that is the first time the little feller have ever smiled. They is things I could tell her, I guess, but we ain't got time.

Anyway, I start to walk away an the little boy done thowed the ping pong ball an bounce it off the back of my head. It were jus my luck that somebody got a photograph right at that moment, an, of course, it wound up in the newspapers. "Young Chinese Displays His Hatred of American Capitalists," the caption said.

Anyway, Mister Wilkins come up an drag me away an fore

I know it, we is on the plane an flyin high. Last thing he says to me afore we land back in Washington is, "Well, Gump, I spose you know about the Chinese custom that if you save a Chinaman's life, you is responsible for it forever." He have a nasty little smile on his face, an he is settin next to me on the plane an they has just tole us not to get up an to fasten our seatbelts. Well, I jus look over at him an cut the biggest fart of my life. It soun somethin like a buzz saw. Mister Wilkins' eyes bugged out an he say, "Argggg!" an start fannin the air an tryin to unloosen his seatbelt.

A pretty stewardess come runnin up to see what all the commotion is about an Mister Wilkins is coughin an choakin an all of a sudden I done started fannin the air mysef an holdin my nose an pointin at Mister Wilkins, an shoutin, "Somebody open a winder," an shit like that. Mister Wilkins, he get all red in the face an begin protestin an pointin back at me, but the stewardess, she jus smiled an gone on back to her seat.

After he quit sputterin an all, Mister Wilkins start adjustin his collar an say to me under his breath, "Gump, that was a extremely crude thing to do." But I jus grinned an looked straight ahead.

They sent me back to Fort Dix after that, but instead of puttin me in the Steam Heat Company, I am tole they is lettin me out of the Army early. It don't take but a day or so, an then I am gone. They give me some money for a ticket home, an I have got a few dollars mysef. Now I got to decide what to do.

I know I ought to go on home an see my mama, cause she's in the po house an all. I think maybe I ought to get started with the little srimp bidness, too, an begin to make somethin of my life, but all this time, in the back of my mind, I have been thinkin of Jenny Curran up at Harvard University. I got a bus to the train station, an all the way there I am tryin to

10

I did not have no address for Jenny cept a post office box, but I did have her letter with the name of the little place where she said she was playin with her band, The Cracked Eggs. It was called the Hodaddy Club. I tried to walk there from the train station, but I kep gettin lost, so I finally took a taxicab. It was in the afternoon an there was nobody in there but a couple of drunk guys an bout a half inch of beer on the floor from the night before. But they was a feller behin the bar say Jenny an them will be there bout nine o'clock. I axed if I can wait, an the guy say, "Sure," so I set down for five or six hours an took a load off my feet.

Directly, the place begun to fill up. They was mostly college-lookin kids but was dressed like geeks at a sideshow. Everbody wearin dirty blue jeans an tee shirts an all the guys had beards an wore glasses an all the girls have hair that look like a bird gonna fly out of it any secont. Presently the band come out on stage an start settin up. They is three or four fellers an they has got all this huge electric stuff, pluggin it in everwhere. It certainly is a far cry from what we done in the Student Union building back at the University. Also, I do not see Jenny Curran noplace.

After they get the electric stuff set up, they start to play, an let me say this: them people was loud! All sorts of colored lights begin to flash an the music they is makin sound sort of like a jet airplane when it takin off. But the crowd lovin it an when they is done, everbody begin to cheer an yell. Then a light fall on a side of the stage an there she is—Jenny hersef!

She is changed from the way I known her. First, she is got hair down to her ass, an is wearin sunglasses inside, at *night!* She is dressed in blue jeans an a shirt with so many spangles on it she look like a telephone switchboard. The band start up again an Jenny begun to sing. She has grapped hole of the microphone an is dancin all aroun the stage, jumpin up an down an wavin her arms an tossin her hair aroun. I am tryin to understan the words to the song, but the band is playin too loud for that, beatin on the drums, bangin on the piano, swattin them electric guitars till it seem like the roof gonna cave in. I am thinkin, what the hell is this?

After a wile they take a break an so I got up an tried to get through a door that go backstage. But they is a feller standing there who say I cannot come in. When I go walkin back to my seat, I notice everbody is starin at my Army uniform. "That is some costume you has got on there," somebody says, an somebody else say, "Far out!" an another one say, "Is he for real?"

I am beginnin to feel like a idiot again, an so I gone on outside, thinkin maybe I can walk aroun an figger things out. I guess I must of walked for haf an hour or so, an when I get back to the place they is a long line of people waitin to get in. I go up to the front an try to splain to the guy that all my stuff is in there, but he say to go wait at the end of the line. I guess I stood there a hour or so, an listened to the music comin from inside, an I have to tell you, it sounded a little better when you got away from it like that.

Anyway, after a wile, I got bored an went down a alley an roun to the back of the club. They was some little steps an I sat down there an watched the rats chasin each other in the garbage. I had my harmonica in my pocket, so's to pass the time, I got it out an started to play a little. I could still hear the music from Jenny's band, an after a wile I foun mysef bein able to play along with them, sort of usin the chromatic stop to get half out of key so it would fit in with what they was playin. I don't know how long it was, but it didn't take much afore I was able to make runs of my own, way up in C major, an to my suprise, it didn't soun half bad when you was playin it—so long as you didn't have to *listen* to it too.

All of a sudden the door behin me bust open an there is Jenny standin there. I guess they had taken their break again, but I wadn't payin no attention an had kep on playin.

"Who is that out there?" she say.

"It's me," I say, but it is dark in the alley an she stick her head out the door an say, "Who is playin that harmonica?"

I stand up an I am kind of embarrassed on account of my clothes, but I say, "It's me. Forrest."

"It is *who?*" she say.

"Forrest."

"Forrest? *Forrest Gump!*" an suddenly she rush out the door an thowed hersef into my arms.

Jenny an me, we set aroun backstage an caught up on things till she had to play her nex set. She had not exactly quit school, she had got thowed out when they foun her in a feller's room one night. That was a thowin-out offense in them days. The banjo player had run off to Canada rather than go in the Army, an the little band had broke up. Jenny had gone out to California for a wile, an weared flowers in her hair, but she say them people is a bunch of freaks who is stoned all the time, an so she met this guy an come with him to Boston, an they had done some peace marches an all, but he turned out to be a fairy, so she split up with him, an took up with a real serious peace marcher who was in to makin bombs an stuff, an blowin up buildins. That didn't work out neither, so she met up with this guy what teached at Harvard University, but it turned out he was married. Next, she went with a guy that had seemed real nice but one day he got both their asses arrested for shoplifting, an she decided it was time to pull hersef together.

She fell in with The Cracked Eggs, an they started playin a new kind of music, an got real popular aroun Boston, an they was even gonna go to New York an make a tape for an album nex week. She say she is seein this guy that goes to Harvard University, an is a student in philosophy, but that after the show tonight, I can come home an stay with them. I am very disappointed that she has got hersef a boyfrien, but I don't have noplace else to go, so that's what I done.

Rudolph is the boyfrien's name. He is a little guy bout a hundrit pounds or so, an has hair like a dustmop an wears a lot of beads aroun his neck an is settin on the floor when we get to their apartment, meditatin like a guru.

"Rudolph," Jenny say, "this is Forrest. He is a friend of mine from home, an he is gonna be stayin with us a wile."

Rudolph don't say nothin, but he wave his hand like the Pope when he is blessin somethin.

Jenny ain't got but one bed, but she made up a little pallet for me on the floor an that is where I slept. It wadn't no worse than a lot of places I slept in the Army, an a damn sight better than some.

Next mornin I get up an there is Rudolph still settin in the middle of the room meditatin. Jenny fixed me some breakfast an we lef ole Rudolph settin there an she took me on a tour of Cambridge. First thing she says is that I have got to get mysef some new clothes, on account of people up here does not understan an will think I am tryin to put them on. So we go to a surplus store an I get me some overalls an a lumber jacket an change into them right there an take my uniform in a paper bag.

We is walkin aroun Harvard University, an who does Jenny run into but the married professor she used to date. She is still friends with him, even tho in private she like to refer to him as a "degenerate turd." Doctor Quackenbush is his name.

Anyway, he is all excited on account of he is beginnin to teach a new course next week that he thunk up all by hissef. It is called the "Role of the Idiot in World Literature."

I pipe up an say I think it sounds pretty interestin, an he say, "Well, Forrest, why don't you sit in on the class? You might enjoy it."

Jenny look at both of us kind of funny-like, but she don't say nothin. We gone on back to the apartment an Rudolph is still squattin on the floor by hissef. We was in the kitchen an I axed her real quiet if Rudolph could talk, an she say, yes, sooner or later.

That afternoon Jenny took me to meet the other guys in the band an she tell them I play the harmonica like heaven itsef, an why don't they let me set in with them at the club tonight. One of the guys axe me what I like to play best, an I say, "Dixie," an he say he don't believe he has heard what I say, an Jenny jump in an say, "It don't matter, he will be fine once he's got a ear for our stuff."

So that night I be playin with the band an everybody agree I am makin a good contribution an it is very enjoyable, gettin to set there an watch Jenny sing an thow hersef all over the stage.

That nex Monday I have decided to go ahead an set in on Doctor Quackenbush's class, "Role of the Idiot in World Literature." The title alone is enough to make me feel sort of important.

"Today," Doctor Quackenbush says to the class, "we has a visitor who is gonna be auditing this course from time to time. Please welcome Mister Forrest Gump." Everbody turn an look at me an I give a little wave, an then the class begin.

"The idiot," Doctor Quackenbush say, "has played an important role in history an literature for many years. I suppose you has all heard of the village idiot, who was usually some retarded individual livin in a village someplace. He was often the object of scorn an mockery. Later, it become the custom of nobility to have in their presence a court jester, a sort of person that would do things to amuse the royalty. In many instances, this individual was actually an idiot or a moron, in others, he was merely a clown or jokester. . . ."

He go on like this for a wile, an it begun to become apparent to me that idiots was not jus useless people, but was put here for a purpose, sort of like Dan had said, an the purpose is to make people laugh. At least that is somethin.

"The object of having a fool for most writers," Doctor Quackenbush say, "is to employ the device of *double entendre,* permittin them to let the fool make a fool of hisself, an at the same time allow the reader the revelation of the greater meaning of the foolishness. Occasionally, a great writer like Shakespeare would let the fool make an ass out of one of his principal characters, thereby providing a twist for the readers' enlightenment."

At this point, I am becomin somewhat confused. But that is normal. Anyhow, Mister Quackenbush say that to demonstrate what he has been talkin about, we is gonna do a scene from the play, *King Lear,* where there is a fool an a madman in disguise an the king hisself is crazy. He tells this guy named Elmer Harrington III to play the part of Mad Tom o'Bedlam, an for this girl called Lucille to play The Fool. Another guy called Horace somebody was to be crazy ole King Lear. An then he say, "Forrest, why doesn't you play the role of the Earl of Gloucester?"

Mister Quackenbush say he will get a few stage props from the drama department, but he want us to get up our own costumes, just so the thing would be more "realistic." How I got into this deal, I do not know, is what I am thinkin.

Meantime, things is happenin with our band, The Cracked Eggs. A feller from New Yawk have flown up an listened to us an says he wants to get us in a recordin studio an make a tape of our music. All the fellers is excited, includin Jenny Curran, an me, of course. The feller from New Yawk, Mister Feeblestein is his name. He say if everthing go well, we could be the hottest thing since the invention of night baseball. Mister Feeblestein say all we got to do is sign a piece of paper an then start gettin rich.

George, the guy who plays keyboard for us, has been teachin me a little bit of how to play it, an Mose, the drummer, is also lettin me beat on his drums some. It is kind of fun, learnin how to play all them things, an my harmonica too. Ever day I practice some, an ever night the band play at the Hodaddy Club.

Then one afternoon I come home from class an there is Jenny settin by hersef on the couch. I axed her where is Rudolph, an she say he has "split." I axed what for, an she say, "Cause he is a nogood bastid like all the rest," an so I says, "Why don't we go out an get ourselfs some supper an talk bout it?"

Naturally, she does most of the talkin, an it is really jus a string of gripes bout men. She say we are "lazy, unresponsible, selfish, low-down lyin shits." She is goin on that way for a wile an then she start to cry. I says, "Awe, Jenny, don't do that. It ain't nothin. That ole Rudolph didn't look like the kinda feller for you no how, squattin on the floor like that an all." An she say, "Yes, Forrest, probly you is right. I'd like to go home now." An so we do.

When we get home, Jenny begun takin off her clothes. She is down to her underpants, an I am jus settin on the couch tryin not to notice, but she come up an stand in front of me an she say, "Forrest, I want you to fuck me now."

You coulda knocked me over with a feather! I jus set there an gawked up at her. Then she set down nex to me an started foolin with my britches, an nex thing I knowed, she'd got off my shirt an was huggin an kissin me an all. At first, it was jus a little odd, her doin all that. Course I had dreamed bout it all along, but I had not expected it quite this way. But then, well I guess somethin come over me, an it didn't matter what I'd expected, cause we was rollin aroun on the couch an had our clothes nearly off an then Jenny pulled down my undershorts an her eyes get big an she say, "Whooo—lookit what you got there!" an she grapped me jus like Miz French had that day, but Jenny never say nothin about me keepin my eyes closed, so I didn't.

Well, we done all sorts of things that afternoon that I never even dreamt of in my wildest imagination. Jenny shown me shit I never could of figgered out on my own—sidewise, crosswise, upside down, bottomwise, lengthwise, dogwise, standin up, settin down, bendin over, leanin back, inside-out an outside-in—only way we didn't try it was apart! We rolled all over the livin room an into the kitchen—stove in furniture, knocked shit over, pulled down drapes, mussed up the rug an even turned the tv set on by accident. Wound up doin it in the sink, but don't axe me how. When we is finally finished, Jenny jus lie there a wile, an then she look at me an say, "Goddamn, Forrest, where is you *been* all my life?"

"I been aroun," I says.

Naturally, things are a bit different between Jenny an me after that. We commenced to sleep in the same bed together, which was also kind of strange for me at first, but I sure got used to it. When we was doin our act at the Hodaddy Club, ever so often Jenny would pass by me an muss up my hair, or run her fingers down the back of my neck. All of a sudden things start to change for me—like my whole life jus begun, an I am the happiest feller in the world.

11

The day arrived when we is to give our little play in Professor Quackenbush's class at Harvard. The scene we is to do is when King Lear an his fool go out onto the heath, which is like a marsh or a field back home, an a big storm done blowed up an everbody run into a shack called a "hovel."

Inside the hovel there is a guy called Mad Tom o'Bedlam who is actually a character name of Edgar disguised up as a crazy person on account of being fucked over by his brother, who is a bastid. Also, the king is gone totally nuts by this time, an Edgar is playin a nut too, an the fool, of course, is actin like one. My part is to be the Earl of Gloucester, who is Edgar's father, an sort of a straight man for them other stooges.

Professor Quackenbush have rigged up a ole blanket or somethin to resemble a hovel an he has got some kind of wind machine to sound like a storm—big electric fan with clothespins holdin pieces of paper to the blades. Anyway, here come Elmer Harrington III as King Lear, dressed in a gunnysack an wearin a colander on his head. The girl they got to play the fool has foun a fool's costume someplace, with a little cap that has bells tied to it, an them kinds of shoes that curl up in front like Arabs wear. The guy playin Tom o'Bedlam has foun hissef a Beatle wig an some clothes out of the garbage an has painted his face with dirt. They is takin it all very seriously.

I am probly the best-lookin of the bunch, tho, cause Jenny done set down an sewed me up a costume out of a sheet an a pillow case that I am wearin like a diaper, an she has also made me a cape out of a tablecloth, just like Superman wears.

Anyway, Professor Quackenbush start up his wind machine an say for us to begin at page twelve, where Mad Tom is tellin us his sad story.

"Do poor Tom some charity, whom the foul fiend vexes," Tom say.

An King Lear say, "What? Have his daughters brought him to this pass? Couldst thou save nothing? Didst thou give them all?"

An the fool say, "Nay, he reserved a blanket, else we had all been shamed."

This shit go on for a wile, then the fool say, "This cold night will turn us all to fools and madmen."

In this, the fool is correct.

Just bout this time, I am sposed to enter into the hovel carrying a torch, which Professor Quackenbush have borrowed from the drama department. The fool call out, "Look! Here come a walking fire!" an Professor Quackenbush light my torch an I go across the room into the hovel.

"This is the foul fiend Flibbertigibbet," Tom o'Bedlam say.

"What's he?" the king axes.

An I say, "What are you there? Your names?"

Mad Tom say he is jus "Po Tom, that eats the swimmin frawg, the toad, the tadpole and the newt . . ." an a bunch of other shit, an then I sposed to suddenly recognize the king, an say:

"What! Hath your grace no better company?"

An Mad Tom, he answer, "The prince of darkness is a gentleman—Modo he's call'd, and Mahu."

The wind machine be blowin hard now, an I reckon Professor Quackenbush have not considered that I am six feet six inches tall when he built the hovel, cause the top of my torch is bumpin against the ceiling.

Mad Tom, he is now sposed to say, "Poor Tom's a-cold," but instead, he say, "Watch that torch!"

I look down at my book to see where that line come from, an Elmer Harrington III say to me, "Look out for that torch, you idiot!" an I say back to him, "For once in my life I am not the idiot—*you* is!" An then all of a sudden the roof to the hovel catch on fire an fall on Mad Tom's Beatle wig an set it on fire too.

"Turn off the goddamn wind machine!" somebody shout, but it is too late. Everthing burning up!

Mad Tom is hollerin an yellin an King Lear take off his colander an jam it on Mad Tom's head to put the fire out. People is jumpin aroun an choakin an coughin an cussin an the girl playin the fool gets hysterical an commence to shriek an cry, "We will all be kilt!" For a moment or two, it actually looks that way.

I turn behin me, an damn if my cape ain't caught on fire, an so I thowed open the winder an grapped the fool aroun her waist an out we leaped. It was only from the secont story winder, an they was a bunch of shrubs down there that broke our fall, but it was also lunchtime an hundrits of people was wanderin aroun the Yard. There we was, all a-fire an smolderin.

Black smoke come pourin from up in the open winder of the class an all of a sudden there is Professor Quackenbush, leanin out an lookin aroun, shakin his fist, face all covered up with soot.

"Gump, you fuckin idiot—you stupid asshole! You will pay for this!" he shoutin.

The fool is grovelin aroun on the groun an bawlin an wringing her hans but she is okay—just singed up a bit—so I just took off—bounded across the Yard fast as I could run, cape still on fire, smoke trailin behin me. I didn't stop till I got home, an when I get into the apartment, Jenny say, "Oh, Forrest, how was it? I bet you was wonderful!" Then she get a peculiar look on her face. "Say, do you smell somethin burnin?" she axes.

"It is a long story," I say.

Anyhow, after that I did not attend the "Role of the Idiot in World Literature" no more, as I have seen quite enough. But ever night I an Jenny are playin with The Cracked Eggs an all day long we is makin love an takin walks an havin picnics on the banks of the Charles River an it is heaven. Jenny has written a nice tender song called "Do It to Me Hard an Fast," in which I get to take bout a five-minute ride on my harmonica. It were a splendid spring an summer, an we went down to New Yawk an made the tapes for Mister Feeblestein an a few weeks later he call up to say we is gonna have a record album. Not too long after that, everbody be callin us up to play in their towns an we took the money we got from Mister Feeblestein an bought us a big bus with beds an shit in it an go on the road.

Now there is somethin else durin that period that played a great role in my life. One night after we is finished the first set at the Hodaddy Club, Mose, the drummer for The Cracked Eggs, take me aside an say, "Forrest, you is a nice clean-cut feller an all, but they is somethin I want you to try that I think will make you play that harmonica better."

I axe what it is, an Mose say, "Here," an he give me a little cigarette. I tell him I don't smoke, but thanks, an Mose say, "It is not a regular cigarette, Forrest. It have got somethin in it to expand your horizons."

I tole Mose I ain't sure I need my horizons expanded, but he sort of insisted. "At least try it," he say, an I thought for a minute, an conclude that one cigarette ain't gonna hurt none, an so I do.

Well let me say this: my horizons indeed become expanded.

Everthing seem to slow down an get rosy keen. That secont set we played that night was the best of my life, I seemed to hear all the notes a hundrit times as I was playin them, an Mose come up to me later an say, "Forrest, you think *that's* good—use it when you're screwin."

I did, an he was right bout that too. I used some of my money to buy me some of that stuff, an before you know it, I was doin it day in an day out. The only problem was, it kind of made me stupider after a wile. I just get up in the mornin an light up one of them joints, which is what they called them, an lie there all day till it was time to go an play. Jenny didn't say nothin for a wile, cause she been known to take a puff or two hersef, but then one day she say to me, "Forrest, don't you think you been doin too much of that shit?"

"I dunno," I says, "how much is too much?"

An Jenny say, "As much as you are doin is too much."

But I didn't want to stop. Somehow, it got rid of everthing I might be worried bout, tho there wadn't too much of that at that time anyway. At night I'd go out between sets at the Hodaddy Club an set in the little alley an look up at the stars. If they weren't any stars, I'd look up anyway, an one night Jenny come out an find me lookin up at the rain.

"Forrest, you has got to quit this," she say. "I am worried bout you, cause you ain't doin nothin cept playin an lyin aroun all day. It ain't healthy. I think you need to get away for a wile. We ain't got no concerts booked after tomorrow down in Provincetown, so I think maybe we ought to go someplace an take a vacation. Go up to the mountains maybe."

I jus nod my head. I ain't even sure I heard all she said.

Well, the nex night in Provincetown, I find the backstage exit an go on outside to lite up a joint. I am settin there by mysef, mindin my business, when these two girls come up. One of them say, "Hey, ain't you the harmonica player with The Cracked Eggs?"

I nod yes, an she jus plop hersef down in my lap. The other girl is grinnin an squealin an suddenly she take off her blouse. An the other girl is tryin to unzip my pants an have her skirt pulled up an I am jus settin there blowed away. Suddenly the stage door open an Jenny call out, "Forrest, it is time to . . ." an she stop for a secont an then she say, "Awe shit," an slam the door.

I jumped up then, an the girl in my lap felled on the groun an the other one is cussin an all, but I went inside an there is Jenny leaned up against the wall cryin. I went up to her but she say, "Keep away from me, you shithead! You men is all alike, jus like dogs or somethin—you got no respect for anybody!"

I ain't never felt so bad. I don't remember much bout that last set we played. Jenny went up to the front of the bus on the trip back an wouldn't speak to me none at all. That night she slep on the sofa an the nex mornin she say maybe it is time for me to find my own place. An so I packed up my shit an left. My head hangin very low. Couldn't explain it to her or nothin. Thowed out again.

Jenny, she took off someplace after that. I axed aroun, but nobody knowed where she was. Mose say I can bunk with him till I find a place, but it is a terrible lonely time. Since we ain't playin none for the moment, there ain't nothin much to do, an I be thinkin maybe it's time I go on back home an see my mama an maybe start up that little srimp bidness down where po ole Bubba used to live. Perhaps I is not cut out to be a rock an roll star. Perhaps, I think, I ain't nothin but a bumblin idiot anyhow.

But then one day Mose come back an he say he was over to a saloon on the corner watchin the tv news, an who should he see but Jenny Curran.

She is down in Washington, he say, marchin in a big demonstration against the Vietnam War, an Mose say he wonderin why she botherin with that shit when she ought to be up here makin us money.

I say I has got to go see her, an Mose say, "Well, see if you can bring her back." He say he knows where she probly is stayin, on account of they is this group from Boston that has taken an apartment in Washington to demonstrate against the war.

I packed up all my shit—everthin I own—an thanked Mose an then I am on my way. Whether I come back or not, I do not know.

When I get down to Washington, everthin is a mess. They is police everwhere an people be shoutin in the streets an thowin things like in a riot. Police be bongin folks on the head what thow things, an the situation look like it be gettin out of han.

I find the address of the place Jenny might be at, an go over there, but ain't nobody home. I waited on the steps for most of the day, then, bout nine o'clock at night, a car pull up an some folks get out an there she is!

I get up from the steps an walk towards her, but she turn away from me an run back to the car. Them other people, two guys an a girl, they didn't know what to do, or who I was, but then one of them say, "Look, I wouldn't fool with her right now—she is awful upset." I axed why, an the feller take me aside an tell me this:

Jenny has done jus got out of jail. She have been arrested the day before, an spent the night in the women's jail, an this mornin, fore anybody could get her out, the people at the jail done said she might have lice or somethin in her hair cause it so long an all, an they had all her hair shaved off. Jenny is bald.

Well, I reckon she don't want me to see her this way, cause she has done got into the back seat of the car an is lyin down. So I crawled up on my hans an knees so I couldn't see in the winder, an I say, "Jenny—it's me, Forrest."

She don't say nothing, so I start tellin her how sorry I am bout what's happened. I tell her I ain't gonna smoke no more dope, nor play in the band no more on account of all the bad temptations. An I say I'm sorry bout her hair. Then I crawled back to the steps where my shit is, an looked in my duffelbag an find a ole watch cap from the Army an crawled back to the car an stuck it on a stick an polked it thru the winder. She took it, an put it on, an come out of the car, an say, "Awe get up off the groun you big Bozo, an come into the house."

We set an talked for a wile, an them other people been smokin dope an drinkin beer, but I ain't havin none. They is all discussin what they is gonna do tomorrow, which is that they is a big demonstration at the U.S. Capitol at which a bunch of Vietnam veterans is gonna take off they medals an thow them on the steps of the Capitol.

An Jenny suddenly say, "Do you know Forrest here done won the Congressional Medal of Honor?" An everbody get completely quiet an be lookin at me, an then at each other, an one of them say, "Jesus Christ have just sent us a present!"

Well, the next mornin, Jenny come into the livin room where I is sleepin on the sofa an say, "Forrest, I want you to go with us today, an I want you to wear your Army uniform." When I axed why, she say, "Because you is gonna do somethin to stop all the sufferin over in Vietnam." An so I get into my uniform, an Jenny come back after a wile with a bunch of chains she has bought at the hardware store, an say, "Forrest, wrap these aroun you."

I axed why again, but she say, "Just do it, you will find out later. You want to make me happy, doesn't you?"

An so off we went, me in my uniform an the chains an Jenny an the other folks. It is a bright clear day an when we get to the Capitol they is a mob there with tv cameras an all the police in the world. Everbody be chantin an hollerin an givin the finger to the police. After a wile, I seen some other guys in Army uniforms an they was bunched together an then, one by one, they commenced to walk as close as they can get to the steps of the Capitol an they took off they medals an thowed them. Some of the fellers was in wheelchairs an some was lame an some was missing arms an legs. Some of them jus tossed they medal on to the steps, but others really thowed them hard. Somebody tap me on the shoulder an say it is my turn now. I look back at Jenny an she nod, so I go on up there mysef.

It get sort of quiet, then somebody on a bullhorn announce my name, an say I is gonna thow away the Congressional Medal of Honor as a token of my support for endin the Vietnam War. Everbody cheer an clap, an I can see the other medals lyin there on the steps. High above all this, up on the porch of the Capitol, is a little bunch of people standin aroun, couple of cops an some guys in suits. Well, I figger I gotta do the best I can, so I take off the medal an look at it for a secon, an I be rememberin Bubba an all, an Dan, an I dunno, somethin come over me, but I got to thow it, so I rare back an heave that medal hard as I can. Couple of seconts later, one of the guys on the porch that is wearin a suit, he jus keel over. Unfortunately, I done thowed the medal too far an knocked him in the head with it.

All hell break loose then. Police be chargin into the crowd an people be shoutin all sorts of things an tear gas bust open an suddenly five or six police pounced on me an commence knockin me with they billy sticks. A bunch more police come runnin up an nex thing you know, I am handcuffed an thowed in a police wagon an hauled off to jail.

I am in jail all night long, an in the mornin they come an take me in front of the judge. I has been there before.

Somebody tell the judge that I is accused of "assault with a dangerous weapon—a medal—an resistin arrest," an so on an han him a sheet of paper. "Mister Gump," the judge say, "do you realize that you have conked the Clerk of the U.S. Senate on the head with your medal?"

I ain't sayin nothin, but it look like I am in serious trouble this time.

"Mister Gump," the judge say, "I do not know what a man of your stature, a man what has served his country so well, is doin mixed up with a bunch of tuity-fruities that is thowin away their medals, but I will tell you what, I is gonna order you committed for psychiatric observation for thirty days to see if they can figger out why you has done such a idiotic thing."

They took me back to my cell after that, an a wile later load me on a bus an truck me off to St. Elizabeth's mental hospital.

Finally, I am "Put Away."

12

This place is a serious loony bin. They put me in a room with a feller called Fred that has been here for almost a year. He begun to tell me right off what kind of nuts I got to contend with. They is one guy that poisoned six people, somebody else that used a meat cleaver on his mama. They is people who have done all sorts of shit—from murder an rape to sayin they is the King of Spain or Napoleon. Finally I axed Fred why he is in here an he say because he is a axe murderer, but they is lettin him out in another week or so.

The secont day I am there, I is tole to report to the office of my psychiatrist, Doctor Walton. Doctor Walton, it turn out, is a woman. First, she say, she is gonna give me a little test, then I is gonna have a physical examination. She set me down at a table an start showin me cards with ink blots on them, axin me what I thought they were. I kep sayin "ink blot" till she finally get mad an tell me I got to say somethin else, an so I started makin things up. Then I am handed a long test an tole to take it. When I am done, she say, "Take off your clothes."

Well, with one or two exceptions, ever time I take off my clothes, somethin bad happen to me, so I says I would rather not, an she make a note of this an then tell me either I do it mysef, or she will get the attendants to hep me. It was that kind of deal.

I go on an do it, an when I is butt neckid, she come into the room an look at me, up an down, an say, "My, my—you is a fine specimen of a man!"

Anyhow, she start bongin me on the knee with a little rubber hammer like they done back at the University, an polkin me in all sorts of places. But she ain't never said for me to "bend over," an for this I am grateful. Afterward, she say I can get dressed an go back to my room. On the way there, I past by a room with a glass door an inside it they is a bunch of little guys, settin an lyin aroun, droolin an spasmoin an beatin on the floor with they fists. I jus stood there for a wile, lookin in, an I'm feelin real sorry for them—kinda remind me of my days back at the nut school.

A couple of days later, I am tole to report to Doctor Walton's office again. When I get there, she is with two other guys dressed up as doctors, an she say they is Doctor Duke and Doctor Earl—both with the National Institute of Mental Health. An they is very interested in my case, she say.

Doctor Duke an Doctor Earl set me down an start axin me questions—all kinds of questions—an both of them took turns bongin me on the knees with the hammer. Then Doctor Duke say, "Look here, Forrest, we has got your test scores, an it is remarkable how well you is done on the math part. So we would like to give you some other tests. They produce the tests, an make me take them, an they is a lot more complicated than the first one, but I figger I done okay. Had I knowed what was gonna happen nex, I would of fucked them up.

"Forrest," Doctor Earl say, "this is phenomenal. You is got

a brain jus like a computer. I do not know how well you can reason with it—which is probly why you is in here in the first place—but I have never seen anything quite like this before."

"You know, George," Doctor Duke say, "this man is truly remarkable. I have done some work for NASA a wile back, an I think we ought to send him down to Houston to the Aeronautics and Space Center an have them check him out. They has been lookin for just this sort of feller."

All the doctors be starin at me, an noddin they heads, an then they bonged me on the knees with a hammer one more time an it look like here I go again.

They flown me down to Houston, Texas, in a big ole plane with nobody on it but me an Doctor Duke, but it is a pleasant sort of trip cept they got me chained to my seat han an foot.

"Look here, Forrest," Doctor Duke say, "the deal is this. Right now you is in a shitpot of trouble for thowin that medal at the Clerk of the U.S. Senate. You can go to jail for ten years for that. But if you cooperates with these people at NASA, I will personally see to it that you is released—okay?"

I nod my head. I knowed I got to get outta jail an find Jenny again. I am missin her somethin terrible.

I am at the NASA place at Houston for about a month. They has examined me an tested me an questioned me so much I feel like I am goin on the Johnny Carson show.

I ain't.

One day they haul me into a big room an tell me what they has in mind.

"Gump," they say, "we wants to use you on a flight to outer space. As Doctor Duke has pointed out, your mind is jus like a computer—only better. If we can program it with the right stuff, you will be extremely useful to America's space program. What do you say?"

I thought for a minute, an then I says I had better axe my

mama first, but they make an even stronger argument—like spendin the next ten years of my life in the slammer.

An so I says yes, which is usually what gets me in trouble ever time.

The idea they has thought up is to put me in a spaceship an shoot me up aroun the earth bout a million miles. They has already shot people up to the moon, but they didn't find nothin there worth a shit, so what they is plannin nex is a visit to Mars. Fortunately for me, Mars is not what they got in mind at the moment—instead, this is to be a sort of trainin mission in which they gonna try to figger out what kind of folks would be suited best for the Mars trip.

Besides me, they has picked a woman an a ape to go along.

The woman is a crabby-lookin lady called Major Janet Fritch, who is sposed to be America's first woman astronaut, only nobody knows bout her cause all this be pretty top secret. She is a sort of short lady with hair look like it been cut by puttin a bowl over her head, an she don't seem to have much use for either me or the ape.

The ape ain't so bad, actually. It is a big ole female orang-utang called Sue, what has been captured in the jungles of Sumatra or someplace. Actually they has got a whole bunch of them apes down here, an have been shootin them up into space for a long wile, but they says Sue will be best on this trip on account of she is a female an will be friendlier than a male ape, an also, this will be her third space flight. When I find this out, I am wonderin how come they gonna send us way up there with the only experienced crew member bein a ape. Kind of makes you think, don't it?

Anyhow, we got to go thru all kinds of trainin before the flight. They puttin us in cyclotrons an spinnin us aroun, an in little rooms with no gravity an such as that. An all day long they be crammin my mind with shit they want me to remember, such as equations to figger the distance between wherever we is, an wherever they want us to go, an how to get back again; all kinds of crap like coaxiel coordinates, co sine computations, spheriod trigonometry, Boolean algebra, antilogarithms, Fourier analysis, quadrats an matrix math. They say I is to be the "backup" for the backup computer.

I have writ a bunch of letters to Jenny Curran but all of them done come back "Addressee not Known." Also I done wrote to my mama, an she send me back a long letter the gist of which is "How can you do this to your po ole mama when she is in the po house an you is all she got lef in the world?"

I dared not tell her that I am facin a jail sentence if I don't, so I jus write her back an say not to worry, on account of we has an experienced crew.

Well, the big day finally come, an let me say this: I am not jus a little bit nervous—I am scarit haf to death! Even tho it was top secret, the story done leaked to the press and now we gonna be on tv an all.

That mornin, somebody brung us the newspapers to show us how famous we was. Here is some of the headlines:

"Woman, Ape and Idiot in Next U.S. Space Effort."

"America Launching Odd Messengers Toward Alien Planets."

"Girl, Goon, and Gorilla to Lift Off Today."

There was even one in the New Yawk *Post* that say, "Up They Go—But Who's in Charge?"

The only one that sounded halfway nice was the headline in the New Yawk *Times,* which say, "New Space Probe Has Varied Crew."

Well, as usual, everthing is all confusion from the minute we get up. We go to get our breakfast an somebody say, "They ain't sposed to eat no breakfast the day of the flight." Then somebody else say, "Yes we is," an then somebody else say, "No they ain't," an it go on like that for a wile till ain't nobody hungry anymore.

They get us into our space suits an take us out there to the launchin pad in a little bus with ole Sue ridin in back in a cage. The spaceship is about a hundrit stories tall an is all foamin an hissin an steamin an look like it bout to eat us alive! A elevator take us to the capsule we is to be in, an they strap us in an load ole Sue in her place in back. Then we wait.

An we wait some more.

An we wait some more.

An we wait some more.

All along, the spaceship be boilin an hissin an growlin an steamin. Somebody say a hundrit million people out there watchin us on television. I reckon they be waitin too.

Anyhow, bout noon, somebody come up an knock on the spaceship door an say, we is temporarily cancelin this mission till they get the spaceship fixed.

So we all get to go back down in the elevator again, me, Sue, an Major Fritch. She be the only one moanin an bitchin, cause Sue an me is very relieved.

Our relief was not to last long, however. Bout a hour later somebody run into the room where we is jus about to set down to lunch an say, "Get in your space suits again right now! They is fixin to shoot you up in space!"

Everbody be hollerin an shoutin again an rushin aroun. I reckon maybe a bunch of the tv viewers have called in to complain or somethin, an so they decided to lite that fire under our asses no matter what. Whatever it is, it don't matter now.

Anyhow, we is put back on the bus an taken to the spaceship an we is halfway up the elevator when somebody suddenly say, "Jesus, we forgot the goddamn ape!" an he start hollerin down to the fellers on the groun to go back an get ole Sue.

We is strapped in again an somebody is countin backwards from one hundrit when they come thru the door with Sue. We is all leaned back in our seats an the count is down to about "ten," when I be hearin some strange growlin noises from behin us where Sue is. I sort of turned aroun, an low an behole, it ain't Sue settin there at all, it is a big ole *male* ape, what got his teeth bared an is grappin holt of his seatbelt straps like he is about to bust loose any secont!

I tell Major Fritch an she look aroun an say, "Oh my God!" an get on the radio to whoever it is in the groun control tower. "Listen," she say, "you has made a mistake an put one of them male apes in here with us, so we better call this thing off till it is straightened out." But all of a sudden the spaceship start to rumblin an quakin an the guy in the control tower says over the radio, "That's *your* problem now, sister, we got a schedule to meet."

An away we go.

13

My first impression is of bein squashed under somethin, such as my daddy was when them bananas fell on him. Can't move, can't yell, can't say nothin, can't do nothin—we is strictly here for the ride. Outside, lookin thru the winder, all I can see is blue sky. The spaceship is movin out.

After a little wile, we seem to slow down some, an things ease up. Major Fritch say we can unbuckle our seatbelts now, an get on bout our bidness, whatever it is. She say we is now travelin at a speed of fifteen thousan miles a hour. I look back an sure enough, the earth is only a little ball behin us, jus like it look in all them pichers from outer space. I look aroun, an there's the big ole ape, all sour-lookin, an glum, glarin at Major Fritch an me. She say maybe he want his lunch or somethin, an for me to go on back there an give him a banana afore he gets angry an does somethin bad.

They has packed a little bag of food for the ape an it contain bananas an some cereals an dried berries an leaves an shit like that. I get it open an start rummagin thru it lookin for somethin that will make the ape happy, an meantime, Major Fritch is on the radio with Houston Groun Control.

"Now listen here," she say, "we has got to do somethin bout this ape. It ain't Sue—it is a male ape, an he don't look none to glad to be here. He might even be violent."

It took a wile for the message to get there an a reply to get back to us, but some feller down there say, "Awe pooh! One ape is jus like any other."

"The hell it is," Major Fritch say. "If you was in this little bitty compartment with that big ole thing you would be singing a different tune."

An after a minute or two a voice come cracklin over the radio, say, "Look, you is ordered not to tell anybody about this, or we will all be made laughing-stocks. As far as you or anybody else is concerned, that ape is Sue—no matter what it's got between its legs."

Major Fritch look at me an shake her head. "Aye, aye, sir," she say, "but I'm gonna keep that fucker strapped in as long as I'm in here with him—you understand that?"

An from the ground control there come back one word: "Roger."

Actually, after you get used to it, bein in outer space is kind of fun. We is without gravity, an so can float all over the spaceship, an the scenery is remarkable—moon an sun, earth an stars. I wonder where Jenny Curran is down there, an what she is doin.

Aroun an aroun the earth we go. Day an night go by ever hour or so an it sort of put a different perspective on things. I mean, here I am doin this, an when I get back—or should I say *if* I get back—what then? Go an start up my little srimp-growin bidness? Go find Jenny again? Play in The Cracked Eggs? Do somethin about my mama bein in the po house? It is all very strange.

Major Fritch be catchin a wink or two of sleep whenever

she can, but when she ain't sleepin, she is bitchin. Crabbin bout the ape, crabbin bout what kind of jackoffs they is down at groun control, crabbin bout she got no place to put on her makeup, crabbin bout me eatin food when it ain't supper or lunchtime. Hell, all we got to eat is Granola bars anyway. I don't want to be complainin too much, but it seem like they might of picked a good-lookin woman or at least one that don't bitch all the time.

An furthermore, let me say this: that ape ain't no dreamboat either.

First I give it a banana—okay? It grapped the banana an started peelin it, but then it put the banana down. Banana started floatin all aroun the cabin of the spaceship an I got to go find it. I give it back to the ape an he start mushin it up an flingin the mush everplace, an I got to go clean that up. Wants attention all the time too. Evertime you leave it alone it commences to put up an enormous racket an clack its jaws together like a set of them wind-up teeth. Drive you nuts after a wile.

Finally I got out my harmonica an started playin a little somethin—"Home on the Range," I think it was. An the ape started to calm down a little. So I played some more—stuff like "The Yellow Rose of Texas" an "I Dream of Jeannie with the Light Brown Hair." Ape is lyin there lookin at me, peaceful as a baby. I forget there is a tv camera in the spaceship an they is pickin all this up down there at groun control. Nex mornin when I wake up somebody hole up a newspaper in front of the camera down in Houston for us to see. The headline say, "Idiot Plays Space Music to Soothe Ape." That is the sort of shit I has got to contend with.

Anyhow, things are goin along pretty good, but I been noticin that ole Sue is lookin at Major Fritch in a kind of strange way. Ever time she get near him, Sue sort of perk up an be reachin out like he wants to grap her or somethin, an she start bitchin at him—"Git away from me you awful thing.

Keep your hans to yoursef!" But ole Sue has got somethin in mind. That much I can tell.

It ain't long before I find out what it is. I have gone behin this little partition to take a pee in a jar in private, when all of a sudden I hear this commotion. I stick my head aroun the partition an Sue has managed to grap a holt of Major Fritch an he has got his han down in her space suit. She is yellin an hollerin to beat the band an is crackin Sue over the head with the radio microphone.

Then it dawns on me what the problem is. Wile we has been up in space for nearly two days, ole Sue been strapped into his seat an ain't had a chance to take a leak or nothin! An I sure remember what that's like. He must be bout to bust! Anyhow, I go over an got him away from Major Fritch an she still hollerin an yellin, callin him a "filthy animal," an shit like that. When she get loose, Major Fritch go up to the front of the cockpit an put her head down an start sobbin. I unstrap Sue an take him behin the partition with me.

I find a empty bottle for him to pee in, but after he finished, he take the bottle an heave it into a panel of colored lights an it bust to pieces an all the pee start floatin aroun in the spaceship. I say, to hell with this, an start leadin Sue back to his seat when I seen a big glob of pee headin straight for Major Fritch. It look like it gonna hit her in the back of the head, so I turn Sue loose an try to head off the pee with a net they have give us for catchin stuff that's floatin aroun. But jus as I am bout to net the glob of pee, Major Fritch sit back up an turn aroun an it caught her right in the face.

She start hollerin an bawlin again an in the meantime, Sue has done gone an started rippin out wires from the control panel. Major Fritch is screamin, "Stop him! Stop him!" but before you know it, sparks an stuff is flyin all aroun inside the spaceship an Sue is jumpin from ceilin to floor tearin shit up. A voice come over the radio wantin to know "What in hell is goin on up there?" but by then it is too late.

The spaceship is weavin all aroun an goin end over end an me, Sue an Major Fritch is tossed aroun like corks. Can't grap holt of nothin, can't turn off nothin, can't stan up or set down. The voice of groun control come over the radio again, say, "We is noticin some kine of minor stabilization trouble with your craft. Forrest, will you manually insert the D-six program into the starboard computer?"

Shit—he got to be jokin! I'm spinnin aroun like a top an I got a wild ape loose in here to boot! Major Fritch is hollerin so loud I cannot hear or even think nothin, but the gist of what she is hollerin seem to be that we is bout to crash an burn. I managed to get a glance out of the winder, an in fact things don't look good. That earth comin up on us mighty fast.

Somehow I managed to get to where the starboard computer is, an hold on to the panel with one han an I'm puttin D-six into the machine. It is a program designed to land the spaceship in the Indian Ocean in case we get in trouble, which we certainly is now.

Major Fritch an ole Sue be holdin on for dear life, but Major Fritch holler out, "What is you doin over there?" When I tole her, she say, "Forgit that, you stupid turd—we is already done passed over the Indian Ocean. Wait till we go roun again an see if you can set us down in the South Pacific."

Believe it or not, it don't take much time to go roun the world when you is in a spaceship, an Major Fritch has grapped holt to the radio microphone an is hollerin at them people at groun control that we is headed for either a splashdown or crash-down in the South Pacific Ocean an to come get us as soon as they can. I'm punchin buttons like crazy an that big ole earth is loomin closer. We fly over somethin Major Fritch thinks look like South America an then there be only water again, with the South Pole off to our left an Australia up ahead.

Then everthing get scorchin hot, an funny little souns are comin from the outside of the spaceship an it start shakin an hissin an the earth is dead up ahead. Major Fritch shout to me, "Pull the parachute lever!" but I am pinned in my seat. An she is pressed up against the ceilin of the cabin, an so it look like it's curtains for us, since we is goin bout ten thousan miles a hour, an headed straight for a big ole green blob of land in the ocean. We hit that goin this fast, ain't even gonna be a grease spot lef.

But then all of a sudden somethin go "pop" an the spaceship slow down. I look over, an damn if ole Sue ain't pulled the parachute lever hissef an saved our asses. I remind mysef then an there to feed him a banana when all this shit is over.

Anyhow, the spaceship be swingin back an forth under the parachute, an it look like we is gonna hit the big ole green blob of land—which apparently ain't so good neither, since we is sposed only to hit water an then ships will pick us up. But ain't nothin gone right from the time we set foot in this contraption, so why should anybody expect it to now?

Major Fritch is on the radio an sayin to groun control, "We is bout to land on someplace north of Australia out in the ocean, but I ain't sure where we is."

Couple of seconts later a voice come back say, "If you ain't sure where you is, why don't you look out the winder, you dumb broad?"

So Major Fritch put the radio down an go look out the winder an she say, "Jesus—this look like Borneo or someplace," but when she try to tell that to groun control, the radio done gone dead.

We be gettin real close to the earth now, an the spaceship still swinging under the parachute. There is nothin but jungle an mountains beneath us cept for a little bitty lake that is kind of brown. We can barely make out somethin goin on nex to the lake down there. The three of us—me, Sue an Major Fritch—all got our noses pressed to the winder lookin down, an all of a sudden Major Fritch cry out, "Good God! This ain't Borneo—this is fuckin New Guinea, an all that shit on the groun must be one of them Cargo Cults or somethin!"

Sue an me lookin down hard, an there on the groun nex to the lake, lookin back at us, is about a thousan natives, all with they arms raised up towards us. They is wearin little grass skirts an has their hair all flayed out, an some is carryin shields an spears.

"Damn," I say, "what you say they is?"

"Cargo Cult," Major Fritch say. "In World War II we used to drop packages of candy an stuff like that on these jungle bunnies to keep em on our side, an they ain't never forgot it. Figgered it was God or somebody doin it, an ever since, they is waiting for us to come back. Even built crude runways an all—see down there? They has got a landin zone all marked off with them big roun black markers."

"Them things look more like cookin pots to me," I says.

"Yeah, they do, sort of," Major Fritch say curiously.

"Ain't this where cannibals come from?" I axed.

"I reckon we will soon find out," she say.

Spaceship is gently swingin towards the lake, an jus afore we hit, they start beatin they drums an movin they mouths up and down. We can't hear nothin on account of bein in the capsule, but our maginations doin just fine.

14

Our landin in the little lake was not too bad. They was a splash an a bounce an then we is back on earth again. Everthin got real quiet, an me an Sue and Major Fritch peek out the winder.

They is a whole tribe of natives standin bout ten feet away on the shore, lookin at us, an they is bout the fiercest-looking folks imaginable—scowlin an leanin forward so's to see what we is. Major Fritch say maybe they is upset cause we didn't thow them nothin from the spaceship. Anyhow, she say she is gonna set down an try to figger out what to do now, on account of we has somehow got this far okay an she don't want to make no false moves with these spooks. Seven or eight of they biggest fellas jumps into the water and begin pushin us over to land.

Major Fritch still be settin there figgerin when there is a big knock at the door of the spaceship. We all look at each other an Major Fritch say, "Don't nobody do nothin."

An I say, "Maybe they be gettin angry if we don't let em in."

"Just be quiet," she say, "an maybe they think nobody's in here an go away."

So we waited, but sure enough, after a wile they is another knock on the spaceship.

I say, "It ain't polite not to answer the door," an Major Fritch hiss back at me, "Shut up your dumbfool ass—can't you see these people is dangerous?"

Then all of a sudden ole Sue go over an open the door hissef. Standin there outside is the biggest coon I has seen since we played them Nebraska corn shucker jackoffs in the Orange Bowl.

He got a bone thru his nose an is wearin a grass skirt an carryin a spear an has a lot of beads strung aroun his neck, an his hair look somethin like that Beatle wig Mad Tom o'Bedlam wore in the Shakespeare play.

This feller seem extremely startled to find Sue starin back at him from inside the spaceship door. As a matter of fact, he is so suprised that he keel over in a dead faint. Major Fritch an me is peepin out the winder again, an when all them other natives seen this feller keel over, they run off in the shrubs an hide—I guess to wait an see what's gonna happen nex.

Major Fritch say, "Hole still now—don't make a move," but ole Sue, he grapped holt of a bottle that was settin there an he jump out on the groun an pour it in the feller's face to revive him. All of a sudden the feller set up an start sputterin an coughin an spittin an shakin his head from side to side. He was revived all right, but what Sue had grapped an poured in his face was the bottle what I used to pee in. Then the feller recognize Sue again, an he thowed his hans up an fall over on his face an begin bowin an scrapin like a Arab.

An then out from the bushes come the rest of them, movin slow an scarit-like, eyes big as saucers, ready to thow they spears. The feller on the groun stop bowin for a moment an

look up an when he seen the others, he holler out somethin
an they put down they spears an come up to the spaceship an
gather aroun it.

"They look friendly enough now," Major Fritch say. "I
spose we better go on out an identify ourselfs. The people
from NASA will be here in a few minutes to pick us up." As
it turns out, that is the biggest piece of bullshit I have ever
heard in my life—before or since.

Anyhow, Major Fritch an me, we walk on out of the spaceship an all them natives goin "ooooh" an "ahhhh." That ole
boy on the groun, he look at us real puzzled-like, but then he
get up an say, "Hello—me good boy. Who you?" an he stick
out his han.

I shake his han, but then Major Fritch start tryin to tell him
who we is, sayin we is, "Participants in the NASA multi-
orbital pre-planetary sub-gravitational inter-spheroid space-
flight trainin mission."

The feller jus stan there gapin at us like we was spacemen,
an so I says, "We is Americans," an all of a sudden his eyes
light up an he say, "Do tell! Americans! What a jolly fine
show—I say!"

"You speak English?" Major Fritch axed.

"Why hell yes," he say. "I've been to America before.
During the war. I was recruited by the Office of Strategic
Services to learn English, and then sent back here to organize
our people in guerrilla warfare against the Japanese." At this,
Sue's eyes get big an bright.

It seem kinda funny to me, though—a big ole boon like
this speaking such good American out in the middle of
noplace, so I says, "Where'd you go t'school?"

"Why, I went to Yale, old sport," he says. "Boola-Boola,
an all that." When he say "boola-boola," all them other
Sambo's start chantin it too, an the drums start up again, until
the big guy wave them quiet.

"My name is Sam," he say. "At least that's what they called

me at Yale. My real name's quite a mouthful. What a delight you dropped in. Would you like some tea?"

Me an Major Fritch be lookin at each other. She is damn near speechless, so I says, "Yeah, that'd be good," an then Major Fritch get her voice back an speak up kind of high-pitched, "You ain't got a phone we can use, do you?" she say.

Big Sam sort of scowl an wave his hans an the drums start up again an we be escorted into the jungle with everbody chantin "boola-boola."

They has got theyselfs a little village set up in the jungle with grass huts an shit jus like in the movies, an Big Sam's hut is the grandest of all. Out in front he got a chair look like a throne, an four or five women wearin nothin on top are doin whatever he say. One of the things he say is for them to get us some tea, an then he point to a couple of big stones for Major Fritch an me to set down on. Sue has been followin along behin us all the way, holdin on to my han, an Big Sam motion for him to set on the groun.

"That's a terrific ape you have there," Sam says. "Where'd you get him?"

"He works for NASA," Major Fritch says. She ain't lookin none too happy bout our situation.

"You don't say?" says Big Sam. "Is he paid?"

"I think he'd like a banana," I says. Big Sam said somethin an one of the woman natives brung Sue a banana.

"I'm awfully sorry," Big Sam say, "I think I haven't asked your names."

"Major Janet Fritch, United States Air Force. Serial number 04534573. That's all I'm going to tell you."

"Oh, my dear woman," says Big Sam. "You are not a prisoner here. We are just poor backward tribesmen. Some say we've not progressed much since the Stone Age. We mean you no harm."

"I ain't got nothin else to say till I can use the phone," Major Fritch say.

"Very well then," says Big Sam. "And what of you, young man?"

"My name is Forrest," I tell him.

"Really," he say. "Is that taken from your famous Civil War General Nathan Bedford Forrest?"

"Yep," I says.

"How very interesting. I say, Forrest, where did you go to school?"

I started to say I went up to the University of Alabama for a wile, but then I decided to play it safe, an so I tole him I went to Harvard, which was not exactly a lie.

"Ah, Harvard—the old Crimson," Big Sam says. "Yes—I knew it well. Lovely bunch of fellows—even if they couldn't get into Yale," an then he start to laugh real loud. "Actually, you do look sort of like a Harvard man at that," he say. Somehow, I figger that trouble lay ahead.

It was late in the afternoon an Big Sam tole a couple of them native women to show us where we is gonna stay. It is a grass hut with a dirt floor an a little entranceway, an it sort of remind me of the hovel where King Lear went. Two big ole fellers with spears come up an be standin guard outside our door.

All night long them natives be beatin on they drums an chantin "boola-boola," an we could see out the entrance that they have set up a great big cauldron an built a fire under it. Me an Major Fritch don't know what to make of all this, but I reckon ole Sue does, cause he settin over in the corner by hissef, lookin glum.

Bout nine or ten o'clock they still ain't fed us no food, an Major Fritch say maybe I ought to go axe Big Sam for our supper. I start to go out the door of the hovel but them two natives cross they spears in front of me, an I get the message an go back inside. Suddenly it dawn on me how come we ain't been invited to supper—we *is* the supper. It is a bleak outlook.

Then the drums quit an they stop chantin "boola-boola." Outside we hear somebody squawkin an he is answered by somebody else squawkin that sound like Big Sam. That go on for a wile, an the argument get real heated up. Just as it seem like they can't shout any louder, we hear this big "conk," which sound like somebody get hit over the head with a board or somethin. Everthing get quiet for a moment, then the drums start up again an everbody chantin "boola-boola" once more.

Next mornin, we settin there an Big Sam come thru the door an he say, "Hello—did you have a nice sleep?"

"Hell no," Major Fritch say. "How in God's name does you expect us to sleep with all that racket out there?"

Big Sam get a pained look on his face, an say, "Oh, I'm sorry about that. But you see, my people were, ah, sort of expectin a gift of some sort when they saw your vehicle drop from the sky. We have been waiting since 1945 for the return of your people an their presents to us. When they saw that you had no presents, naturally they assumed that *you* were the present, and they were prepared to cook you and eat you until I persuaded them otherwise."

"You're shittin me, buster," Major Fritch say.

"To the contrary," says Big Sam. "You see, my people are not exactly what you would call *civilized*—at least by your standards—as they have a particular affection for human flesh. Especially white meat."

"Do you mean to tell me you people are cannibals?" Major Fritch say.

Big Sam shrug his shoulders. "That's bout the size of it."

"That's disgusting," says Major Fritch. "Listen, you has got to see to it that we is not harmed, an that we get out of here an back to civilization. There is probably a search party from

NASA about to arrive any minute. I demand that you treat us with the dignity you would accord any allied nation."

"Ah," Big Sam say, "that was precisely what they had in mind last night."

"Now see here!" says Major Fritch. "I demand that we be set free this instant, and allowed to make our way to the nearest city or town where there is a telephone."

"I am afraid," Big Sam say, "that would be impossible. Even if we did turn you loose, the pygmies would get you before you went a hundred yards into the jungle."

"Pygmies?" say Major Fritch.

"We have been at war with the pygmies for many generations. Somebody stole a pig once, I think—nobody remembers who or where—it is lost in legend. But we are virtually surrounded by the pygmies, and have been ever since anyone can remember."

"Well," says Major Fritch, "I'd rather us take our chances with pygmies than with a bunch of fucking cannibals—the pygmies ain't cannibals, is they?"

"No, madam," Big Sam say, "they are headhunters."

"Terrific," Major Fritch say sourly.

"Now last night," Big Sam says, "I managed to save you from the cooking pot, but I am not sure how long I can keep my people at bay. They are determined to turn your appearance into some sort of gain."

"Is that so?" Major Fritch says. "Like what?"

"Well, for one thing, your ape. I think they would at least like to be able to eat him."

"That ape is the sole property of the United States of America," says Major Fritch.

"Nonetheless," Big Sam says, "I think it would be a diplomatic gesture on your part."

Ole Sue be frownin an noddin his head slowly an lookin sorrowfully out the door.

"And then," Big Sam continue, "I think that wile you are here, you could perhaps do some work for us."

"What sort of work?" Major Fritch say suspiciously.

"Well," say Big Sam, "farming work. Agriculture. You see, I have been trying to improve the ignominious lot of my people for many years. And not too long ago I stumbled on an idea. If we can simply turn the fertile soil here to our advantage, and bring to it some of the modern techniques of agronomy, we might thus begin to haul ourselves out of our tribal predicament and assume a role in the world market-place. In short, turn ourselves away from this backward and stale economy and become a viable, cultured race of peoples."

"What kind of farming?" Major Fritch axed.

"Cotton, my dear woman, cotton! King of cash crops! The plant that built an empire in your own country some years ago."

"You expectin us to grow cotton!" Major Fritch squawked.

"You bet your sweet ass I do, sister," Big Sam say.

15

Well, here we is, plantin cotton. Acres an acres an acres of it. All up an down the whole creation. If they is anythin sure in my life, it is that if we ever get our asses outta here, I don't never want to be no cotton farmer.

Several things done happened after that first day in the jungle with Big Sam an the cannibals. First, Major Fritch an me has convinced Big Sam not to make us give po ole Sue to his tribe to eat. We has persuaded him that Sue would be of a lot more use heppin us plant the cotton than he would be as a meal. An so ever day there is ole Sue out there with us, wearin a big straw hat an carryin a gunnysack, plantin cotton.

Also, bout the third or forth week we was there, Big Sam come into our hovel an say, "Look here, Forrest old boy, do you play chess?"

An I says, "No."

An he say, "Well, you're a Harvard man, you might like to learn."

An I nod my head, an that's how I learnt to play chess.

Ever evenin when we is thru work in the cotton fields, Big Sam'd get out his chess set an we'd set aroun the fire an play till late at night. He showed me all the moves, an for the first few days he taught me strategy. But after that, he quit doin it cause I beat him a game or two.

After a wile, the games get longer. Sometime they last for several days, as Big Sam can not make up his mind where to move to. He'd sit an study them chessmen an then he'd do somethin with one of them, but I always managed to beat him. Sometimes he'd get real angry with hissef, an pound on his foot with a stick or butt his head against a rock or somethin.

"For a Harvard man, you is a pretty good chess player," he'd say, or he'd say, "See here, Forrest—why did you make that last move?" I wouldn't say nothin, or jus shrug my shoulders, an that woud send Big Sam into a rage.

One day he say, "You know, Forrest, I am surely glad you have come here, so I can have somebody to play chess with, an I am glad I have saved you from that cooking pot. Only thing is, I really would like to win jus one chess game from you."

At that, Big Sam be lickin his chops, an it didn't take no idiot to figger out that if I let him win jus one game, he was gonna be satisfied, an have me for his supper, then an there. Kinda kep me on my toes, if you know what I mean.

Meantime, a very strange thing has happened with Major Fritch.

One day she is walkin back from the cotton fields with Sue an me, when a big ole black arm poke out from a clump of bushes an beckon her over. Me an Sue stopped, an Major Fritch walk over to the clump of bushes an say, "Who's that in there?" All of a sudden, the big ole arm reached out an grapped a holt of Major Fritch an snatched her into the bush. Sue an me looked at each other an then run over to where she was. Sue got there first an I was about to leap into the

bushes mysef, when Sue stop me. He start shakin his head an
wavin me away, an we walked off a little bit an waited. They
was all sorts of souns comin from in there, an the bushes is
shakin like crazy. I finally figgered out what was goin on, but
from the soun of Major Fritch's voice, it didn't appear she
was in no danger or nothin, so Sue an me went on back to the
village.

Bout a hour later, here come Major Fritch an this great big
ole feller who is grinnin ear-to-ear. She has got him by the
han, leadin him along. She bring him into the hovel an say to
me, "Forrest, I want you to meet Grurck," an she lead him
forward.

"Hi," I say. I had seen this feller aroun the village before.
Grurck be grinnin an noddin an I nodded back. Sue, he be
scratchin his balls.

"Grurck done axed me to move in with him," she say, "an
I think I will, since it is sort of crowded in here for the three
of us, wouldn't you say?"

I nod my head.

"Forrest. You wouldn't tell nobody bout this, would you?"
Major Fritch axed.

Now who in hell was she thinkin I would tell, is what I
want to know? But I just shook my head, an Major Fritch got
her shit an went off with Grurck to his place. An that's the
way it was.

The days an months an finally the years come an go, an
ever day me an Sue an Major Fritch be workin in the cotton
fields, an I am beginnin to feel like Uncle Remus or somebody. At night, after I finish wuppin Big Sam at chess, I go
into the hovel with ole Sue an we set aroun for a wile. It has
got to where Sue an me can sort of talk to each other, gruntin
an makin faces an wavin our hans. After a long time I am able
to piece together his life story, an it turn out to be bout as
sorry as mine.

When he was jus a little bitty ape, Sue's mama an poppa was walkin in the jungle one day when these guys come along an thowed a net over them, an drug them off. He managed to get on with an aunt an uncle till they kicked him out for eatin too much, an then he was on his own.

He was okay, jus swingin in the trees an eatin bananas till one day he got curious bout what is goin on in the rest of the world, an he swang hissef thru tree after tree till he come on a village near the edge of the jungle. He is thirsty an come down an set by a stream to drink some water when this feller come by paddlin a canoe. Sue ain't never seen a canoe, so he set there watchin it an the feller paddle over to him. He think the feller want to give him a ride, but instead, the feller conked Sue over the head with his oar an hog-tied him an nex thing he knew, he was sold to some guy that put him in a exhibit in Paris.

There was this other orangutang in the exhibit, name of Doris, what was one of the finest-looking apes he had ever seed, an after a wile, they fell in love. The guy that had the exhibit took them aroun the world, an everplace he'd go, the main attraction was to put Doris an Sue together in a cage so's everbody could watch them screw—that was the kind of exhibit it was. Anyway, it was kinda embarrassin for ole Sue, but it were the only chance they had.

Then one time they was on exhibit in Japan, an some guy come up to the feller running the show an offer to buy Doris. So off she went, Sue knowed not where, an he was by hissef.

That caused a definate change in Sue's attitude. He got grouchy, an when they put him on display, he took to growlin an snarlin an finally he begun takin a shit an then flingin the shit thru the cage bars all over them people what had paid their good money to see what an orangutang acts like.

After a wile of this, the exhibit feller got fed up an sold Sue to the NASA people an that's how come he wind up here. I know how he feels a little, cause he's still lonesome for Doris, an I'm still lonesome for Jenny Curran, an ain't a day go by I ain't wonderin what's become of her. But here we both is, stuck out in the middle of nowhere.

The cotton farmin adventure of Big Sam's is beyon anyone's wildest dreams. We has sowed an harvested bale after bale, an they is storin it in big grass shacks built up off the groun. Finally one day, Big Sam say they is fixin to construct a big boat—a barge—to load up the cotton an fight our way thru pygmy country down to where we can sell the cotton an make a fortune.

"I have got it all figured out," Big Sam says. "First we auction off the cotton and get our money. Then we will use it to buy the kinds of things my people need."

I axed him what was that, an he say, "Oh, you know, old sport, beads and trinkets, perhaps a mirror or two—a portable radio and maybe a box of good Cuban cigars—and a case or two of booze."

So this is the kind of deal we is in.

Anyhow, the months go by, an we is harvesting the last cotton crop of the season. Big Sam has done just bout finished the river barge that is to take us thru pygmy country to the town, an the night before we is to leave, they hold a big hoedown to celebrate everthin an also ward off evil spirits.

All the tribe be settin aroun the fire chantin "boola-boola" and beatin on they drums. They has also drug out that big cauldron an got it on the fire steamin an boilin, but Big Sam say it is only a "symbolic gesture."

We is settin there playin chess, an let me tell you this—I am so excited I am bout to bust! Just let us get near a town or city, an we is long gone. Ole Sue knows the deal too, cause he's settin over there with a big grin on his face, ticklin hissef under the arms.

We has played one or two games of chess an is bout to

finish another, when I suddenly look down, an damned if Big Sam ain't got me in check. He is smilin so big, all I can see in the dark is his teeth, an I figger I had better get outta this situation quick.

Only problem is, I can't. Wile I've been assin aroun countin my chickens afore they're hatched, I have put mysef in a impossible position on the chessboard. They ain't no way out.

I studied that thing for a wile, my frown lit up plain as day from the fire's reflection off Big Sam's smilin teeth, an then I says, "Ah, look here—I got to go pee." Big Sam nod, still grinnin, an I'll tell you this, it was the first time I can remember when sayin somethin like that got me *out* of trouble instead of in it.

I went on back behin the hovel an took a pee, but then instead of goin back to the chess game, I went in an got ole Sue an splained to him what the deal was. Then I snuck up on Grurck's hut an whispered for Major Fritch. She come out, an I tole her too, an say we'd better get our butts outta here afore we is all parboiled or somethin.

Well, we all decided to make a break for it. Grurck, he say he's comin with us on account of he's in love with Major Fritch—or however he expressed it. Anyway, the four of us started creepin out of the village an we got down to the edge of the river an was jus bout to get in one of the native canoes, when all of a sudden I look up an standin there over me is Big Sam with about a thousan of his natives, lookin mean an disappointed.

"Come now, old sport," he say, "did you really think you could outsmart this old devil?" An I tell him, "Oh, we was jus goin for a canoe ride in the moonlite—you know what I mean?"

"Yeah," he say, he knowed what I meant, an then his men grapped us up an haul us back to the village under armed guard. The cookin cauldron is bubblin an steamin to beat the band an they has got us tied to stakes in the groun an the outlook is somethin less than rosy.

"Well, old sport," Big Sam say, "this is a unfortunate turn of events indeed. But look at it this way, you will at least be able to console yourself by the knowledge that you have fed a hungry mouth or two. And also, I must tell you this—you are without a doubt the best chess player I have ever encountered, and I was the chess champion of Yale for three of the four years I was there.

"As for you, madam," Big Sam say to Major Fritch, "I am sorry to have to bring your little *affaire d'amour* with old Grurck here to an end, but you know how it is."

"No I *don't* know how it is, you despicable savage," Major Fritch say. "Where do you get off, anyway? You oughta be ashamed of yoursef!"

"Perhaps we can serve you an Grurck on the same platter," Big Sam chuckled, "a little light an dark meat—myself, I'll take a thigh, or possibly a breast—now that would be a nice touch."

"You vile, unspeakable ass!" say Major Fritch.

"Whatever," Big Sam says. "And now, let the feast begin!"

They begun untyin us an a bunch of them jiggaboos hauled us towards the cookin pot. They lifted up po ole Sue first, cause Big Sam say he will make good "stock," an they was holdin him above the cauldron about to thow him in, when lo an behole, a arrow come out of noplace an strike one of the fellers hoistin up Sue. The feller fall down an Sue drop on top of him. Then more arrows come rainin down on us from the edge of the jungle, an everybody is in a panic.

"It is the pygmies!" shout Big Sam. "Get to your arms!" an everybody run to get they spears an knives.

Since we ain't got no spears or knives, Major Fritch, me an Sue an Grurck start runnin down towards the river again, but we ain't no more than ten feet down the path when all of a sudden we is snatched up feet first by some kind of snares set in the trees.

We is hangin there, upside down like bats, an all the blood rushin to our heads, when this little guy come out of the brush an he be laughin an gigglin at us all trussed up. All sorts of savage sounds are comin from the village, but after a wile, everthing quiet down. Then a bunch of other pygmies come an cut us down an tie our hans an feet an lead us back to the village.

It is a sight! They has captured Big Sam an all his natives an has them tied up han an foot too. Look like they is bout to thow them into the boilin pot.

"Well, old sport," Big Sam say, "seems like you were saved in the nick of time, doesn't it?"

I nod my head, but I ain't sure if we isn't jus out of the fryin pan an into the fire.

"Tell you what," says Big Sam, "looks like it's all over for me an my fellers, but maybe you have a chance. If you can get to that harmonica of yours an play a little tune or two, it might save your life. The king of the pygmies is crazy for American music."

"Thanks," I say.

"Don't mention it, old sport," Big Sam say. They lifted him up high an was holdin him over the boilin cauldron, an suddenly he call out to me, "Knight to bishop three—then rook ten to king seven—that's how I beat you!"

They was a big splash, and then all Big Sam's trussed-up natives begun chantin "boola-boola" again. Things are lookin down for us all.

16

After they done finished cookin Big Sam's tribe, an shrinkin they heads, the pygmies slung us between long poles an carried us off like pigs into the jungle.

"What do you spose they intend to do with us?" Major Fritch call out to me.

"I don't know, an I don't give a shit," I call back, an that were about the truth. I'm tired of all this crappola. A man can take jus so much.

Anyhow, after about a day or so we come to the village of the pygmies, an as you might expec, they has got a bunch of little tiny huts in a clearin in the jungle. They truck us up to a hut in the center of the clearin where there is a bunch of pygmies standin aroun—an one little ole feller with a long white beard an no teeth settin up in a high chair like a baby. I figger him to be the king of the pygmies.

They tumped us out onto the groun an untied us, an we stood up an dusted ourselfs off an the king of the pygmies commence jabberin some gibberish an then he get down from his chair an go straight up to Sue an kick him in the balls.

"How come he done that?" I axed Grurck, who had learnt to speak some English wile he was livin with Major Fritch.

"Him want to know if ape is boy or girl," Grurck say.

I figger there must be a nicer way to find that out, but I ain't sayin nothin.

Then the king, he come up to me an start talkin some of that gibberish—pygmalion, or whatever it is—an I'm preparing to get kicked in the balls too, but Grurck say, "Him want to know why you livin with them awful cannibals."

"Tell him it weren't exactly our idea," Major Fritch pipe up an say.

"I got a idea," I says. "Tell him we is American musicians."

Grurck say this to the king an he be peerin at us real hard, an then he axe Grurck somethin.

"What's he say?" Major Fritch want to know.

"Him axe what the ape plays," say Grurck.

"Tell him the ape plays the spears," I say, an Grurck do that, an then the king of the pygmies announce he want to hear us perform.

I get out my harmonica an start playin a little tune—"De Camptown Races." King of the pygmies listen for a minute, then he start clappin his hans an doin what look to be a clog dance.

After I'm finished, he say he wants to know what Major Fritch an Grurck plays, an I tell Grurck to say Major Fritch plays the knives an that Grurck don't play nothin—he is the manager.

King of the pygmies look sort of puzzled an say he ain't never heard of anybody playin knives or spears before, but he tell his men to give Sue some spears an Major Fritch some knives an let's see what sort of music we come up with.

Soon as we get the spears an knives, I say, "Okay—now!"

an ole Sue conk the king of the pygmies over the head with
his spear an Major Fritch threatened a couple of pygmies with
her knives an we run off into the jungle with the pygmies in
hot pursuit.

The pygmies be thowin all sorts of rocks an shit at us from
behin, an shootin they bows an arrows an darts from blow-
guns an such. Suddenly we come out on the bank of a river
an ain't no place to go, an the pygmies are catchin up fast. We
is bout to jump into the river an swim for it, when suddenly
from the opposite side of the river a rifle shot ring out.

The pygmies are right on top of us, but another rifle shot
ring out an they turn tail an run back into the jungle. We be
lookin across the river an lo an behole on the other bank they
is a couple of fellers wearin bush jackets an them white pith
helmets like you used to see in *Ramar of the Jungle*. They step
into a canoe an be paddlin towards us, an as they get closer, I
seen one of them is got NASA stamped on his pith helmet.
We is finally rescued.

When the canoe reach our shore, the guy with NASA
stamped on his helmet get out an come up to us. He go right
up to ole Sue an stick out his han an say, "Mister Gump, I
presume?"

"Where the fuck has you assholes been?" hollared Major
Fritch. "We been stranded in the jungle nearly four goddamn
years!"

"Sorry bout that, ma'am," the feller say, "but we has got
our priorities, too, you know."

Anyway, we is at last saved from a fate worse than death,
an they loaded us up in the canoe an started paddlin us
downriver. One of the fellers say, "Well folks, civilization is
just aroun the corner. I reckon you'll all be able to sell your
stories to a magazine an make a fortune."

"Stop the canoe!" Major Fritch suddenly call out.

The fellers look at one another, but they paddle the canoe over to the bank.

"I have made a decision," Major Fritch say. "For the first time in my life, I have found a man that truly understands me, an I am not going to let him go. For nearly four years, Grurck an I have lived happily in this land, an I have decided to stay here with him. We will go off in the jungle an make a new life for ourselfs, an raise a family an live happily ever after."

"But this man is a cannibal," one of the fellers say.

"Eat your heart out, buster," says Major Fritch, an she an Grurck get out of the canoe an start back into the jungle again, han in han. Jus before they disappeared, Major Fritch turn aroun an give Sue an me a little wave, an then off they go.

I looked back to the end of the canoe, an ole Sue is settin there twistin his fingers.

"Wait a minute," I says to the fellers. I go back an set down on the seat nex to Sue an say, "What you thinkin bout?"

Sue ain't sayin nothin, but they is a little bitty tear in his eye, an I knowed then what was bout to happen. He grapped me aroun the shoulders in a big hug, an then leaped out of the boat an ran up a tree on the shore. Last we seen of him, he is swingin away thru the jungle on a vine.

The feller from NASA be shakin his head. "Well, what about you, numbnuts? You gonna follow your friends there into Bonzoland?"

I looked after them for a minute, then I said, "Uh, uh," an set back down in the canoe. Wile they was paddlin us away, don't you believe I didn't think bout it for a moment. But I jus couldnt do it. I reckon I got other weenies to roast.

They flown me back to America an tole me on the way how there was to be a big welcome home reception for me, but seems like I have heard that before.

Sure enough tho, soon as we landed in Washington bout a million people was on han, cheerin an clappin an actin like they is glad to see me. They drove me into town in the back seat of a big ole black car an said they was takin me to the White House to see the President. Yep, I been there before too.

Well, when we get to the White House, I'm expectin to see the same ole President what fed me breakfast an let me watch "The Beverly Hillbillies," but they is got a new President now—feller with his hair all slicked back, puffy little cheeks an a nose look like Pinocchio's.

"Tell me now," this President say, "did you have an exciting trip?"

A feller in a suit standin next to the President lean over an whisper somethin to him, an suddenly the President say, "Oh, ah, accually what I meant was, how great it is that you have escaped from your ordeal in the jungle."

The feller in the suit whisper somethin else to the President, an he say to me, "Er, now what about your companion?"

"Sue?" I say.

"Was that her name?" Now he be lookin at a little card in his han. "Says here it was a Major Janet Fritch, and that even as you were being rescued she was dragged off into the jungle by a cannibal."

"Where it say that?" I axed.

"Right here," the President say.

"That's not so," I says.

"Are you suggesting I am a liar?" say the President.

"I'm jus sayin it ain't so," I says.

"Now look here," say the President, "I am your commander in chief. I am not a crook. I do not lie!"

"I am very sorry," I says, "but it ain't the truth bout Major Fritch. You jus take that off a card, but—"

"Tape!" the President shout.

"Huh?" I says.

"No, no," says the feller in the suit. "He said *'take'*—not 'tape'—Mister President."

"TAPE!" scream the President. "I told you never to mention that word in my presence again! You are all a bunch of disloyal Communist swines." The President be poundin hisself on the knee with his fist.

"None of you understand. I don't know anything bout anything! I never heard of anything! And if I did, I either forgot it, or it is top secret!"

"But Mister President," say the feller in the suit, "he didn't say it. He only said—"

"Now *you* are calling me a liar!" he say. "You're fired!"

"But you can't fire me," the feller say. "I am the Vice President."

"Well, pardon me for saying so," says the President, "but you are never going to make President if you go aroun calling your commander in chief a liar."

"No, I guess you're right," say the Vice President. "I beg your pardon."

"No, I beg yours," the President say.

"Whatever," say the Vice President, kinda fiddlin with hisself. "If you will all excuse me now, I have to go pee."

"That's the first sensible idea I have heard all day," say the President. Then he turn to me an axe, "Say, aren't you the same fellow that played ping-pong and saved the life of old Chairman Mao?"

I says, "Yup," an the President say, "Well what did you want to do a thing like that for?"

An I says, "Cause he was drownin," an the President say, "You should have held him under, instead of saving him. Anyway, it's history now, because the son of a bitch died while you were away in the jungle."

"You got a tv set?" I axed.

The President look at me kind of funny. "Yeah, I have

141

one, but I don't watch it much these days. Too much bad news."

"You ever watch 'The Beverly Hillbillies'?" I say.

"It's not on yet," he say.

"What is?" I axed.

" 'To Tell the Truth'—but you don't want to look at that—it's a bunch of shit." Then he say, "Look here, I have a meeting to go to, why don't I walk you to the door?" When we get outside on the porch, an the President say in a very low voice, "Listen, you want to buy a watch?"

I say, "Huh?" an he step over close to me an shove up the sleeve on his suit an lo an behole he must of had twenty or thirty wristwatches aroun his arm.

"I ain't got no money," I says.

The President, he roll down his sleeve an pat me on the back. "Well, you come back when you do and we'll work something out, okay?"

He shook my han an a bunch of photographers come up an start takin our picher an then I'm gone. But I'll say this, that President seem like a nice feller after all.

Anyhow, I'm wonderin what they gonna do with me now, but I don't have to wonder long.

It took bout a day or so for things to quiet down, an they had put me up in a hotel, but then a couple of fellers come in one afternoon an say, "Listen here, Gump, the free ride's over. The government ain't payin for none of this anymore—you're on your own now."

"Well, okay," I say, "but how bout givin me a little travelin money to get home on. I'm kinda light right now."

"Forget it, Gump," they say. "You is lucky not to be in jail for conkin the Clerk of the Senate on the head with that medal. We done you a favor to get you off that rap—but we is washin our hans of your ass as of right now."

So I had to leave the hotel. Since I ain't got no things to

pack, it wadn't hard, an I just went out on the street. I walked a wile, down past the White House where the President live, an to my suprise they is a whole bunch of people out front got on rubber masks of the President's face an they is carryin some kind of signs. I figger he must be pleased to be so popular with everbody.

17

Even tho they said they wouldn't give me no money, one of
the fellers did loan me a dollar before I lef the hotel. First
chance I got, I phoned home to the po house where my
mama was stayin to let her know I'm okay. But one of them
nuns says, "We ain't got no Mrs. Gump here no longer."

When I axed where she was, the nun say, "Dunno—she
done run off with some protestant." I thanked her an hanged
up the phone. In a way, I'm sort of relieved. At least mama
done run off with *somebody,* an ain't in the po house no more.
I figger I got to find her, but to tell the truth, I ain't in no big
hurry, cause sure as it's gonna rain, she'll be bawlin an hollerin an fussin at me on account of I lef home.

It did rain. Rained cats an dogs an I foun me a awnin to
stand under till some guy come out an run me off. I was
soakin wet an cold an walkin past some government buildin
in Washington when I seen a big ole plastic garbage bag
settin in the middle of the sidewalk. Just as I get close to it,

the bag commenced to move a little bit, like there is somethin in there!

I stopped an went up to the bag an nudged it a little with my toe. Suddenly the bag jump bout four feet back an a voice come out from under it, say, "Git the fuck away from me!"

"Who is that in there?" I axed, an the voice say back, "This is *my* grate—you go find your own."

"What you talkin bout?" I say.

"My grate," the voice say. "Git off my grate!"

"What grate?" I axed.

All of a sudden the bag lift up a little an a feller's head peek out, squintin up at me like I'm some kinda idiot.

"You new in town or somethin?" the feller says.

"Sort of," I answered. "I'm jus tryin to get outta the rain."

The feller under the bag is pretty sorry-lookin, half bald-headed, ain't shaved in months, eyes all red an bloodshot an most of his teeth gone.

"Well," he say, "in that case I reckon it okay for a little wile—here." He reach up an han me another garbage bag, all folded up.

"What I'm sposed to do with this?" I axed.

"Open it up an git under it, you damn fool—you said you wanted to git outta the rain." An then he pull his bag back down over hissef.

Well, I did what he said, an to tell you the truth, it wadn't so bad, really. They was some hot air comin up outta the grate an it make the bag all warm an cozy inside an kep off the rain. We be squattin side-by-side on the grate with the bags over us an after a wile the feller says over to me, "What's your name anyway?"

"Forrest," I says.

"Yeah? I knew a guy named Forrest once. Long time ago."

"What's your name?" I axed.

"Dan," he say.

"Dan? *Dan?*—hey, wait a minute," I says. I thowed off my

garbage bag an went an lifted up the bag off the feller an it was him! Ain't got no legs, an he is settin on a little wood cart with roller-skate wheels on the bottom. Must of aged twenty years, an I could hardly recognize him. But it was him. It was ole Lieutenant Dan!

After he had got out of the Army hospital, Dan went back to Connecticut to try to get back his ole job teachin history. But they wadn't no history job available, so they made him teach math. He hated math, an besides, the math class was on the secont floor of the school an he had a hell of a time makin it up the stairs with no legs an all. Also, his wife done run off with a tv producer that lived in New Yawk an she sued him for divorce on grounds of "incompatibility."

He took to drinkin an lost his job an jus didn't do nothin for a wile. Thieves robbed his house of everthin he had an the artificial legs they had give him at the VA hospital were the wrong size. After a few years, he said, he jus "give up," an took to livin like a bum. There's a little money ever month from his disability pension, but most of the time he jus give it away to the other bums.

"I dunno, Forrest," he say, "I guess I'm jus waitin to die or somethin."

Dan han me a few bucks an say to go aroun the corner an git us a couple of bottles of Red Dagger wine. I jus got one bottle tho, an used the money for mine to git one of them ready-made sambwiches, cause I ain't had nothin to eat all day.

"Well, old pal," Dan say after he has polished off half his wine, "tell me what you been doin since I saw you last."

So I did. I tole him about goin to China an playin ping-pong, an findin Jenny Curran again, an playin in The Cracked Eggs band an the peace demonstration where I thowed my medal away an got put in jail.

"Yeah, I remember that one all right. I think I was still

here in the hospital. I thought bout going down there mysef, but I guess I wouldn't have thowed my medals away. Look here," he say. He unbutton his jacket an inside, on his shirt, is all his medals—Purple Heart, Silver Star—must of been ten or twelve of them.

"They remind me of somethin," he said. "I'm not quite sure what—the war, of course, but that's jus a part of it. I have suffered a loss, Forrest, far greater than my legs. It's my spirit, my soul, if you will. There is only a blank there now—medals where my soul used to be."

"But what about the 'natural laws' that's in charge of everthin?" I axe him. "What about the 'scheme of things' that we has all got to fit ourself into?"

"Fuck all that," he say. "It was just a bunch of philosophic bullshit."

"But ever since you tole it to me, that's what I been goin by. I been lettin the 'tide' carry me an tryin to do my best. Do the right thing."

"Well, maybe it works for you, Forrest. I thought it was working for me too—but look at me. Just *look* at me," he say. "What good am I? I'm a goddamn legless freak. A bum. A drunkard. A thirty-five-year-old vagrant."

"It could be worse," I says.

"Oh yeah? How?" he say, an I reckon he got me there, so I finished tellin him bout mysef—gettin thowed in the loony bin an then bein shot up in the rocket an landin down with the cannibals an bout ole Sue an Major Fritch an the pygmies.

"Well my God, Forrest my boy, you sure as hell *have* had some adventures," Dan say. "So how come you are sittin here with me on the grates under a garbage bag?"

"I dunno," I says, "but I ain't plannin to stay here long."

"What you got in mind then?"

"Soon as this rain stops," I say, "I'm gonna get off my big fat butt an go lookin for Jenny Curran."

"Where is she?"

"Dunno that either," I says, "but I'll find out."

"Sounds like you might need some help," he say.

I look over at Dan an his eyes is gleamin from behin his beard. Somethin is tellin me *he* is the one needs some hep, but that's okay with me.

Ole Dan an me, we went to a mission flophouse that night on account of it didn't stop rainin, an Dan, he paid them fifty cents apiece for our suppers an a quarter for our beds. You could of got supper free for settin an listenin to a sermon or somesuch, but Dan say he'd sleep out in the rain afore wastin our precious time hearin a Bible-thumper give us his view of the world.

Nex mornin Dan loaned me a dollar an I foun a pay phone an called up to Boston to ole Mose, that used to be the drummer for The Cracked Eggs. Sure enough, he still there in his place, an is damn suprised to hear from me.

"Forrest—I don't believe it!" Mose say. "We had given your ass up for lost!"

The Cracked Eggs, he says, have broken up. All the money that Mister Feeblestein have promised them is eaten up by expenses or somethin, an after the secont record they didn't get no more contracts. Mose say people is listenin to a new kind of music now—Rollin Stoned's or the Iggles or somethin—an most of the fellers in The Cracked Eggs is gone someplace an foun real jobs.

Jenny, Mose say, is not been heard of in a long wile. After she had gone down to Washington for the peace demonstration where I was arrested, she went back with The Cracked Eggs for a few months, but Mose say somethin in her jus wadn't the same. One time he say, she broke up cryin on the stage an they had to play a instrumental to get thru the set. Then she started drinkin vodka an showin up late for performances an they was bout to speak to her bout it when she jus done up an quit.

Mose say he personally feel her behavior has somethin to
do with me, but she never would talk bout it. She moved out
of Boston a couple of weeks later, sayin she was goin to
Chicago, an that is the last he seen of her in nearly five years.

I axed if he knew any way for me to reach her, an he say
maybe he have a ole number she give him jus before she lef.
He leave the phone an come back a few minutes later an give
the number to me. Other than that, he say, "I ain't got a
clue."

I tole him to take care, an if I ever get up to Boston I will
look him up.

"You still playin your harmonica?" Mose axed.

"Yeah, sometimes," I say.

I went an borrowed another dollar from Dan an called the
number in Chicago.

"Jenny Curran—Jenny?" a guy's voice say. "Oh, yeah—I
remember her. Nice little piece of ass. Been a long time."

"You know where she's at?"

"Indianapolis is where she say she was goin when she lef
here. Who knows? Got herself a job at Temperer."

"At what?"

"Temperer—the tire factory. You know, they make tires—
for cars."

I thank the guy an went back an tole Dan.

"Well," he say, "I never been to Indianapolis. Heard it's
nice there in the fall."

We started tryin to thumb a ride out of Washington, but
didn't have no luck to speak of. A guy gave us a ride to the
city limits on the back of a brick truck, but after that, nobody
didn't want to pick us up. I guess we was too funny-lookin or
somethin—Dan settin on his little roller dolly an my big ole
ass standin nex to him. Anyhow, Dan say why don't we take a
bus, cause he's got enough money for that. To tell you the

truth, I felt bad about takin his money, but somehow I figgered that he wanted to go, and it would be good to get him
outta Washington too.

An so we caught a bus to Indianapolis an I put Dan in the
seat nex to me an stowed his little cart in the shelf up above.
All the way there he be sluggin down Red Dagger wine an
sayin what a shitty place the world is to live in. Maybe he's
right. I don't know. I'm just a idiot anyhow.

The bus left us off in the middle of Indianapolis an Dan an
me is standin on the street tryin to figger out what to do nex
when a policeman come up an say, "Ain't no loiterin on the
street," an so we moved on. Dan axed a feller where is the
Temperer Tire Company an it is way outside of town so we
started headin in that direction. After a wile there ain't no
sidewalks an Dan can't push his little cart along, so I picked
him up under one arm and the cart under the other an we
kep on goin.

Bout noon, we seed a big sign say "Temperer Tires," an
figger this be the place. Dan say he will wait outside an I go
on in an they is a woman at the desk an I axed if I could see
Jenny Curran. Woman look at a list an say Jenny is workin in
"re-treads," but ain't nobody allowed to go there cept'n if
they works in the plant. Well, I'm just standin there, tryin to
decide what to do, an the woman say, "Look, honey, they is
bout to get a lunch break in a minute or so, why don't you go
roun to the side of the buildin. Probly she'll come out," so
that's what I did.

They was a lot of folks come out an then, all by hersef, I
seen Jenny walk thru a door an go over to a little spot under a
tree an pull a sambwich out of a paper bag. I went over an
sort of creeped behin her, an she's settin on the groun, an I
says, "That shore look like a tasty sambwich." She didn't
even look up. She kep starin right ahead, an say, "Forrest, it
has to be you."

18

Well, let me tell you—that were the happiest reunion of my life. Jenny is cryin an huggin me an I'm doin the same an everbody else in re-treads is standin there wonderin what is goin on. Jenny say she is off work in bout three hours, an for me an Dan to go over to this little tavern across the street an have a beer or somethin an wait for her. Then she will take us to her place.

We go to the tavern an Dan is drinkin some Ripple wine on account of they got no Red Dagger, but he say Ripple is better anyhow cause it got a nicer "bouquet."

Bunch of other fellers is in there too, playin darts an drinkin an arm rasslin each other at a table. One big ole guy seem to be the bes arm rassler of the tavern, an ever once in a wile some feller would come up an try to beat him but couldn't. They be bettin on it too, five an ten dollars a whack.

After a little bit, Dan whisper over to me, "Forrest, you think you could beat that big bozo over there at arm rasslin?"

An I say I dunno, an Dan say, "Well, here's five bucks, cause I'm bettin you can."

So I go up an say to the feller, "Would you mine if I set down an arm rassle with you?"

He look up at me, smilin, an say, "Long as you got money, you is welcome to try."

So I set down an we grapped each other's hans an somebody say, "Go!" an the rassle is on. Other feller be gruntin an strainin like a dog tryin to shit a peach seed, but in about ten secons I had smushed his arm down on the table an whipped him at arm rasslin. All the other fellers had come gatherin aroun the table an were goin "oooh" an "ahh" an I could hear ole Dan shoutin an cheerin.

Well, the other feller ain't none too happy but he paid me five dollars an got up from the table.

"My elbow slipped," he say, "but nex time you come back here I want to have a go at you again, hear?" I nodded an went back to the table Dan was at an give him the money.

"Forrest," he say, "we may have foun a easy way to make ourselfs some bread." I axed Dan if I could have a quarter to git me a pickled egg from the jar on the counter, an he han me a dollar an say, "You git anything you want, Forrest. We is now got a way to earn a livelyhood."

After work, Jenny come over to the tavern an take us to her place. She is livin in a little apartment not too far from the Temperer Tire Company an has got it all fixed up nice with things like stuffed animals an strings of colored beads hangin from the bedroom door. We went out to a grocery an bought some chicken an Jenny cooked supper for Dan an me an I tole her all that had happened since I seen her last.

Mostly, she is curious about Major Fritch, but when I say she run off with a cannibal, Jenny seemed more relaxed bout it. She say life has not exactly been a bowl of cherries for her either durin the past few years.

After she lef The Cracked Eggs, Jenny done gone to Chicago with this girl she met in the peace movement. They had demonstrated in the streets an got thowed in jail a bunch of times an Jenny say she is finally gettin tired of havin to appear in court an besides, she is concerned that she is developin a long police record.

Anyhow, she is livin in this house with about fifteen people an she says they is not exactly her type of persons. Didn't wear no underwear or nothin, an nobody flushed the toilets. She an this guy decided to take an apartment together, cause he didn't like where they was livin neither, but that didn't work out.

"You know, Forrest," she say, "I even tried to fall in love with him, but I jus couldn't because I was thinkin of you."

She had wrote to her mama an axed her to get in touch with my mama to try an find out where I was bein kept, but her mama write her back sayin our house done burnt up an my mama is now livin in the po house, but by the time the letter get to Jenny, Mama done already run off with the protestant.

Anyhow, Jenny said she didn't have no money an so she heard they is hirin people at the tire company an she come down to Indianapolis to get a job. Bout that time she seen on the television that I am bout to be launched into space, but they is no time for her to get down to Houston. She say she watched, "with horror," as my spaceship crashed, an she give me up for dead. Ever since, she jus been puttin in her time makin re-treads.

I took her an hole her in my arms an we stayed like that for a wile. Dan rolled hissef into the bathroom, say he's got to take a pee. When he's in there, Jenny axe how he gonna do that, an don't he need hep? an I say, "No, I seen him do it before. He can manage."

She shake her head an say, "This is where the Vietnam War have got us."

There ain't much disputin that either. It is a sad an sorry spectacle when a no-legged man have got to pee in his shoe an then dump it over into the toilet.

The three of us settle into Jenny's little apartment after that. Jenny fixed up Dan a place in a corner of the livin room with a little mattress an she kep a jar on the bathroom floor so he wouldn't have to use his shoe. Ever mornin she'd go off to the tire company an Dan an me would set aroun the house an talk an then go down to the little tavern near where Jenny worked to wait till she got off.

First week we started doin that, the guy I beat arm rasslin wanted a chance to git back his five bucks an I gave it to him. He tried two or three times more an in the end lost bout twenty-five dollars an after that he didn't come back no more. But they was always some other feller wanted to try his luck an after a month or two they was guys comin from all over town an from other little towns too. Dan an me, we is pullin in bout a hundrit fifty or two hundrit dollars a week, which weren't bad, let me tell you. An the owner of the tavern, he is sayin he gonna hole a national contest, an git the tv there an everthing. But before that happen, another thing come along that changed my life for sure.

One day a feller come into the tavern that was wearin a white suit an a Hiwaian shirt an a lot of gold jewelry aroun his neck. He set up at the bar wile I was finishin off some guy at arm rasslin an then he come an set down at our table.

"Name's Mike," he say, "an I have heard bout you."

Dan axed what has he heard, an Mike say, "That this feller here is the strongest man in the world."

"What of it?" Dan says, an the feller say, "I think I got a idea how you can make a hell of a lot more money than this nickel an dime shit you're doin here."

"How's that?" Dan say.

"Rasslin," says Mike, "but not this piss-ant stuff—I mean

the real thing. In a ring with hundrits of thousands of payin customers."

"Rasslin who?" Dan axed.

"Whoever," says Mike. "They is a circuit of professional rasslers—The Masked Marvel, The Incredible Hulk, Georgeous George, Filthy McSwine—you name em. The top guys make a hundrit, two hundrit thousand dollars a year. We's start your boy here off slow. Teach him some of the holds, show him the ropes. Why, I bet in no time he'd be a big star —make everybody a pile of money."

Dan look at me, say, "What you think, Forrest?"

"I dunno," I says. "I was kinda thinkin bout goin back home an startin a little srimp bidness."

"Shrimp!" says Mike. "Why boy, you can make fifty times more money doing this than shrimpin! Don't have to do it all your life—just a few years, then you'll have something to fall back on, money in the bank, a nest egg."

"Maybe I ought to axe Jenny," I say.

"Look," Mike say, "I come here to offer you a chance of a lifetime. You don't want it, jus say so, an I'll be on my way."

"No, no," Dan say. Then he turn to me. "Listen, Forrest, some of what this feller say make sense. I mean, how else you gonna earn enough money to start a srimp bidness?"

"Tell you what," Mike say, "you can even take your buddy here with you. He can be your manager. Anytime you want to quit, you're free to do it. What do you say?"

I thought bout it for a minute or so. Sounded pretty good, but usually they is some catch. Nevertheless, I open my big mouth an say the fatal word: "Yes."

Well, that's how I become a professional rassler. Mike had his office in a gymnasium in downtown Indianapolis an ever day me an Dan would catch the bus down there so's I could get taught the proper way to rassle.

In a nutshell, it was this: nobody is sposed to get hurt, but it sposed to look like they do.

They be teachin me all sorts of things—half-nelsons, the airplane spin, the Boston crab, the pile driver, hammerlocks an all such as that. Also, they taught Dan how to yell an scream at the referee, so as to cause the greatest commotion.

Jenny is not too keen on the rasslin bidness on account of she say I might git hurt, an when I say nobody gits hurt cause it's all put-on, she say, "Then what's the point of it?" It is a good question that I cannot rightly answer, but I am lookin foward to makin us some money anyhow.

One day they is tryin to show me somethin called "the belly flop," where I is sposed to go flyin thru the air to lan on top of somebody but at the last minute he rolls away. But somehow, I keep screwin it up, an two or three times I lan right on the feller afore he gits a chance to move out the way. Finally Mike come up into the ring an say, "Jesus, Forrest— you some kind of idiot or somethin! You coud hurt somebody that way, a big ole moose like you!"

An I says, "Yep—I *am* a idiot," an Mike say, "What you mean?" an then Dan, he say for Mike to come over to him for a secont an he splain somethin to him, an Mike say, "Good God! Is you kiddin?" an Dan shake his head. Mike look at me an shrug his shoulders an say, "Well, I guess it takes all kinds."

Anyway, bout a hour later Mike come runnin out of his office up to the ring where Dan an me is.

"I've got it!" he shoutin.

"Got what?" Dan axed.

"His name! We have to give Forrest a name to rassle under. It just came to me what it is."

"What might that be?" Dan say.

"The Dunce!" says Mike. "We will dress him up in diapers an put a big ole dunce cap on his head. The crowd will love it!"

Dan think for a minute. "I dunno," he says, "I don't much like it. Sounds like you are tryin to make a fool out of him."

"It's only for the crowd," Mike say. "He has to have a gimmick of some sort. All the big stars do it. What could be better than The Dunce!"

"How about callin him The Spaceman?" say Dan. "That would be appropriate. He could wear a plastic helmet and some antennas."

"They already got somebody called The Spaceman," Mike says.

"I still don't like it," Dan say. He looks at me, an axed, "What you think, Forrest?"

"I don't really give a shit," I says.

Well, that was the way it was. After all them months of trainin I am finally bout to make my debut as a rassler. Mike come in to the gym the day before the big match an he has a box with my diaper an a big ole black dunce cap. He say to be back at the gym at noon tomorrow so he can drive us to my first rasslin match which is in Muncie.

That night when Jenny get home I gone into the bathroom an put on the diaper an the dunce cap an come out into the livin room. Dan is settin on his little platform cart watchin tv an Jenny is readin a book. Both of them look up when I walk thru the door.

"Forrest, what on earth?" Jenny says.

"It's his costume," say Dan.

"It makes you look like a fool," she say.

"Look at it this way," Dan says. "It's like he is in a play or somethin."

"He still looks like a fool," says Jenny. "I can't believe it! You'd let them dress him up like that an go out in public?"

"It's only to make money," Dan say. "They got one guy called 'The Vegetable' that wears turnip greens for a jock-strap an puts a hollowed-out watermelon over his head with little eyes cut out for him to see thru. Another guy calls himself 'The Fairy,' an has wings on his back an carries a wand. Sumbitch probly weighs three hundred pounds—you oughta see him."

"I don't care what the rest of them do," Jenny says, "I don't like this one bit. Forrest, you go an get out of that outfit."

I gone on back to the bathroom an took off the costume. Maybe Jenny is right, I'm thinkin—but a feller's got to make a livin. Anyhow, it ain't near as bad as the guy I got to rassle tomorrow night in Muncie. He calls hissef "The Turd," an dresses in a big ole body stockin that is painted to look like a piece of shit. Lord knows what he gonna smell like.

19

The deal in Muncie is this: I am to get whupped by The Turd.

Mike tell me that on our ride up there. It seem that The Turd has got "seniority" over me an therefore he is due for a win, an bein that it's my first appearance, it is necessary for me to be on the losin end. Mike say he jus want to tell me how it is from the beginnin so there won't be no hard feelins.

"That is rediculous," Jenny say, "somebody callin theyself 'The Turd.' "

"He probly is one," Dan say, tryin to cheer her up.

"Just remember, Forrest," Mike says, "it's all for show. You can't lose your temper. Nobody is to be hurt. The Turd must win."

Well, when we finally git to Muncie, they is a big ole auditorium where the rasslin is to be helt. One bout is already in progress—The Vegetable is rasslin a guy that calls hisself "The Animal."

The Animal is hairy as a ape, an is wearin a black mask over his eyes, an the first thing he does is to snatch off the hollered-out watermelon that The Vegetable is got over his head an drop kick it into the upper bleachers. Nex, he grapped The Vegetable by his head an ram him into the ring post. Then he bite The Vegetable on the han. I was feelin kinda sorry for the po ole Vegetable, but he got a few tricks hissef—namely, he reached down into the collard green leaves he is wearin for a jockstrap an grapped a hanful of some kind of shit an rub it in The Animal's eyes.

The Animal be bellowin an staggerin all over the ring rubbin his eyes to git the stuff out, an The Vegetable come up behin him an kick him in the ass. Then he thowed The Animal into the ropes an wind them up aroun him so's he can't move an start to beatin the hell outta The Animal. The crowd be booin The Vegetable an thowin paper cups an stuff at him an The Vegetable be givin them back the finger. I was gettin kinda curious how it was gonna wind up, but then Mike come up to me an Dan an say for us to go on back into the dressin room an get into my costume cause I'm on nex against The Turd.

After I get into my diapers an the dunce cap, somebody knock on the door an axe, "Is The Dunce in there?" an Dan say, "Yes," an the feller say, "You is on now, c'mon out," an off we go.

The Turd is already in the ring when I come down the aisle with Dan pushin hissef along behin me. The Turd is runnin aroun the ring makin faces at the crowd an damn if he don't actually look somethin like a turd in that body stockin. Anyhow, I climbed up in the ring an the referee get us together an say, "Okay, boys, I want a good clean match here—no gougin eyes or hittin below the belt or bitin or scratchin or any kind of shit like that. I nod an say, "Uh-huh," an The Turd be glarin at me fiercely.

When the bell rung, me an The Turd be circlin each other an he reached out with his foot to trip me but missed an I grapped him by the shoulders an slung him into the ropes. It was then I foun out he have greased hissef up with some kinda slippery shit that make him hard to hold on to. I tried to grap him aroun his waist but he shot out from my hans like a eel. I took a holt of his arm, but he squished away from that too, an be grinnin an laughin at me.

Then he come runnin at me head on to butt me in the stomach but I stepped aside an The Turd go flyin thru the ropes an land in the front row. Everbody be booin an cat-callin him, but he climbed on back up in the ring an brung with him a foldup chair. He start chasin me aroun with the chair an since I got nothin to defend mysef with, I start to run away. But The Turd, he hit me in the back with the chair, an let me tell you, that hurt. I tried to get the chair away from him, but he conked me on the head with it, an I was in a corner an there wadn't no place to hide. Then he kicked me in the shin an when I bend over to hole my shin, he kick me in the other shin.

Dan is settin on the ring apron yellin at the referee to make The Turd put down the chair, but it ain't doin no good. The Turd hit me four or five times with the chair an knock me down an get on top of me an grap my hair an start bangin my head on the floor. Then he grap holt to my arm an begun twistin my fingers. I look over at Dan an say, "What the hell is this?" an Dan be tryin to get thru the ring ropes but Mike, he stand up an pull Dan back by his shirt collar. Then all of a sudden the bell rung, an I get to go to my corner.

"Listen," I says, "this bastid is tryin to kill me, beatin me on the head with a chair an all. I is gonna have to do somethin bout it."

"What you is gonna do is *lose,*" Mike say. "He ain't tryin to hurt you—he is just tryin to make it look good."

"It sure don't *feel* good," I say.

"Jus stay in there for a few more minutes an then let him

pin you down," Mike says. "Remember, you is makin five hundrit dollars for comin here an losin—not winnin."

"He hits me with that chair again, I don't know what I'm gonna do," I says. I am lookin out in the audience an there is Jenny lookin upset an embarrassed. I am beginnin to think this is not the right thing to do.

Anyhow, the bell rung again an out I go. The Turd try to grap me by the hair but I flung him off an he go spinnin into the ropes like a top. Then I picked him up aroun the waist an lif him up but he slid out of my grip an land on his ass an be moanin an complainin an rubbin his ass, an the nex thing I knew, his manager done handed him one of them "plumber's helpers" with the rubber thing on the end an he commence to beat me on the head with that. Well, I grapped it away from him an busted it in two over my knee an start goin after him, but I see Mike there, shakin his head, an so I let The Turd come an take holt of my arm an twist it in a hammer-lock.

The sumbitch damn near broke my arm. Then he shoved me down on the canvas an begun to hit me in the back of the head with his elbow. I coud see Mike over there, noddin an smilin his approval. The Turd get off me an commenced to kickin me in the ribs an stomach, then he got his chair again an wacked me over the head with it eight or nine times an finally he kneed me in the back an there wadn't a thing I coud do bout it.

I jus lay there, an he set on my head an the referee counted to three an it was sposed to be over. The Turd get up an look down at me an he spit in my face. It was awful an I didn't know what else to do, an I jus couldn't hep it, an I started to cry.

The Turd was prancin aroun the ring an then Dan come up an rolled himsef over to me an started wipin my face with a towel, an nex thing I knew, Jenny had come up in the ring

too an was huggin me an cryin hersef an the crowd was hollerin an yellin an thowin stuff into the ring.

"C'mon, let's get outta here," Dan say, an I got to my feet
an The Turd be stickin out his tongue at me an makin faces.

"You is certainly correctly named," Jenny says to The Turd
as we was leavin the ring. "That was disgraceful."

She could of said it bout both of us. I ain't never felt so
humiliated in my life.

The ride back to Indianapolis was pretty awkward. Dan an
Jenny ain't sayin nothin much an I am in the back seat all sore
an skint up.

"That was a damn good performance you put on out there
tonight, Forrest," Mike says, "especially the cryin at the end
—crowd loved it!"

"It wadn't no performance," Dan says.

"Oh, shucks," Mike say. "Look—somebody's always got to
lose. I'll tell you what—nex time, I will make sure Forrest
wins. How's that make you feel?"

"Ought not to be any 'nex time,' " Jenny says.

"He made good money tonight, didn't he?" Mike say.

"Five hundrit dollars for gettin the shit beat out of him
ain't so good," Jenny says.

"Well it was his first match. Tell you what—nex time, I'll
make it six hundrit."

"How about twelve hundrit?" Dan axed.

"Nine hundrit," Mike says.

"How bout lettin him wear a bathin suit instead of that
dunce cap an diapers?" says Jenny.

"They loved it," Mike says. "It's part of his appeal."

"How would you like to have to dress up in somethin like
that?" Dan says.

"I ain't a idiot," says Mike.

"You shut the fuck up bout that," Dan say.

Well, Mike was good for his word. Nex time I rassled, it was against a feller called "The Human Fly." He was dressed up in somethin with a big pointed snout like a fly have, an a mask with big ole bugged-out eyes. I got to thow him bout the ring an finally set on his head an I collected my nine hundrit dollars. Furthermore, everbody in the crowd cheered wildly an kep hollerin, "We want The Dunce! We want The Dunce!" It wadn't such a bad deal.

Nex, I got to rassle The Fairy, an they even let me bust his wand over his head. After that, they was a hole bunch of guys I come up against, an Dan an me had managed to save up about five thousan dollars for the srimp bidness. But also let me say this: I was gettin very popular with the crowds. Women was writin me letters an they even begun to sell dunce caps like mine as souvenirs. Sometimes I'd go into the ring an they would be fifty or a hundrit people settin there in the audience wearin dunce caps, all clappin an cheerin an callin out my name. Kinda made me feel good, you know?

Meantime, me an Jenny is gettin along fairly good cept for my rasslin career. Ever night when she get back to the apartment we cook ourselfs some supper an her an me an Dan set aroun in the livin room an plan bout how we gonna start the srimp bidness. The way we figger it, we is gonna go down to Bayou La Batre, where po ole Bubba come from, an get us some marsh land off the Gulf of Mexico someplace. We has got to buy us some mesh wire an nets an a little rowboat an somethin to feed the srimp wile they growin, an they will be other things too. Dan say we has also got to be able to have us a place to live an buy groceries an stuff wile we wait for our first profits an also have some way to git them to the market. All tole, he figgers it is gonna take bout five thousan dollars to set everthing up for the first year—after that, we will be on our own.

The problem I got now is with Jenny. She say we already got the five thousan an so why don't we jus go ahead an pack up an go down there? Well, she have a point there, but to be perfectly truthful, I jus ain't quite ready to leave.

You see, it ain't really been since we played them Nebraska corn shucker jackoffs at the Orange Bowl that I has really felt like I done accomplished somethin. Maybe for a little bit durin the ping-pong games in Red China, but that lasted just for a few weeks. But now, you see, ever Saturday night ever week, I am goin out there an hearin them cheer. An they is cheerin *me*—idiot or not.

You should of heard them cheer when I whupped The Grosse Pointe Grinder, who come into the ring with hundrit dollar bills glued to his body. An then they was "Awesome Al from Amarillo," that I done put a Boston Crab hold on an won mysef the Eastern Division champeenship belt. After that, I got to rassle Juno the Giant, who weighed four hundrit pounds an dressed in a leopard skin an carried a papier-maché club.

But one day when Jenny come home from work she say, "Forrest, you an me has got to have a talk."

We went outside an took a walk near a little creek an Jenny foun a place to set down, an then she say, "Forrest, I think this rasslin business is gone far enough."

"What you mean?" I axed, even though I kind of knew.

"I mean we have got nearly ten thousan dollars now, which is more than twice what Dan says we need to start the srimp business. And I am beginnin to wonder jus why you are continuin to go up there ever Saturday night an make a fool of yoursef."

"I ain't makin no fool of mysef," I says, "I has got my fans to think of. I am a very popular person. Cain't jus up an leave like that."

"Bullshit," Jenny say. "What you callin a 'fan,' an what you mean by 'popular'? Them people is a bunch of screwballs to be payin money to watch all that shit. Bunch of grown men gettin up there in they jockstraps an pretendin to hurt each

other. An whoever heard of people callin theyselfs 'The Vegetable,' or 'The Turd,' an such as that—an *you,* callin yoursef
'The Dunce'!"

"What's wrong with that?" I axed.

"Well how do you think it makes me feel, the feller I'm in
love with bein known far an wide as 'The Dunce,' an makin a
spectacle of hissef ever week—an on television, too!"

"We get extra money for the television," I says.

"Screw the extra money," Jenny says. "We don't need no
extra money!"

"Whoever heard of nobody didn't need any extra
money?" I say.

"We don't need it that bad," Jenny say. "I mean, what I
want is to find a little quiet place for us to be in an for you to
get a respectable job, like the srimp business—for us to get us
a little house maybe an have a garden an maybe a dog or
somethin—maybe even kids. I done had my share of fame
with The Cracked Eggs, an it didn't get me nowhere. I
wadn't happy. I'm damned near thirty-five years old. I want
to settle down. . . ."

"Look," I says, "it seem to me that *I* oughta be the one
what say if I quit or not. I ain't gonna do this forever—jus till
it is the right time."

"Well I ain't gonna wait aroun forever, neither," Jenny
say, but I didn't believe she meant it.

20

I had a couple of matches after that an won both of them, naturally, an then Mike call Dan an me in his office one day an says, "Look here, this week you are gonna rassle The Professor."

"Who is that?" Dan axed.

"He comes from California," says Mike, "an is pretty hot stuff out there. He is runner up to the Western Division champion."

"Okay by me," I say.

"But there is just one other thing," say Mike. "This time, Forrest, you got to lose."

"Lose?" I says.

"Lose," say Mike. "Look, you been winnin ever week for months an months. Don't you see you got to lose ever once in a wile to keep up your popularity?"

"How you figger that?"

"Simple. People like a underdog. Makes you look better the nex time."

"I don't like it," I say.

"How much you payin?" Dan axed.

"Two thousan."

"I don't like it," I says again.

"Two thousan's a lot of money," Dan say.

"I still don't like it," I says.

But I took the deal.

Jenny is been actin sort of peculiar lately, but I put it down to nerves or somethin. Then one day she come home an say, "Forrest, I'm at the end of my rope. Please don't go out there an do this."

"I got to," I says. "Anyhow, I is gonna lose."

"Lose?" she say. I splain it to her jus like Mike splain it to me, an she say, "Awe shit, Forrest, this is too much."

"It's my life," I says—whatever that meant.

Anyway, a day or so later, Dan come back from someplace an says him an me got to have a talk.

"Forrest, I think I got the solution to our problems."

I axed what it was.

"I think," says Dan, "we better be bailin out of this business pretty soon. I know Jenny don't like it, an if we are gonna start our srimp thing, we best be on bout it. But," he say, "I think I got a way to bail out an clean up at the same time."

"How's that?" I axed.

"I been talkin to a feller downtown. He runs a bookie operation an the word is out you gonna lose to The Professor this Saturday."

"So?" I says.

"So what if you win?"

"Win?"

"Kick his ass."

"I get in trouble with Mike," I says.

"Screw Mike," Dan say. "Look, here's the deal. Spose we

take the ten thousan we got an bet it on you to *win?* Two-to-
one odds. Then you kick his ass an we got *twenty* grand."

"But I'll be in all sorts of trouble," I says.

"We take the twenty grand an blow this town," Dan say.
"You know what we can do with twenty grand? We can start
one hell of a srimp business an have a pile left over for ourselves. I'm thinkin maybe it's time to get out of this rasslin
stuff anyway."

Well, I'm thinkin Dan is the manager, an also that Jenny
has said I gotta get out of rasslin too, an twenty grand ain't a
bad deal.

"What you think?" Dan says.

"Okay," I say. "Okay."

The day come for me to rassle The Professor. The bout is
to be helt up at Fort Wayne, an Mike come by to pick us up
an is blowin the horn outside, an I axed Jenny if she is ready.

"I ain't goin," she say. "I'll watch it on television."

"But you got to go," I says, an then I axed Dan to splain
why.

Dan tole Jenny what the plan was, an that she had to go, on
account of we needed somebody to drive us back to Indianapolis after I done whupped The Professor.

"Neither of us can drive," he say, "an we gonna have to
have a fast car right outside the arena when it's over to get us
back here to collect the twenty grand from the bookie an
then hightail it out of town."

"Well, I ain't havin nothin to do with a deal like that,"
Jenny say.

"But it's twenty grand," I says.

"Yeah, an it's dishonest too," she says.

"Well, it's dishonest what he's been doin all the time,"
Dan says, "winnin an losin all planned out beforehand."

"I ain't gonna do it," Jenny said, an Mike was blowin his

horn again, an Dan say, "Well, we gotta go. We'll see you back here sometime after it's over—one way or the other."

"You fellers oughta be ashamed of yourselfs," Jenny say.

"You won't be so high-falutin when we come back with twenty thousan smackeroos in our pocket," Dan says.

Anyhow, off we go.

On the ride to Fort Wayne, I ain't sayin much on account of I'm kinda embarrassed bout what I'm fixin to do to ole Mike. He ain't treated me so badly, but on the other han, as Dan have splained, I has made a lot of money for him too, so it gonna come out aroun even.

We get to the arena an the first bout is already on—Juno the Giant is gettin the hell kicked out of him by The Fairy. An nex up is a tag team match between lady midgets. We gone on into the dressin room an I put on my diapers an dunce cap. Dan, he get somebody to dial the number of the taxicab company an arrange for a cab to be there outside with its motor runnin after my match.

They beat on my door an it's time to go on. Me an The Professor is the feature bout of the evenin.

He is already there in the ring when I come out. The Professor is a little wiry guy with a beard an wearin spectacles an he have on a black robe an morter-board hat. Damn if he don't look like a professor at that. I decided right then to make him eat that hat.

Well, I climb on up in the ring an the announcer say, "Ladies an Gentlemen." At this there be a lot of boos, an then he say, "We is proud tonight to have as our main attraction for the North American Professional Rasslin Association title bout two of the top contenders in the country—The Professor versus The Dunce!"

At this, they is so much booin an cheerin that it is impossible to say if the crowd is happy or angry. It don't matter nohow, cause then the bell ring an the match is on.

The Professor has taken off his robe, glasses, an the morter-board hat an is circlin me, shakin his finger at me like I'm bein scolded. I be tryin to grap a holt of him, but ever time, he jump out of the way an keep shakin his finger. This go on for a minute or two an then he make a mistake. He run aroun behin me an try to kick me in the ass, but I done snatched a holt of him by the arm an slung him into the ropes. He come boundin off the ropes like a slingshot ball an as he go past me I trip him up an was bout to pounce on him with the Bellybuster maneuver, but he done scrambled out of the way to his corner an when I look up, he is got a big ole ruler in his han.

He be whoppin the ruler in his palm like he gonna spank me with it, but instead, when I grapped for him this time, he done jam the ruler in my eye, like to gouge it out. I'll tell you this—it hurt, an I was stumblin aroun tryin to get my sight back when he run up behin me an put somethin down my diapers. Didn't take long to find out what it was—it was ants! Where he got them, lord knows, but the ants commence to bitin me an I was in a awful fix.

Dan is there, hollerin for me to finish him off, but it ain't no easy thing with ants in your pants. Anyhow, the bell rung an that was the end of the roun an I go on back to my corner an Dan be tryin to get the ants out.

"That was a dirty trick," I say.

"Just finish him," Dan says, "we can't afford no screw-ups."

The Professor come out for the secont round an be makin faces at me. Then he get close enough for me to snatch him up an I lifted him over my head an begun doin the Airplane Spin.

I spinned him aroun bout forty or fifty times till I was pretty sure he was dizzy an then heaved him hard as I could over the ropes into the audience. He land up in bout the fifth row of bleachers in the lap of a ole woman who is knittin a sweater, an she start beatin him with a umbrella.

Trouble is, the Airplane Spin have taken its toll on me too. Everthin spinnin aroun but I figger it don't matter cause it'll stop pretty soon, an The Professor, he is finished anyway. In this, I am wrong.

I am almost recovered from the spinnin when all of a sudden somethin got me by the ankles. I look down, an damn if The Professor ain't climbed back in the ring an brought with him the ball of yarn the ole lady was knittin with, an now he done rapped it aroun my feet.

I started tryin to wriggle out, but The Professor be runnin circles aroun me with the yarn, rappin me up like a mummy. Pretty soon, I am tied up han an foot an cain't move or nothin. The Professor stop an tie the yarn up in a little fancy knot an stand in front of me an take a bow—like he is a magician just done some trick or somethin.

Then he saunter over to his corner an get a big ole book— look like a dictionary—an come back an take another bow. An then he crack me on the head with the book. Ain't nothin I can do. He must of cracked me ten or twelve times before I gone down. I am helpless an I am hearin everbody cheer as The Professor set on my shoulders an pin me—an win the match.

Mike an Dan, they come in the ring an unraveled the yarn off me an heped me up.

"Terrific!" Mike say, "Just terrific! I couldn't of planned it better mysef!"

"Oh shut up," Dan say. An then he turn to me. "Well," he say, "this is a fine state of affairs—gettin yoursef outsmarted by The Professor."

I ain't sayin nothin. I am miserable. Everthin is lost an the one thing I know for sure is that I ain't gonna rassle never again.

We didn't need the getaway cab after that, so Dan an me rode back to Indianapolis with Mike. All the drive back, he be sayin how great it was that I lost to The Professor that way, an how nex time I gonna get to win an make everbody thousans of dollars.

When he pull up in front of the apartment, Mike reach back an han Dan a envelope with the two thousan dollars he was gonna pay me for the match.

"Don't take it," I says.

"What?" says Mike.

"Listen," I say. "I got to tell you somethin."

Dan cut in. "What he wants to say is, he ain't gonna be rasslin no more."

"You kiddin?" Mike say.

"Ain't kiddin," says Dan.

"Well how come?" Mike axed. "What's wrong, Forrest?"

Before I could say anythin, Dan say, "He don't want to talk about it now."

"Well," says Mike, "I understan, I guess. You go get a good night's sleep. I'll be back first thing in the mornin an we can talk bout it, okay?"

"Okay," Dan says, an we get out of the car. When Mike is gone, I says, "You shouldn't of took the money."

"Well it's all the hell we got left now," he say. Everthin else is gone. I didn't realize till a few minutes later how right he was.

We get to the apartment an lo an behole, Jenny is gone too. All her things is gone, cept she lef us some clean sheets an towels an some pots an pans an stuff. On the table in the livin room is a note. Dan foun it first, an he read it out loud to me.

Dear Forrest, [it says]

I am just not able to take this anymore. I have tried to talk to you about my feelings, and you don't seem to care. There is something particularly bad about what you are gonna do tonight, because it isn't honest, and I am afraid I cannot go on with you any longer.

Maybe it is my fault, partly, because I have gotten to an age where I need to settle down. I think about having a house and a family and goin to church and things like that. I have known you since the first grade, Forrest—nearly thirty years—and have watched you grow up big and strong and fine. And when I finally realized how much I cared for you—when you came up to Boston—I was the happiest girl in the world.

And then you took to smoking too much dope, and you fooled with those girls down in Provincetown, an even after that, I missed you, and was glad you came to Washington during the peace demonstration to see me.

But when you got shot up in the spaceship and were lost in the jungle nearly four years, I think maybe I changed. I am not as hopeful as I used to be, and think I would be satisfied with just a simple life somewhere. So, now I must go an find it.

Something is changed in you, too, dear Forrest. I don't think you can help it exactly, for you were always a "special" person, but we no longer seem to think the same way.

I am in tears as I write this, but we must part now. Please don't try to find me. I wish you well, my darling— good-bye.

love,
Jenny

Dan handed the note to me but I let it drop on the floor an just stood there, realizin for the first time in my life what it is truly like to be a idiot.

21

Well, after that I was one sorry bastid.

Dan an me stayed at the apartment that nite, but the nex mornin started packin up our shit an all, cause there wadn't no reason to be in Indianapolis no longer. Dan, he come to me an say, "Here, Forrest, take this money," an helt out the two thousand dollars Mike had give us for rasslin The Professor.

"I don't want it," I says.

"Well you better take it," says Dan, "cause it's all we got."

"You keep it," I says.

"At least take haf of it," he say. "Look, you gotta have some travelin money. Get you to wherever your goin."

"Ain't you goin with me?" I axed.

"I'm afraid not, Forrest," he says. "I think I done enough damage already. I didn't sleep none last night. I'm thinkin about how I got you to agree to bet all our money, an how I got you to keep on rasslin when it oughta have been apparent Jenny was about to freak out on us. An it wadn't your fault

you got whupped by The Professor. You did what you could.
I am the one to blame. I jus ain't no good."

"Awe, Dan, it wadn't your fault neither," I says. "If I
hadn't of got the big head bout bein The Dunce, an begun to
believe all that shit they was sayin bout me, I wouldn't of got
in this fix in the first place."

"Whatever it is," Dan say, "I jus don't feel right taggin
along anymore. You got other fish to fry now. Go an fry em.
Forget about me. I ain't no good."

Well, me an Dan talked for a long time, but there wadn't
no convincin him, an after a wile, he got his shit an I hepped
him down the steps, an the last I seen of him, he was pushin
hissef down the street on his little cart, with all his clothes an
shit piled in his lap.

I went down to the bus station an bought a ticket to Mobile. It was sposed to be a two day an two nite trip, down thru
Louisville, to Nashville, to Birmingham an then Mobile, an I
was one miserable idiot, settin there wile the bus rolled
along.

We passed thru Louisville durin the nite, an the nex day we
stopped in Nashville an had to change busses. It was about a
three hour wait, so I decided to walk aroun town for a wile. I
got me a sambwich at a lunch counter an a glass of iced tea an
was walkin down the street when I seen a big sign in front of
a hotel say, "Welcome Grandmaster's Invitational Chess
Tournament."

It sort of got my curiosity up, on account of I had played all
that chess back in the jungle with Big Sam, an so I went on
into the hotel. They was playin the chess game in the ball-
room an had a big mob of people watchin, but a sign say,
"Five dollars admission," and I didn't want to spend none of
my money, but I looked in thru the door for a wile, an then
jus went an set down in the lobby by mysef.

They was a chair across from me with a little ole man settin in it. He was all shriveled up an grumpy-lookin an had on a black suit with spats an a bow tie an he had a chessboard set out on a table in front of him.

As I set there, ever once in a wile he would move one of the chessmen, an it begun to dawn on me that he was playin by hissef. I figgered I had bout another hour or so fore the bus lef, so I axed him if he wanted somebody to play with. He jus looked at me an then looked back down at his chessboard an didn't say nothin.

A little bit later, the ole feller'd been studyin the chessboard for most of a half hour an then he moved his white bishop over to black square seven an was jus bout to take his han off it when I says, " 'scuse me."

The feller jumped like he'd set on a tack, an be glarin across the table at me.

"You make that move," I says, "an you be leavin yoursef wide open to lose your knight an then your queen an put your ass in a fix."

He look down at his chessboard, never takin his han off the bishop, an then he move it back an say to me, "Possibly you are right."

Well, he go on back to studyin the chessboard an I figger it's time to get back to the bus station, but jus as I start to leave, the ole man say, "Pardon me, but that was a very shrewd observation you made."

I nod my head, an then he say, "Look, you've obviously played the game, why don't you sit down an finish this one with me? Just take over the white in their positions now."

"I cain't," I says, cause I got to catch the bus an all. So he jus nods an gives me a little salute with his han an I went on back to the bus station.

Time I get there, the damn bus done lef anyway, an here I am an ain't no other bus till tomorrow. I jus cain't do nothin right. Well, I got a day to kill, so I walked on back to the hotel an there is the little ole man still playin against hissef, an he seems to be winnin. I went on up to him an he look up an motion for me to set down. The situation I have come into is pretty miserable—haf my pawns gone an I ain't got but one bishop an no rooks an my queen is about to be captured nex.

It took me most of a hour to git mysef back in a even position, an the ole man be kinda gruntin an shakin his head evertime I improve my situation. Finally, I dangle a gambit in front of him. He took it, an three moves later I got him in check.

"I will be damned," he say. "Just who *are* you, anyway?"

I tole him my name, an he say, "No, I mean, where have you played? I don't even recognize you."

When I tole him I learnt to play in New Guinea, an he say, "Good heavens! An you mean to say you haven't even been in regional competition?"

I shook my head an he says, "Well whether you know it or not, I am a former international grand master, and you have just stepped into a game you couldn't possibily have won, and totally annihilated me!"

I axed how come he wadn't playin in the room with the other people, an he says, "Oh, I played earlier. I'm nearly eighty years old now, an there is a sort of senior tournament. The real glory is to the younger fellows now—their minds are jus sharper."

I nodded my head an thanked him for the game an got up to go, but he says, "Listen, have you had your supper yet?"

I tole him I had a sambwich a few hours ago, an he say, "Well how about letting me buy you dinner? After all, you gave me a superb game."

I said that woud be okay, an we went into the hotel dinin room. He was a nice man. Mister Tribble was his name.

"Look," Mister Tribble say wile we is havin dinner, "I'd have to play you a few more games to be sure, but unless your playing this evening was a total fluke, you are perhaps one of the brightest unrecognized talents in the game. I would like to sponsor you in a tournament or two, and see what happens."

I tole him about headin home an wantin to get into the srimp bidness and all, but he say, "Well, this could be the opportunity of a lifetime for you, Forrest. You could make a lot of money in this game, you know." He said for me to think it over tonight, an let him know somethin in the mornin. So me an Mister Tribble shook hans, an I went on out in the street.

I done wandered aroun for a wile, but they ain't a lot to see in Nashville, an finally I wound up settin on a bench in a park. I was tryin to think, which don't exactly come easy to me, an figger out what to do now. My mind was mostly on Jenny an where she is. She say not to try to find her or nothin, but they is a feelin down deep in me someplace that she ain't forgot me. I done made a fool of mysef in Indianapolis, an I know it. I think it was that I wadn't tryin to do the right thing. An now, I ain't sure what the right thing is. I mean, here I am, ain't got no money to speak of, an I got to have some to start up the srimp bidness, an Mister Tribble say I can win a good bit on the chess circuit. But it seem like ever time I do somethin besides tryin to get home an get the srimp bidness started, I get my big ass in hot water—so here I am again, wonderin what to do.

I ain't been wonderin long when up come a policeman an axe me what I'm doin.

I says I'm jus settin here thinkin, an he say ain't nobody allowed to set an think in the park at night an for me to move along. I go on down the street, an the policeman be followin me. I didn't know where to go, so after a wile I saw an alley an walked on back in it an foun a place to set down an rest my feet. I ain't been settin there more'n a minute when the same ole policeman come by an see me there.

"All right," he say, "come on outta there." When I get out to the street, he say, "What you doin in there?"

I says, "Nothin," an he say, "That's exactly what I thought —you is under arrest for loiterin."

Well, he take me to the jail an lock me up an then in the mornin they say I can make one phone call if I want. Course I didn't know nobody to phone but Mister Tribble, so that's what I did. Bout haf a hour later, he shows up at the police station an springs me out of jail.

Then he buys me a big ole breakfast at the hotel an says, "Listen, why don't you let me enter you in the interzonal championships next week in Los Angeles? First prize is ten thousan dollars. I will pay for all your expenses an we will split any money you win. Seems to me you need a stake of some sort, and, to tell you the truth, I would enjoy it immensely mysef. I will be your coach and adviser. How bout it?"

I still had some doubts, but I figgered it wouldn't hurt to try. So I said I woud do it for a wile. Till I got enough money to start the srimp thing. An me an Mister Tribble shook hans an become partners.

Los Angeles was quite a sight. We got there a week early an Mister Tribble would spend most of the day coachin me an honin down my game, but after a wile of this, he jus shook his head an say there ain't no sense in tryin to coach me, cause I got "every move in the book" already. So what we did was, we went out on the town.

Mister Tribble took me to Disneyland an let me go on some rides an then he arranged to get us a tour of a movie lot. They is got all sorts of movies goin on, an people is runnin aroun shoutin "take one," an "cut," an "action," an shit like that. One of the movies they was doin was a Western an we seen a feller get hissef thowed thru a plate glass winder about ten times—till he got it right.

Anyway, we was jus standin there watchin this, when some guy walk up an says, "I beg your pardon, are you an actor?"

I says, "Huh?" An Mister Tribble, he says, "No, we are chess players."

An the feller say, "Well that's kind of a shame, because the big guy here, he looks ideal for a role in a movie I'm doing." And then he turn to me an feel of my arm an say, "My, my, you *are* a big strong feller—are you sure you don't act?"

"I did once," I says.

"Really!" the feller says. "What in?"

"King Lear."

"Marvelous, baby," he says, "that's just marvelous—do you have your SAG card?"

"My what?"

"Screen Actors Guild—oh, no matter," he say. "Listen, baby, we can get that, no trouble. What I want to know is, where have they been hiding you? I mean, just look at you! A perfect big strong silent type—another John Wayne."

"He is no John Wayne," Mister Tribble say sourly, "he is a world-class chess player."

"Well all the better," the feller say, "a *smart* big, strong, silent type. Very unusual."

"Ain't as smart as I look," I says, tryin to be honest, but the feller say none of that matters anyhow, cause actors ain't sposed to be smart *or* honest or nothin like that—just be able to get up there an say they lines.

"My name's Felder," he says, "an I make movies. I want you to take a screen test."

"He has to play in a chess tournament tomorrow," Mister Tribble say. "He has no time for acting or screen tests."

"Well, you could squeeze it in, couldn't you? After all, it might be the break you've been looking for. Why don't you come along, too, Tribble, we'll give you a screen test as well."

22

The nex mornin is when the chess tournament is bein helt out at the Beverly Hills Hotel. Me an Mister Tribble is there early an he has me signed up for matches all day.

Basically, it ain't no big deal. It took me about seven minutes to whup the first guy, who was a regional master an also a professor in some college, which made me secretly feel kind of good. I had beat a professor after all.

Nex was a kid about seventeen, an I wiped him out in less than half a hour. He thowed a tantrum an then commenced to bawlin an cryin an his mama had to come drag him off.

They was all sorts of people I played that day an the nex, but I beat em all pretty fast, which was a relief since when I played against Big Sam I had to keep settin there an not go to the bathroom or nothin, cause if I got up from the chessboard he would move the pieces aroun an try to cheat.

Anyhow, by that time I had got my way into the finals an they was a day's rest in between. I gone on back to the hotel with Mister Tribble an found a message to us from Mister

Felder, the movie guy. It say, "Please call my office this afternoon an arrange for a screen test tomorrow morning," an it give a telephone number to call.

"Well, Forrest," Mister Tribble say, "I don't know bout this. What do you think?"

"I dunno either," I says, but to tell the truth, it soun sort of excitin, bein in the movies an all. Maybe I even get to meet Raquel Welch or somebody.

"Oh, I don't suppose it would hurt anything," Mister Tribble say. "I guess I'll call an set up an appointment." So he call Mister Felder's office an be findin out when an where for us to go an all of a sudden he cup his hand over the phone an say to me, "Forrest, can you swim?" An I say, "Yup," an he say back into the phone, "Yes, he can."

After he done hung up, I axed why they want to know if I can swim, an Mister Tribble say he don't know, but he recon we will find out when we get there.

The movie lot we gone to is a different place than the other one, an we was met at the gate by a guard that took us to where the screen test is bein helt. Mister Felder is there arguin with a lady that actually look somethin like Raquel Welch, but when he seen me, he is all smiles.

"Ah, Forrest," he say, "Terrific you came. Now what I want you to do is go thru that door to Makeup and Costuming, and then they will send you back out when they are finished."

So I gone on thru the door an there is a couple of ladies standin there an one of em say, "Okay, take off your clothes." Here I go again, but I do as I am tole. When I get thru takin off my clothes, the other lady han me this big blob of rubber-lookin clothes with scales an shit all over it an funny-lookin webbed feet an hans. She say to put it on. It take the three of us to get me in the thing but after bout a hour we manage. Then they point me in the direction of Makeup an I is tole to set in a chair wile a lady an a feller commence to jam down this big rubber mask over my head an fit it to the costume an start paintin over the lines where it showed. When they is thru, they say for me to go back out to the movie set.

I can hardly walk on account of the webbed feet an it is hard to get the door open with a webbed han, but finally I do an I suddenly find mysef in a outdoor place with a big lake an all sorts of banana trees an tropical-lookin shit. Mister Felder is there an when he seen me, he jump back an say, "Terrific, baby! You is perfect for the part!"

"What part is that?" I axed, an he say, "Oh, didn't I tell you? I am doing a remake of *The Creature from the Black Lagoon.*" Even a idiot like me could guess what part he have in mind for me to play.

Mister Felder motion for the lady he had been arguin with to come over. "Forrest," he say, "I want you to meet Raquel Welch."

Well, you coudda knocked me over with a feather! There she were, all dressed up in a low-cut gown an all. "Please to meet you," I says thru the mask, but Raquel Welch turn to Mister Felder lookin mad as a hornet.

"What'd he say? Something about my tits, wasn't it!"

"No, baby, no," say Mister Felder. "He just said he was glad to meet you. You can't hear him too well because of that mask he's got on."

I stuck out my webbed han to shake hans with her, but she jump back about a foot, an say, "Uggh! Let's get this goddamn thing over with."

Anyhow, Mister Felder say the deal is this: Raquel Welch is to be flounderin in the water an then she faints, an then I am to come up from under her an pick her up an carry her outta the water. But when she revives, she looks up at me an is scared an commences to scream, "Put me down! Help! Rape!" an all that shit.

But, Mister Felder say, I am not to put her down, cause some crooks is sposed to be chasin us; instead, I am to carry her off into the jungle.

Well, we tried the scene, an the first time we done it, I thought it come off pretty well, an it is really excitin to actually be holdin Raquel Welch in my arms, even tho she be hollerin, "Put me down! Help, police!" an so on.

But Mister Felder say that ain't good enough, an for us to do it again. An that wadn't good enough either, so we be doin that same scene bout ten or fifteen times. In between doin the scene, Raquel Welch is crabbin an bitchin an cussin at Mister Felder, but he just kep on sayin, "Beautiful, baby, beautiful!" an that sort of thing.

Mysef, I'm startin to have a real problem tho. On account of I been in the creature suit nearly five hours now, an they ain't no zipper or nothin to pee thru, an I'm bout to bust. But I don't wanta say nothin bout that, cause this is a real movie an everthin, an I don't want to make nobody mad.

But I gotta do *somethin,* so's I decide that the nex time I get in the water, I will jus pee in the suit, an it will run out my leg or somethin into the lagoon. Well, Mister Felder, he say, "Action!" an I go in the water an start to pee. Raquel Welch be flounderin aroun an then she faints, an I dive under an grap her an haul her onto shore.

She wakes up an start to beatin on me an hollerin, "Help! Murder! Put me down!" an all, but then she suddenly stop hollerin an she say, "What is that smell?"

Mister Felder holler, "Cut!" an he stand up an say, "What was that you said, baby? That ain't in the script."

An Raquel Welch say, "Shit on the script! Somethin stinks aroun here!" Then she suddenly look at me an say, "Hey, you—whoever you are—did you take a leak?"

I was so embarrassed, I did not know what to do. I just stood there for a secont, holdin her in my arms, an then I shake my head an say, "Uh uh."

It was the first lie I ever tole in my life.

"Well somebody sure did," she say, "cause I know pee when I smell it! An it wadn't me! So it *has* to be you! How dare you pee on me, you big oaf!" Then she start beatin on me with her fists an hollerin to "Put me down!" and "Get away from me!" an all, but I jus figgered the scene is startin up again an so I begun to carry her back into the jungle.

Mister Felder shout, *"Action!"* The movie cameras begun to rollin once more, an Raquel Welch is beatin an clawin an yellin like she never done before. Mister Felder is back there hollerin, "That's it, baby—terrific! Keep it up!" I coud see Mister Tribble back there too, settin in a chair, kinda shakin his head an tryin to look the other way.

Well, when I get back in the jungle a little ways, I stopped an turned aroun to see if that's where Mister Felder is fixin to yell "Cut," like he had before, but he was jumpin aroun like a wild man, motionin to keep on goin, an shoutin, "Perfect, baby! That's what I want! Carry her off into the jungle!"

Raquel Welch is still scratchin an flailin at me an screamin, "Get away from me you vulgar animal!" an such as that, but I kep on goin like I'm tole.

All of a sudden she screech, "Oh my god! My dress!"

I ain't noticed it till now, but when I look down, damn if her dress ain't caught on some bush back there an done totally unravel itself. Raquel Welch is butt neckid in my arms!

I stopped an said, "Uh oh," an started to turn aroun to carry her back, but she begin shriekin, "No, no! You idiot! I can't go back there like this!"

I axed what she wanted me to do, an she say we gotta find someplace to hide till she gets things figgered out. So I keep on goin deeper into the jungle when all of a sudden out of noplace come a big object thru the trees, swingin towards us on a vine. The object swung past us once an I coud tell it was a ape of some sort, an then it swung back again an dropped off the vine at our feet. I almost fainted dead away. It was ole Sue, hissef!

Raquel Welch begun to bawlin an hollerin again an Sue has grapped me aroun the legs an is huggin me. I don't know how he recognized me in my creature suit, cept I guess he smelt me or somethin. Anyhow, Raquel Welch, she finally say, "Do you *know* this fucking baboon?"

"He ain't no baboon," I says, "He's a orangutang. Name's Sue."

She look at me kinda funny an say, "Well if it's a *he*, then how come its name is Sue?"

"That is a long story," I say.

Anyhow, Raquel Welch is tryin to cover hersef up with her hans, but ole Sue, he knows what to do. He grapped holt of a couple of big leaves off one of them banana trees an han them up to her an she partly covered hersef up.

What I find out later is that we have gone across our jungle location onto another set where they is filmin a Tarzan movie, an Sue is being used as a extra. Not long after I got rescued from the pygmies in New Guinea, white hunters come along an captured ole Sue an shipped his ass to some animal trainer in Los Angeles. They been usin him in movies ever since.

Anyway, we ain't got time to jack aroun now, on account of Raquel Welch is screechin an bitchin again, say, "You gotta take me someplace where I can get me some clothes!" Well, I don't know where you can find no clothes in the jungle, even if it *is* a movie set, so we jus keep movin along, hopin somethin will happen.

It does. We suddenly come to a big fence, an I figger there probly be someplace on the other side of it to get her some clothes. Sue finds a loose board in the fence an lifts it up so's we can get thru, but as soon as I step on the other side, ain't nothin to step on, an me an Raquel go tumblin head over heels down the side of this hill. We finally rolled all the way to the bottom an when I look aroun, damn if we ain't landed right on the side of a big ole road.

"Oh my God!" Raquel Welch yell. "We're on the Santa Monica Freeway!"

I look up, an here come ole Sue, lopin down the hillside. He finally get down to us, an the three of us be standin there. Raquel Welch is movin the banana leaves up an down, tryin to cover herself up.

"What we gonna do now?" I axed. Cars are wizzin by, an even tho we must of been a odd-lookin sight, ain't nobody even payin us the slightest attention.

"You gotta take me someplace!" she hollers. "I got to get some clothes on!"

"Where?" I says.

"Anywhere!" she screams, an so we started off down the Santa Monica Freeway.

After a wile, up in the distance, we seen a big white sign up in some hills say "HOLLYWOOD," an Raquel Welch say, "We got to get off this damn freeway and get to Rodeo Drive, where I can buy me some clothes." She is keepin pretty busy tryin to cover herself up—ever time a car come towards us, she put the banana leaves in front, an when a car come up from behin, she move em back there to cover her ass. In mixed traffic, it is quite a spectacular sight—look like one of them fan dancers or somethin.

So we got off the freeway an went across a big field. "Has that fuckin monkey got to keep follown us?" Raquel Welch say. "We look rediculous enough as it is!" I ain't sayin nothin, but I look back, an ole Sue, he got a pained look on his face. He ain't never met Raquel Welch before, neither, an I think his feelins is hurt.

Anyhow, we kep goin along an they still ain't nobody payin us much mind. Finally we come to a big ole busy street an Raquel Welch say, "Goodgodamighty—this is Sunset

Boulevard! How am I gonna explain goin across Sunset Boulevard butt neckid in broad daylight!" In this, I tend to see her point, an I am sort of glad I got on the creature suit so's nobody will recognize me—even if I *am* with Raquel Welch.

We come to a traffic light an when it turn green, the three of us walked on across the street, Raquel Welch doin her fan dance to beat the band an smilin at people in cars an stuff like she was on stage. "I am totally humiliated!" she hisses at me under her breath. "I am violated! Just wait till we get outta this. I am gonna have your big ass, you goddamn idiot!"

Some of the people waitin in their cars at the traffic light commence to honkin they horns and wavin, on account of they must of recognized Raquel Welch, an when we get across the street, a few cars turn our way an start to followin after us. By the time we get to Wilshire Boulevard we have attracted quite a sizable crowd; people come out of they houses an stores an all to follow us—look like the Pied Piper or somethin—an Raquel Welch's face is red as a beet.

"You'll never work in this town again!" she say to me, flashin a smile to the crowd, but her teeth is clenched tight.

We gone on a bit further, an then she say, "Ah—finally—here is Rodeo Drive." I look over at a corner an, sure enough, there is a woman's clothing store. I tap her on the shoulder an point at it, but Raquel Welch say, "Uggh—that's Popagallo. Nobody would be caught dead these days wearing a Popagallo dress."

So we walked some more an then she say, "There—Giani's—they got some nice things in there," an so we go inside.

They is a sales feller at the door with a little moustache an a white suit with a handkerchief stickin out of the coat pocket, an he is eyein us pretty carefully as we come thru the door.

"May I help you, madam?" he axed.

"I want to buy a dress," Raquel Welch say.

"What did you have in mind?" say the feller.

"Anything, you fool—can't you see what's going on!"

Well, the sales feller point to a couple of racks of dresses an say there might be somethin in there her size, so Raquel Welch go over an begin to look thru the dresses.

"An is there somethin I can do for you gentlemen?" the feller says to me an Sue.

"We is just with her," I say. I look back, an the crowd is all gathered outside, noses pressed to the winder.

Raquel Welch took about eight or nine dresses into the back an tried them on. After a wile she come out an say, "What do you think about this one?" It is a sort of brown-lookin dress with a bunch of belts an loops all over it an a low neckline.

"Oh, I'm not so sure, dear," say the salesman, "somehow it—it just isn't *you.*" So she go back an try on another one an the salesman say, "Oh, wonderful! You look absolutely precious."

"I'll take it," say Raquel Welch, an the salesman say, "Fine —how would you like to pay for it?"

"What do you mean?" she axed.

"Well, cash, check, credit card?" he say.

"Look you bozo—can't you see I don't have anything like that with me? Where the hell do you think I'd *put* it?"

"Please, madam—don't let's be vulgar," the salesman say.

"I am Raquel Welch," she tell the man. "I will send somebody around here to pay you later."

"I am terribly sorry, lady," he say, "but we don't do business that way."

"But I'm *Raquel Welch!*" she shout. "Don't you recognize me?"

"Listen lady," the man say, "Half the people that come in here say they are Raquel Welch or Farrah Fawcett or Sophia Loren or somebody. You got any ID?"

"ID!" she shout. "Where do you think I would keep ID?"

"No ID, no credit card, no money—no dress," say the salesman.

"I'll prove who the hell I am," Raquel Welch say, an all of a sudden she pull down the top of the dress. "Who else is got tits like these in this one-horse town!" she screech. Outside, the crowd all be beatin on the winders an hollerin an cheerin. But the salesman, he punched a little button an some big guy what was the security detective come over an he say, "Okay, your asses is all under arrest. Come along quietly an there won't be no trouble."

23

So here I am, thowed in jail again.

After the security feller corralled us at Giani's, two car-loads of cops come screamin up an this one cop come up to the salesman an say, "Well, what we got here?"

"This one says she's Raquel Welch," the salesman say. "Come in here wearin a bunch of banana leaves an wouldn't pay for the dress. I don't know bout these other two—but they look pretty suspicious to me."

"I *am* Raquel Welch!" she shout.

"Sure, lady," the cop say. "An I am Clint Eastwood. Why don't you go along with these two nice fellers here." He point to a couple of other cops.

"Now," says the head cop, an he be lookin at me an Sue, "what's your story?"

"We was in a pitcher," I says.

"That why you're wearin that creature suit?" he axe.

"Yup," I says.

"An what bout him?" he say, pointin to Sue. "That's a pretty realistic costume, if I say so myself."

"Ain't no costume," I says. "He's a purebread orangutang."

"Is that so?" the cop say. "Well I'll tell you what. We got a feller down to the station who makes pitchers, too, an he would love to get a couple of shots of you clowns. So you jus come along too—an don't make no sudden moves."

Anyhow, Mister Tribble has got to come down an bail me out again. An Mister Felder showed up with a whole platoon of lawyers to git out Raquel Welch, who by this time is hysterical.

"You jus wait!" she shriek back at me as they turnin her loose. "When I git finished, you won't be able to find a job as a spear carrier in a nightmare!"

In this, she is probly correct. It look like my movie career is over.

"That's life, baby—but I'll call you for lunch sometime," Mister Felder says to me as he is leavin. "We'll send somebody by later to pick up the creature suit."

"C'mon, Forrest," say Mister Tribble. "You and I have got other fish to fry."

Back at the hotel, Mister Tribble an me an Sue is settin in our room havin a conference.

"It is going to pose a problem, with Sue here," Mister Tribble says. "I mean, look how we had to sneak him up the stairs and everthin. It is very difficult to travel with an orangutan, we have to face that."

I tole him how I felt bout Sue, bout how he saved my ass more than once in the jungle an all.

"Well, I think I understand your feelings," he says. "And I'm willing to give it a try. But he's going to have to behave himself, or we'll be in trouble for sure."

"He will," I say, an ole Sue be noddin an grinnin like a ape.

Anyhow, nex day is the big chess match between me an the International Grand Master Ivan Petrokivitch, also known as Honest Ivan. Mister Tribble have taken me to a clothes store an rented me a tuxedo on account of this is to be a big fashionable deal, an a lot of muckity-mucks will be on han. Furthermore, the winner will get ten thousan dollars, an my haf of that ought to be enough to get me started in the srimp bidness, so I cannot afford to make no mistakes.

Well, we get to the hall where the chess game is to take place an there is bout a thousan people millin aroun an already settin at the table is Honest Ivan, glarin at me like he's Muhammad Ali or somebody.

Honest Ivan is a big ole Russian feller with a high forehead, jus like the Frankenstein monster, an long black curly hair such as you might see on a violin player. When I go up an set down, he grunt somethin at me an then another feller say, "Let the match begin," an that was it.

Honest Ivan is got the white team an he get to make the first move, startin with somethin call The Ponziani Opening.

I move nex, using The Reti Opening, an everthin is goin pretty smooth. Each of us make a couple of more moves, then Honest Ivan try somethin known as The Falkbeer Gambit, movin his knight aroun to see if he can take my rook.

But I seed that comin, an set up somethin called The Noah's Ark Trap, an got his knight instead. Honest Ivan ain't lookin none too happy but he seem to take it in stride an employed The Tarrasch Threat to menace my bishop.

I ain't havin none of that, tho, an I thowed up The Queen's Indian Defense an that force him to use The Schevenigen Variation, which lead me to utilize The Benoni Counter.

Honest Ivan appear to be somewhat frustrated, an was twistin his fingers an bitin on his lower lip, an then he done tried a desperation move—The Fried Liver Attack—to which I applied Alekhine's Defense an stopped his ass cold.

It look for a wile like it gonna be a stalemate, but Honest Ivan, he went an applied The Hoffman Maneuver an broke out! I look over at Mister Tribble, an he sort of smile at me, an he move his lips an mouth the word *"Now,"* an I knowed what he mean.

You see, they was a couple of tricks Big Sam taught me in the jungle that was not in the book an now was the time to use them—namely, The Cookin Pot Variation of The Coconut Gambit, in which I use my queen as bait an sucker that bastid into riskin his knight to take her.

Unfortunately, it didn't work. Honest Ivan must of seen that comin an he snapped up my queen an now my ass is in trouble! Nex I pull somethin called The Grass Hut Ploy, in which I stick my last rook out on a limb to fool him, but he wadn't fooled. Took my rook an my other bishop too, an was ready to finish me off with The Petroff Check, when I pulled out all the stops an set up The Pygmie Threat.

Now the Pygmie Threat was one of Big Sam's specialties, an he had taught it to me real good. It depends a lot on suprise an usin several other pieces as bait, but if a feller falls victim to The Pygmie Threat, he might as well hang up his jockstrap an go on home. I was hopin an prayin it woud work, cause if it didn't, I ain't got no more bright ideas an I'm just about done for already.

Well, Honest Ivan, he grunt a couple of times an pick up his knight to move it to square eight, which meant that he would be suckered in by The Pygmie Threat an in two more moves I would have him in check an he would be powerless to do anythin about it!

But Honest Ivan must of smelt somethin fishy, cause he moved that piece from square five to square eight an back again nine or ten times, never takin his han off it, which would have meant the move was final.

The crowd was so quiet you coulda heard a pin drop, an I am so nervous an excited I am bout to bust. I look over an Mister Tribble is rollin his eyes up in the air like he's prayin an a feller what come with Honest Ivan is scowlin an lookin sour. Honest Ivan move the piece back to square eight two or three more times, but always he put it back on square five. Finally, it look like he gonna do somethin else, but then he lif up the piece one more time an have it hoverin above square eight an I be holdin my breath an the room is quiet as a tomb. Honest Ivan still be hoverin with the piece an my heart is beatin like a drum, an all of a sudden he look straight at me— an I don't know what happened, I guess I was so excited an all—but suddenly I cut a humongus baked-bean fart that sound like somebody is rippin a bedsheet in haf!

Honest Ivan get a look of suprise on his face, an then he suddenly drop his chess piece an thowed up his hans an say, "Uggh!" an start fannin the air an coughin an holdin his nose. Folks standin aroun us begun to move back an was mumblin an takin out they handkerchiefs an all, an I am so red in the face I look like a tomato.

But when it all settle down again, I look at the chessboard an damn if Honest Ivan ain't lef his piece right on square eight. So I reached out an snap it up with my knight, an then I grapped two of his pawns an his queen an finally his king— checkmate! I done won the match an the five thousan dollars! The Pygmie Threat done come thru again.

All the wile, Honest Ivan be makin loud gestures an protestin an all an him an the feller that come with him immediately file a formal complaint against me.

The guy in charge of the tournament be thumbin thru his rule book till he come to where it say, "No player shall knowingly engage in conduct that is distractive to another player while a game is in progress."

Mister Tribble step up an say, "Well, I don't think you can

prove that my man did what he did *knowingly.* It was a sort of involuntary thing."

Then the tournament director thumb thru his book some more, an come to where it say, "No player shall behave in a manner that is rude or offensive to his opponent."

"Listen," Mister Tribble say, "haven't you ever had the need to break wind? Forrest didn't mean anything by it. He's been sitting there a long time."

"I don't know," the tournament director say, "on the face of it, I think I'm going to have to disqualify him."

"Well can't you give him another chance at least?" Mister Tribble axed.

The tournament director scratched his chin for a minute. "Well, perhaps," he say, "but he is gonna have to contain hissef because we cannot tolerate this sort of thing here, you know?"

An so it was beginnin to look like I might be allowed to finish the game, but all of a sudden they is a big commotion at one end of the room, an ladies are screaming an shrieking an all an then I look up an here come ole Sue, swingin towards me on a chandelier.

Jus as the chandelier got overhead Sue let go an dropped right on top of the chessboard, scatterin all the pieces in a dozen directions. Honest Ivan fell over backwards across a chair an on the way down ripped haf the dress off a fat lady that looked like a advertisement for a jewelry store. She commenced to flailin an hollerin an smacked the tournament director in the nose an Sue was jumpin up an down an chatterin an everbody is in a panic, stompin an stumblin an shoutin to call the police.

Mister Tribble grapped me by the arm an say, "Let's get out of here, Forrest—you have already seen enough of the police in this town."

This I coud not deny.

Well, we get on back to the hotel, an Mister Tribble say we got to have another conference.

"Forrest," he say, "I just do not believe this is going to work out anymore. You can play chess like a dream, but things have gotten too complicated otherwise. All that stuff that went on this afternoon was, well, to put it mildly, it was bizarre."

I am noddin an ole Sue is lookin pretty sorrowful too.

"So, I'll tell you what I'm going to do. You're a good boy, Forrest, and I can't leave you stranded out here in California, so I am going to arrange for you and Sue to get back to Alabama or wherever it is you came from. I know you need a little grubstake to start your shrimp business, and your share of the winnings, after I deduct expenses, comes to a little under five thousand dollars."

Mister Tribble hand me a envelope an when I look inside it, there is a bunch of hundrit dollar bills.

"I wish you all the best in your venture," he say.

Mister Tribble phone for a taxicab an got us to the railroad station. He has also arranged for Sue to ride in the baggage car in a crate, and says I can go back there an visit with him an take him food an water when I want. They brung out the crate an Sue got on inside it an they took him off.

"Well, good luck, Forrest," Mister Tribble say, an he shake my han. "Here's my card—so stay in touch and let me know how it's going, okay?"

I took the card an shook his han again an was sorry to be leavin cause Mister Tribble was a very nice man, an I had let him down. I was settin in my seat on the train, lookin out the winder, an Mister Tribble was still standin on the platform. Jus as the train pulled out, he raised up his han at me an waved goodbye.

So off I went again, an for a long time that night my head

was full of dreams—of going back home again, of my mama, of po ole Bubba an of the srimp bidness an, of course, of Jenny Curran too. More than anythin in the world, I wished I were not such a loony tune.

24

Well, finally, I done come home again.

The train got into the Mobile station bout three o'clock in the mornin an they took off ole Sue in his crate an lef us standin on the platform. Ain't nobody else aroun cept some feller sweepin the floor an a guy snoozin on a bench in the depot, so Sue an me walked on downtown an finally foun a place to sleep in a abandoned buildin.

Nex mornin, I got Sue some bananas down by the wharf an found a little lunch counter where I bought a great big breakfast with grits an eggs an bacon an pancakes an all, an then I figgered I had to do *somethin* to get us squared away, so I begun to walk out to where the Little Sisters of the Poor home was located. On the way, we passed by where our ole house used to be, an it wadn't nothin lef but a field of weeds an some burnt up wood. It was a very strange feelin, seein that, an so we kep on goin.

When I got to the po house, I tole Sue to wait in the yard

so as not to startle them sisters none, an I went in an axed about my mama.

The head sister, she was real nice, an she say she don't know where Mama is, cept she went off with the protestant, but that I might try axin aroun in the park cause mama use to go an set there in the afternoons with some other ladies. So I got Sue an we gone on over there.

They was some ladies settin on the benches an I went up an tole one of them who I was, an she looked at ole Sue, an say, "I reckon I might of guess it."

But then she say she has heard that Mama was workin as a pants presser in a dry cleanin store on the other side of town, an so me an Sue went over there an sho enough, there is po ole Mama, sweatin over a pair of pants in the laundry.

When she seen me, Mama drop everthin an thowed hersef into my arms. She is cryin an twistin her hans an snifflin jus like I remembered. Good ole Mama.

"Oh, Forrest," she say. "You have come home at last. There wadn't a day gone by I didn't think bout you, an I done cried mysef to sleep ever night since you been gone." That didn't suprise me none tho, an I axed her bout the protestant.

"That low-down polecat," mama say. "I should of knowed better than to run off with a protestant. Wadn't a month went by before he chucked me for a sixteen-year-ole girl—an him bein nearly sixty. Let me tell you, Forrest, protestants ain't got no morals."

Just then a loud voice come from inside the dry cleanin stow, say, "Gladys, have you done lef the steam press on somebody's pants?"

"Oh my God!" Mama shout, an run back inside. All of a sudden a big column of black smoke blowed out thru the winder an people inside is bawlin an hollerin an cussin an nex thing I knowed, Mama is bein hauled out of the stow by a big old ugly bald-headed guy that is shoutin an manhandlin her.

"Git out! Git out!" he holler. "This is the last straw! You done burnt up your last pair of pants!"

Mama be cryin an weepin an I stepped up to the feller an say, "I think you better be takin your hans off my mama."

"Who the hell is you?" he axed.

"Forrest Gump," I says back, an he say, "Well you git your ass outta here too, an take your mama with you, cause she don't work here no more!"

"You best not be talkin that way aroun my mama," I says, an he say back, "Yeah? What you gonna do about it?"

So I showed him.

First, I grapped him an picked him up in the air. Then I carried him into where they was washin all these clothes in a big ole oversize laundry machine they use for quilts and rugs, an I open the top an stuff him in an close the lid shut an turned the dial to "Spin." Last I seen of him, his ass were headed for the "Rinse" cycle.

Mama is bawlin an dawbin at her eyes with a handkerchief an say, "Oh, Forrest, now I done lost my job!"

"Don't worry none, Mama," I tole her, "everthin gonna be okay, cause I have got a plan."

"How you gonna have a plan, Forrest?" she say. "You is a idiot. How is a po idiot gonna have a plan?"

"Jus wait an see," I says. Anyhow, I am glad to have got off on the right foot my first day home.

We got outta there, an started walkin towards the roomin house where Mama stayin. I had done introduced her to Sue an she say she was pleased that at least I have got *some* kinda friend—even if he is a ape.

Anyhow, Mama an me ate supper at the roomin house an she got Sue a orange from the kitchen, an afterwards, me an Sue went down to the bus station an got the bus to Bayou La Batre, where Bubba's folks lived. Sure as rain, last thing I saw of Mama she was standin on the porch of the roomin house wipin her eyes an sobbin as we lef. But I had give her haf the five thousan dollars to sort of tide her over an pay her rent an all till I could get mysef established, so I didn't feel so bad.

Anyhow, when the bus get to Bayou La Batre we didn't have no trouble findin Bubba's place. It's about eight o'clock at night an I knocked on the door an after a wile an ole feller appears an axed what I want. I tole him who I was an that I knowed Bubba from playin football an from the Army, an he got kinda nervous but he invited me inside. I had tole ole Sue to stay out in the yard an kinda keep outta sight since they probly hasn't seen nothin look like him down here.

Anyhow, it was Bubba's daddy, an he got me a glass of iced tea an started axin me a lot of questions. Wanted to know bout Bubba, bout how he got kilt an all, an I tole him the best I could.

Finally, he say, "There's somethin I been wonderin all these years, Forrest—what do you think Bubba died for?"

"Cause he got shot," I says, but he say, "No, that ain't what I mean. What I mean is, why? Why was we over there?"

I thought for a minute, an say, "Well, we was tryin to do the right thing, I guess. We was jus doin what we was tole."

An he say, "Well, do you think it was worth it? What we did? All them boys gettin kilt that way?"

An I says, "Look, I am jus a idiot, see. But if you want my real opinion, I think it was a bunch of shit."

Bubba's daddy nod his head. "That's what I figgered," he say.

Anyhow, I tole him why I had come there. Tole him bout me an Bubba's plan to open up a little srimp bidness, an how I had met the ole gook when I was in the hospital an he showed me how to grow srimp, an he was gettin real interested an axin a lot of questions, when all of a sudden they is a tremendous squawkin set up out in the yard.

"Somethin's after my chickens!" Bubba's daddy shout, an

he went an got a gun from behin the door an go out on the porch.

"They is somethin I got to tell you," I says, an I tole him bout Sue bein there, cept we don't see hide nor hair of him.

Bubba's daddy go back in the house an get a flashlight an shine it aroun in the yard. He shine it under a big tree an down at the bottom is a goat—big ole billy goat, standin there pawin the groun. He shine it up in the tree an there is po Sue, settin on a limb, scared haf to death.

"That goat'll do it ever time," say Bubba's daddy. "Git on away from there!" he shout, an he thow a stick at the goat. After the goat was gone, Sue come down from the tree an we let him inside the house.

"What is that thing?" Bubba's daddy axed.

"He is a orangutang," I says.

"Looks kinda like a gorilla, don't he?"

"A little bit," I says, "but he ain't."

Anyway, Bubba's daddy say we can sleep there that night, an in the mornin, he will go aroun with us an see if we can find some place to start the srimp bidness. They was a nice breeze blowin off the bayou an you coud hear frawgs an crickets an even the soun of a fish jumpin ever once in a wile. It was a nice, peaceful place, an I made up my mind then an there that I was not gonna get into no trouble here.

Nex mornin brite an early we get up an Bubba's daddy done fixed a big breakfast with homemade sausage an fresh yard eggs an biscuits an molasses, an then he take me an Sue in a little boat an pole us down the Bayou. It is calm an they is a bit of mist on the water. Ever once in a wile a big ole bird would take off outta the marsh.

"Now," say Bubba's daddy, "here is where the salt tide comes in," an he point to a slew that runs up in the marsh. "There's some pretty big ponds up in there, an if I was gonna do what you plannin to do, that's where I'd do it."

He pole us up into the slew. "Now you see there," he say, "that is a little piece of high groun an you can jus see the roof of a little shack in there."

"It used to be lived in by ole Tom LeFarge, but he been dead four or five years now. Ain't nobody own it. You wanted, you could fix it up a little an stay there. Last time I looked, he had a couple of ole rowboats pulled up on the bank. Probly ain't worth a damn, but you caulk em up, they'd probly float."

He pole us in further, an say, "Ole Tom used to have some duckboards runnin thru the marsh down to the ponds. Used to fish an shoot ducks in there. You could probly fix em up. It'd be a way of gettin aroun in there."

Well, let me tell you, it looked ideal. Bubba's daddy say they get seed srimp up in them slews an bayou's all the time, an it wouldn't be no trouble to net a bunch of em to start off the bidness with. Another thing he say is that in his experience, a srimp will eat cottonseed meal, which is good on account of it is cheap.

The main thing we got to do is block off them ponds with mesh nets an get the little cabin fixed up to live in an get some supplies like peanut butter an jelly an bread an all that kind of shit. Then we be ready to start growin our srimp.

So we got started that very day. Bubba's daddy took me back to the house an we gone into town an begun buyin supplies. He say we can use his boat till we get ours fixed up, an that night me an Sue stayed in the little fishin shack for the first time. It rained some an the roof leaked like crazy, but I didn't mind. Nex mornin I jus went out an fixed it up.

It took almost a month to get things goin—makin the shack nice an fixin up the rowboats an the duckboards in the marsh an layin the mesh nets aroun one of them ponds. Finally the day come when we is ready to put in some srimp. I have bought a srimp net an me an Sue went on out in the rowboat an dragged it aroun for most of the day. By that night, we had probly fifty pounds of srimp in the bait well an we rowed up an dumped em into the pond. They be crackin an swim- min aroun an dancin on top of the water. My, my, it was a lovely site.

Nex mornin we got us five hundrit pounds of cottonseed meal an thowed a hundrit pounds of it in the pond for the srimp to eat an the nex afternoon we set about nettin-in an- other pond. We done that all summer an all fall an all winter an all spring an by that time we has got four ponds operatin an everthin is lookin rosy. At night I would set out on the porch of the shack an play my harmonica an on Saturday night I would go into town an buy a six-pack of beer an me an Sue would get drunk. I finally feel like I belong some- place, an am doin a honest day's work, an I figger that when we get the first srimp harvested an sold, maybe then it will be all right to try to find Jenny again, an see if she is still mad at me.

25

It was a very nice day in June when we figgered it was time to start our first srimp harvest. Me an Sue got up with the sun an went down to the pond an dragged a net acrost it till it got stuck on somethin. Sue tried to pull it loose first, then I tried, then we tried together till we finally figgered out the net wadn't stuck—it was jus so full of srimp we couldn't move it!

By that evenin we had pulled in about three hundrit pouns of srimp, an we spent the night sortin em out in various sizes. Nex mornin we put the srimp in baskets an took em down to our little rowboat. They weighed so much we damn near tumped over on the way up to Bayou La Batre.

They was a seafood packin house there an Sue an me hauled the srimp from the dock to the weighin room. After everthin is toted up, we got ourselfs a check for eight hundrit, sixty-five dollars! It is about the first honest money I ever made since I played harmonica for The Cracked Eggs.

Ever day for nearly two weeks Sue an me harvested srimp an brought em in to the packin house. When it was finally over, we had made a total of nine thousand, seven hundrit dollars an twenty-six cents. The srimp bidness was a success!

Well, let me tell you—it were a happy occasion. We took up a bushel basket of srimp to Bubba's daddy an he was real happy an say he is proud of us an that he wished Bubba were there too. Then me an Sue caught the bus up to Mobile to celebrate. First thing I done was gone to see my mama at the roomin house, an when I tole her about the money an all, sure enough, she be cloudin up again. "Oh, Forrest," she say, "I am so proud of you—doin so good an all for bein retarded."

Anyhow, I tole Mama about my plan, which was that nex year we was gonna have three times as many srimp ponds, an that we needed somebody to watch over the money an look after our expenses an all, an I axed if she would do that.

"You mean I gotta move all the way down to Bayou La Batre?" Mama say. "Ain't nothin goin on down there. What am I gonna do with mysef?"

"Count money," I says.

After that, me an Sue went downtown an got ourselfs a big meal. I gone down to the docks an bought Sue a big bunch of bananas, an then went an got mysef the biggest steak dinner I could find, with mashed potatoes an green peas an everthin. Then I decided to go drink me a beer someplace an jus as I am walkin by this dark ole saloon near the waterfront, I hear all this loud cussin an shoutin an even after all these years, I knowed that voice. I stuck my head in the door, an sure enough, it were ole Curtis from the University!

Curtis were very happy to see me, callin me a asshole an a cocksucker an a motherfucker an everthin else nice he could think of. As it turns out, Curtis had gone on to play pro football with the Washington Redskins after he lef the University, an then he done got put on waivers after bitin the team owner's wife on the ass at a party. He played for a couple of other teams for a few years, but after that he got hissef a job on the docks as a longshoreman which, he say, was suitable for the amount of education he got at the University.

Anyway, Curtis bought me a couple of beers an we talked about ole times. The Snake, he say, had played quarterback for the Green Bay Packers till he got caught drinkin a entire quart of Polish vodka durin halftime in the Minnesota Vikings game. Then Snake went an played for the New Yawk Giants till he called a Statue-of-Liberty play in the third quarter of the Rams game. The Giants' coach say ain't nobody used a Statue-of-Liberty play in pro ball since nineteen hundrit thirty-one, an that Snake ain't got no bidness callin one now. But actually, Curtis say, it wadn't no Statue-of-Liberty play at all. The truth, accordin to Curtis, was that Snake was so spaced out on dope that when he faded back for a pass he done completely forgot to thow the ball, an the lef end jus happen to see what is goin on, an run aroun behin him an take the ball away. Anyhow, Curtis say the Snake is now assistant coach for a tinymight team someplace in Georgia.

After a couple of beers, I got a idea, an tole Curtis about it.

"How'd you like to come work for me?" I axed.

Curtis be cussin an hollerin but after a minute or two I figger out he is tryin to axe me what I want him to do, so I tole him about the srimp bidness an that we was gonna expand our operation. He cuss an holler some more, but the gist of what he is sayin is "yes."

So all thru that summer an fall an the next spring we be workin hard, me an Sue an Mama an Curtis—an I even had a job for Bubba's daddy. That year we made nearly thirty thousan dollars an are gettin bigger all the time. Things couldn't of been goin better—Mama ain't bawlin hardly at all, an one day we even seen Curtis smile once—altho he stopped an started cussin again soon as he saw us watchin. For me, tho, it ain't quite as happy as it might be, cause I am thinkin a lot about Jenny an what has become of her.

One day, I jus decided to do somethin bout it. It was a Sunday, an I got dressed up an caught the bus up to Mobile an went over to Jenny's mama's house. She was settin inside, watchin tv, when I knocked on the door.

When I tole her who I was, she say, "Forrest Gump! I jus can't believe it. C'mon in!"

Well, we set there a wile an she axed bout Mama an what I'd been doin an everthin, an finally I axed about Jenny.

"Oh, I really don't hear from her much these days," Mrs. Curran say. "I think they livin someplace in North Carolina."

"She got a roomate or somethin?" I axed.

"Oh, didn't you know, Forrest?" she say. "Jenny got married."

"Married?" I say.

"It was a couple of years ago. She'd been livin in Indiana. Then she went to Washington an nex thing I knew, I got a postcard sayin she was married, an they was movin to North Carolina or someplace. You want me to tell her anythin if I hear from her?"

"No'm," I says, "not really. Maybe jus tell her I wish her good luck an all."

"I sure will," Mrs. Curran say, "an I'm so glad you came by."

I dunno, I reckon I ought to of been ready for that news, but I wadn't.

I could feel my heart poundin, an my hans got cold an damp an all I coud think of was goin someplace an curlin up into a ball the way I had that time after Bubba got kilt, an so that's what I did. I foun some shrubs in back of somebody's yard an I crawled under there an jus got mysef into a ball. I think I even commenced to suck my thumb, which I ain't done in a long wile since my mama always said it was a sure sign that somebody's a idiot, unless they are a baby. Anyhow, I don't know how long I stayed there. It was most of a day an a haf I guess.

I didn't feel no blame for Jenny, she done what she had to. After all, I am a idiot, an wile a lot of people *say* they is married to idiots, they couldn't never imagine what would be in store if they ever married a real one. Mostly, I guess, I am jus feelin sorry for mysef, because somehow I had actually got to where I *believed* that Jenny an me would be together someday. An so when I learnt from her mama that she is married, it was like a part of me has died an will never be again, for gettin married is not like runnin away. Gettin married is a very serious deal. Sometime durin the night I cried, but it did not hep much.

It was later that afternoon when I crawled out of the shrubs an gone on back to Bayou La Batre. I didn't tell nobody what had happened, cause I figgered it wouldn't of done no good. They was some work I needed to do aroun the ponds, mendin nets an such, an I went on out by mysef an done it. By the time I get finished it is dark, an I done made a decision—I am gonna thow mysef into the srimp bidness an work my ass off. It is all I can do.

An so I did.

That year we made seventy-five thousan dollars before expenses an the bidness is gettin so big I got to hire more people to hep me run it. One person I get is ole Snake, the quarterback from the University. He is not too happy with his present job with the tinymight football team an so I put him to work with Curtis in charge of dredgin an spillway duties. Then I find out that Coach Fellers from the highschool is done retired an so I give him a job, along with his two goons who has also retired, workin on boats an docks.

Pretty soon the newspapers get wind of what is goin on an send a reporter down to interview me for a sort of "local boy

makes good" story. It appears the nex Sunday, with a photo
of me an Mama an Sue, an the headline say, "Certifiable Idiot
Finds Future in Novel Marine Experiment."

Anyhow, not too long after that, Mama say to me that we
need to get somebody to hep her with the bookkeepin part of
the bidness an give some kind of advice on financial things on
account of we is makin so much money. I done thought bout
it a wile, an then I decided to get in touch with Mister Tribble, cause he had made a bunch of money in bidness before
he retired. He was delighted I had called, he say, an will be
on the nex plane down.

A week after he gets here, Mister Tribble say we got to set
down an talk.

"Forrest," he say, "what you have done here is nothing
short of remarkable, but you are at a point where you need to
begin some serious financial planning."

I axed him what bout, an he say this: "Investments! Diver-
sification! Look, as I see it, this next fiscal year you are going
to have profits at about a hundred and ninety thousand dollars. The following year it will bear near a quarter of a million. With such profits you must reinvest them or the IRS will
tax you into oblivion. Reinvestment is the very heart of
American business!"

An so that's what we did.

Mister Tribble took charge of all that, an we formed a
couple of corporations. One was "Gump's Shellfish Company." Another was called "Sue's Stuffed Crabs, Inc.," an
another was "Mama's Crawfish Étouffée, Ltd."

Well, the quarter of a million become haf a million an the
year followin that, a million, an so on, till after four more
years we done become a five million dollar a year bidness.
We got nearly three hundred employees now, includin The
Turd an The Vegetable, whose rasslin days were over, an we
got them loadin crates at the warehouse. We tried like hell to
find po Dan, but he done vanished without a trace. We did

find ole Mike, the rasslin promoter, an put him in charge of public relations an advertisin. At Mister Tribble's suggestion, Mike done even hired Raquel Welch to do some television ads for us—they dressed her up to look like a crab, an she dance aroun an say, "You ain't never had crabs till you try Sue's!"

Anyhow, things has gotten real big-time. We got a fleet of refrigerator trucks an a fleet of srimp, oyster an fishin boats. We got our own packin house, an a office buildin, an have invested heavily in real estate such as condominiums an shoppin centers an in oil an gas leases. We done hired ole Professor Quackenbush, the English teacher from up at Harvard University, who have been fired from his job for molestin a student, an made him a cook in Mama's étouffée operation. We also hired Colonel Gooch, who got drummed out of the Army after my Medal of Honor tour. Mister Tribble put him in charge of "covert activities."

Mama has gone an had us a big ole house built cause she say it ain't right for a corporate executive like me to be livin in no shack. Mama say Sue can stay on in the shack an keep an eye on things. Ever day now, I got to wear a suit an carry a briefcase like a lawyer. I got to go to meetins all the time an listen to a bunch of shit that sound like pygmie talk, an people be callin me "Mister Gump," an all. In Mobile, they done give me the keys to the city an axed me to be on the board of directors of the hospital an the symphony orchestra.

An then one day some people come by the office an say they want to run me for the United States Senate.

"You're an absolute natural," this one feller say. He is wearing a searsucker suit an smokin a big cigar. "A former star football player for Bear Bryant, a war hero, a famous astronaut and the confidant of Presidents—what more can you ask?!" he axe. Mister Claxton is his name.

"Look," I tell him, "I am just a idiot. I don't know nothin bout politics."

"Then you will fit in perfectly!" Mister Claxton say. "Listen, we need good men like you. Salt of the earth, I tell you! Salt of the earth!"

I did not like this idea any more than I like a lot of the other ideas people have for me, on account of other people's ideas are usually what get me into trouble. But sure enough, when I tole my mama, she get all teary-eyed an proud an say it would be the answer to all her dreams to see her boy be a United States Senator.

Well, the day come when we is to announce my candidacy. Mister Claxton an them others hired the auditorium up in Mobile an hauled me out on the stage in front of a crowd that paid fifty cents apiece to come listen to my shit. They begin with a lot of long-winded speeches an then it come my turn.

"My feller Americans," I begin. Mister Claxton an the others have writ me a speech to give an later they will be questions from the audience. Tv cameras are rollin an flashbulbs are poppin an reporters are scribblin in their notebooks. I read the whole speech, which ain't very long an don't make much sense—but what do I know? I am jus a idiot.

When I am finished talkin, a lady from the newspaper stand up an look at her notepad.

"We are currently on the brink of nuclear disaster," she say, "the economy is in ruins, our nation is reviled throughout the world, lawlessness prevails in our cities, people starve of hunger every day, religion is gone from our homes, greed and avarice is rampant everywhere, our farmers are going broke, foreigners are invading our country and taking our jobs, our unions are corrupt, babies are dying in the ghettos, taxes are unfair, our schools are in chaos and famine, pestilence and war hang over us like a cloud—in view of all this, Mister Gump," she axe, "what, in your mind, is the most pressing issue of the moment?" The place was so quiet you coulda heard a pin drop.

"I got to pee," I says.

At this, the crowd went wile! People begun hollerin an cheerin an shoutin an wavin they hands in the air. From the back of the room somebody started chantin an pretty soon the whole auditorium was doin it.

"WE GOT TO PEE! WE GOT TO PEE! WE GOT TO PEE!" they was yellin.

My mama had been settin there behind me on the stage an she got up an come drug me away from the speaker's stand.

"You ought to be ashamed of yoursef," she say, "talkin like that in public."

"No, no!" Mister Claxton says. "It's perfect! They love it. This will be our campaign slogan!"

"What will?" Mama axed. Her eyes narrowed down to little beads.

"*We Got to Pee!*" Mister Claxton say. "Just listen to them! No one has ever had such a rapport with the common people!"

But mama ain't buyin none of it. "Whoever heard of anybody usin a campaign slogan like that!" she says. "It's vulgar an disgusting—besides, what does it mean?"

"It's a symbol," Mister Claxton says. "Just think, we'll have billboards and placards and bumper stickers made up. Take out television and radio ads. It's a stroke of genius, that's what it is. *We Got to Pee* is a symbol of riddance of the yoke of government oppression—of evacuation of all that is wrong with this country . . . It signifies frustration and impending relief!"

"What!" Mama axed suspiciously. "Is you lost your mind?"

"Forrest," Mister Claxton says, "You are on your way to Washington."

An so it seemed. The campaign was goin along pretty good an "We Got to Pee," had become the byword of the day. People shouted it on the street an from cars an busses. Televi-

sion commentators an newspaper columnists spent a lot of
time trying to tell folks what it meant. Preachers yelled it
from their pulpits an children chanted it in school. It was
beginnin to look like I was a shoo-in for the election, an, in
fact, the candidate runnin against me, he got so desperate he
made up his own slogan, *"I Got to Pee, Too,"* an plastered it all
over the state.

Then it all fell apart, jus like I was afraid it would.

The "I Got to Pee" deal done come to the attention of the
national media an pretty soon the Washington *Post* an the
New Yawk *Times* sent down their investigating reporters to
look into the matter. They axed me a lot of questions an was
real nice an friendly-sounding, but then they went back an
begun to dig up my past. One day the stories broke on the
front page of ever newspaper in the country. "Senatorial
Candidate Has Checkered Career," say the headlines.

First, they write that I done flunked out of the University
my first year. Then they dug up that shit about me an Jenny
when the cops hauled me in from the movie theater. Next
they drag out the photograph of me showin my ass to President Johnson in the Rose Garden. They axed aroun about my
days in Boston with The Cracked Eggs an quote people sayin
that I done smoked marijuana an also mention "a possible
arson incident" at Harvard University.

Worst—they done find out about the criminal charges I got
for thowin my medal at the U.S. Capitol an that I been sen-
tenced by a judge to a loony asylum. Also, they knew all
about my rasslin career, too, an that I was called The Dunce.
They even ran a photo of me being tied up by The Professor.
Finally, they mention several "unnamed sources" sayin I was
involved in a "Hollywood sex scandal with a well-known
actress."

That did it. Mister Claxton come rushin into campaign
headquarters screamin, "We are ruint! We have been stabbed
in the back!" an shit like that. But it was over. I had no choice

cept to withdraw from the race, an the next day Mama an me an Mister Tribble set down for a talk.

"Forrest," Mister Tribble say, "I think it might be good for you to lay low for a while."

I knowed he was right. An besides, there is other things that been naggin at my mind for a long time now, though I ain't said nothin about them before.

When the srimp bidness first started up, I kind of enjoyed the work, gettin up at dawn an goin down to the ponds an puttin up the nets an then harvestin the srimp an all, an me an Sue settin at night on the porch of the fishin shack playin the harmonica, an gettin a six-pack of beer on Saturday an gettin drunk.

Now it ain't nothing like that. I got to go to all sorts of dinner parties where people servin a lot of mysterious-lookin food an the ladies wearin big ole earrings an shit. All day long the phone don't never stop ringin an people be wantin to axe me bout everthin under the sun. In the Senate, it would have jus been worse. Now I ain't got no time to mysef as it is, an somehow, things are slippin past me.

Furthermore, I look in the mirror now an I got wrinkles on my face, an my hair is turnin gray at the edges an I ain't got as much energy as I used to. I know things are movin along with the bidness, but mysef, I feel like I'm jus spinnin in place. I'm wonderin jus why am I doin all this for? A long time ago, me an Bubba had a plan, which has now gone beyon our wildest dreams, but so what? It ain't haf as much fun as the time I played against them Nebraska corn shucker jackoffs in the Orange Bowl, or took a ride on my harmonica up at Boston with The Cracked Eggs, or, for that matter, watched "The Beverly Hillbillies" with ole President Johnson.

An I spose Jenny Curran has somethin to do with it, too, but since ain't nobody can do nothin bout that, I might as well forget it.

Anyhow, I realize I got to get away. Mama be weepin an bawlin an daubbin at her eyes with the handkerchief like I figgered she woud, but Mister Tribble understan completely.

"Why don't we jus tell everbody you are taking a long vacation, Forrest," he say. "An of course your share of the bidness will be here whenever you want it."

So that's what I done. One mornin a few days later I got a little cash, an thowed a few things in a dufflebag an then gone down to the plant. I tole Mama an Mister Tribble goodbye an then went aroun an shook hans with everbody else—Mike an Professor Quackenbush an The Turd an The Vegetable an Snake an Coach Fellers an his goons an Bubba's daddy an all the rest.

Then I gone to the shack an foun ole Sue.

"What you gonna do?" I axed.

Sue grapped holt of my han an then he picked up my bag an carried it out the door. We got in the little rowboat an paddled up to Bayou La Batre an caught the bus to Mobile. A lady in the ticket office there say, "Where you want to go?" an I shrugged my shoulders, so she say, "Why don't you go to Savannah? I been there once an it is a real nice town."

So that's what we did.

26

We got off the bus at Savannah, where it was rainin to beat the band. Sue an me went in the depot an I got a cup of coffee an took it out under the eaves an tried to figger out what we gonna do nex.

I ain't got no plan, really, so after I finish my coffee I took out my harmonica an begun to play. I played a couple of songs, an lo an behole, a feller that was walkin by, he thowed a quarter in my coffee cup. I played a couple of more songs, an after a wile the coffee cup is bout haf full of change.

It done quit rainin so Sue an me walked on off an in a little bit come to a park in the middle of town. I set down on a bench an played some more an sure enough, people begun to drop quarters an dimes an nickels in the coffee cup. Then ole Sue, he caught on, an when folks would pass by, he'd take the coffee cup an go up to them with it. At the end of the day, I'd got nearly five dollars.

We slep in the park that night on a bench an it was a fine, clear night an the stars an moon was out. In the mornin we got some breakfast an I begun to play the harmonica again as folks started showin up for work. We made eight bucks that day an nine the nex, an by the end of the week we had done pretty good, considerin. After the weekend, I foun a little music shop an went in there to see if I could find another harmonica in the key of G on account of playing in C all the time was gettin monotonous. Over in a corner I seen that the feller had a used keyboard for sale. It look pretty much like the one ole George used to play with The Cracked Eggs an that he had taught me a few chords on.

I axed how much he wanted for it, an the feller say two hundrit dollars, but he will make me a deal. So I bought the keyboard an the feller even rigged up a stand on it so's I could play my harmonica too. It definately improved our popularity with the people. By the end of the nex week we was makin almost ten bucks a day, so I gone on back to the music shop an bought a set of used drums. After a few days practice, I got to where I could play them drums pretty good too. I chucked out the ole Styrofoam coffee cup an got a nice tin cup for Sue to pass aroun an we was doin pretty good for ourselfs. I was playin everthing from "The Night They Drove Ole Dixie Down" to "Swing Lo, Sweet Chariot," an I had also foun a roomin house that let ole Sue stay there, an served breakfast an supper too.

One morning Sue an me is going to the park when it started to rain again. One thing about Savannah—it rains buckets ever other day there, or so it seems. We was walking down the street in front of a office building when suddenly I seen something that looked vaguely familiar.

There is a man in a business suit standing on the sidewalk with a unbrella an he is standin right in front of a big plastic garbage bag. Somebody is under the garbage bag, keepin out of the rain, an all you can see is a pair of hands reachin out from under the bag, shinin the shoes of the man in the suit. I gone acrost the street and looked closer, an lo and behol, I can just make out the little wheels of one of them dolly-wagons stickin out from under the bag too. I was so happy I could of just about bust, an I went up an thowed the garbage bag off an sure enough, it was ole Dan hissef, shinin shoes for a livin!

"Gimme that bag back you big oaf," Dan say, "I'm gettin soakin wet out here." Then he saw Sue. "So you finally got married, huh?" Dan say.

"It's a *he,*" I tole him. "You remember—from when I went to space."

"You gonna shine my shoes, or what?" say the feller in the suit.

"Fuck off," Dan says, "before I chew your soles in half." The feller, he walked away.

"What you doin here, Dan?" I axed.

"What does it look like I'm doing?" he say. "I've become a Communist."

"You mean like them we was fightin in the war?" I axed.

"Nah," says he, "them was gook Communists. I'm a real Communist—Marx, Lennin, Trotsky—all that bullshit."

"Then what you shinin shoes for?" I say.

"To shame the imperialist lackeys," he answers. "The way I got it figured, nobody with shined shoes is worth a shit, so the more shoes I shine, the more I'll send to hell in a handbasket."

"Well, if you say so," I says, an then Dan thowed down his rag an wheel himself back under the awnin to git outta the rain.

"Awe hell, Forrest, I ain't no damned Communist," he say, "They wouldn't want nobody like me anyhow, way I am."

"Sure they would, Dan," I says, "You always tole me I could be anythin I wanted to be an do anythin I want to do—an so can you."

"You still believin that shit?" he axed.

"I got to see Raquel Welch butt neckit," I says.

"Really?" Dan say, "what was it like?"

Well, after that, Dan an Sue an me kinda teamed up. Dan didn't want to stay in the boardin house, so he slep outside at night under his garbage bag. "Builds character," was how he put it. He tole bout what he'd been doin since he left Indianapolis. First, he'd lost all the money from the rasslin business at the dog track an what was lef he drank up. Then he got a job at a auto shop working under cars cause it was easy for him with the little dolly-wagon an all, but he said he got tired of oil an grease bein dripped on him all the time. "I may be a no-legged, no-good, drunken bum," he say, "but I ain't never been no greaseball."

Nex, he gone back to Washington where they's havin a big dedication for some monument for us what went to the Vietnam War, an when they seen him, an foun out who he was, they axed him to make a speech. But he got good an drunk at some reception, an forgot what he was gonna say. So he stole a Bible from the hotel they put him up in, an when it come his time to speak, he read them the entire book of Genesis an was fixin to do some excerpts from Numbers when they turned off his mike an hauled his ass away. After that, he tried beggin for a wile, but quit because it was "undignified."

I tole him about playin chess with Mister Tribble an about the srimp bidness bein so successful an all, an about runnin for the United States Senate, but he seemed more interested in Raquel Welch.

"You think them tits of hers are real?" he axed.

We had been in Savannah about a month, I guess, an was doin pretty good. I done my one-man band act an Sue collected the money an Dan shined people's shoes in the crowd. One day a guy come from the newspaper an took our pitchers an ran them on the front page.

"Derelicts Loitering in Public Park," says the caption.

One afternoon I'm settin there playin an thinkin maybe we outta go on up to Charleston when I notice a little boy standin right in front of the drums, jus starin at me.

I was playin "Ridin on the City of New Orleans," but the little feller kep lookin at me, not smilin or nothin, but they was somethin in his eyes that kinda shined an glowed an in a wierd way reminded me of somethin. An then I look up, an standin there at the edge of the crowd was a lady, an when I saw her, I like to fainted.

Lo an behole, it was Jenny Curran.

She done got her hair up in rollers an she looked a bit older, too, an sort of tired, but it is Jenny all right. I am so surprised, I blowed a sour note on my harmonica by mistake, but I finished the song, an Jenny come up an take the little boy by the han.

Her eyes was beamin, an she say, "Oh, Forrest, I knew it was you when I heard the harmonica. Nobody plays the harmonica like you do."

"What you doin here?" I axed.

"We live here now," she say. "Donald is assistant sales manager with some people make roofin tiles. We been here bout three years now."

Cause I quit playin, the crowd done drifted off an Jenny set down on the bench nex to me. The little boy be foolin aroun with Sue, an Sue, he done started turnin cartwheels so's the boy would laugh.

"How come you playin in a one-man band?" Jenny axed. "Mama wrote me you had started a great big ole srimp bidness down at Bayou La Batre an was a millionaire."

"It's a long story," I says.

"You didn't get in trouble again, did you, Forrest?" she say.

"Nope, not this time," I says. "How bout you? You doin okay?"

"Oh, I reckon I am," she say. "I spose I got what I wanted."

"That your little boy?" I axed.

"Yep," she say, "ain't he cute?"

"Shore is—what you call him?"

"Forrest."

"Forrest?" I say. "You name him after me?"

"I ought to," she say sort of quietly. "After all, he's haf yours."

"Haf what!"

"He's your son, Forrest."

"My what!"

"Your son. Little Forrest." I looked over an there he was, gigglin an clappin cause Sue was now doin han-stands.

"I guess I should of tole you," Jenny say, "but when I lef Indianapolis, you see, I was pregnant. I didn't want to say anything, I don't know just why. I felt like, well, there you was, callin yourself 'The Dunce' an all, an I was gonna have this baby. An I was worried, sort of, bout how he'd turn out."

"You mean, was he gonna be a idiot?"

"Yeah, sort of," she say. "But look, Forrest, can't you see! He ain't no idiot at all! He's smart as a whip—gonna go into second grade this year. He made all 'A's' last year. Can you believe it!"

"You sure he's mine?" I axed.

"Ain't no question of it," she say. "He wants to be a football player when he grows up—or a astronaut."

I look over at the little feller again an he is a strong, fine-lookin boy. His eyes is clear an he don't look like he afraid of nothin. Him an Sue is playin tic-tac-toe in the dirt.

"Well," I says, "now what about, ah, your . . ."

"Donald?" Jenny says. "Well, he don't know bout you. You see, I met him just after I left Indianapolis. An I was bout to start showin an all, an I didn't know what to do. He's a nice, kind man. He takes good care of me an little Forrest. We got us a house an two cars an ever Saturday he takes up someplace like the beach or out in the country. We go to church on Sunday, an Donald is savin up to send little Forrest to college an all."

"Coud I see him—I mean, jus for a minute or two?" I axed.

"Sure," Jenny say, an she call the little feller over.

"Forrest," she says, "I want you to meet another Forrest. He's a ole friend of mine—an he is who you are named after."

The little guy come an set down by me an say, "What a funny monkey you got."

"That is a orangutang," I say. "His name is Sue."

"How come you call him Sue, if it's a *he?*"

I knowed right then that I didn't have no idiot for a son. "Your mama say you want to grow up to be a football player, or a astronaut," I says.

"I sure would," he say. "You know anything about football or astronauts?"

"Yep," I say, "a little bit, but maybe you ought to axe your daddy bout that. I'm sure he knows a lot more than me."

Then he give me a hug. It weren't a big hug, but it was enough. "I want to play with Sue some more," he say, an jump down from the bench, an ole Sue, he done organized a game where little Forrest could thow a coin into the tin cup an Sue would catch it in the air.

Jenny come over an set nex to me an sighed, an she pat me on the leg.

"I can't believe it sometimes," she say. "We've knowed each other nearly thirty years now—ever since first grade."

The sun is shinin thru the trees, right on Jenny's face, an they might of been a tear in her eyes, but it never come, an yet they is somethin there, a heartbeat maybe, but I really couldn't say what it was, even tho I knowed it was there.

"I just can't believe it, that's all," she say, an then she lean over an kiss me on the forehead.

"What's that?" I axed.

"Idiots," Jenny says, an her lips is tremblin. "Who ain't a idiot?" An then she is gone. She got up an fetched little Forrest an took him by the han an they walked on off.

Sue come over an set down in front of me an drawed a tic-tac-toe thing in the dirt at my feet. I put a X to the upper right corner, an Sue put a 0 in the middle, an I knowed right then an there ain't nobody gonna win.

Well, after that, I done a couple of things. First, I called Mister Tribble an tole him that anything I got comin in the srimp bidness, to give ten percent of my share to my mama an ten percent to Bubba's daddy, an the rest, send it all to Jenny for little Forrest.

After supper, I set up all night thinkin, altho that is not somethin I am sposed to be particularly good at. But what I was thinkin was this: here I have done foun Jenny again after all this time. An she have got our son, an maybe, somehow, we can fix things up.

But the more I think about this, the more I finally understan it cannot work. And also, I cannot rightly blame it on my bein a idiot—tho that would be nice. Nope, it is jus one of them things. Jus the way it is sometimes, an besides, when all is said an done, I figger the little boy be better off with Jenny an her husband to give him a good home an raise him right so's he won't have no peabrain for a daddy.

Well, a few days later, I gone on off with ole Sue an Dan. We went to Charleston an then Richmond an then Atlanta an then Chattanooga an then Memphis an then Nashville an finally down to New Orleans.

Now they don't give a shit what you do in New Orleans, an the three of us is havin the time of our lifes, playin ever day in Jackson Square an watchin the other fruitcakes do they thing.

I done bought a bicycle with two little sidecars for Sue an Dan to ride in, an ever Sunday we peddle down to the river an set on the bank an go catfishin. Jenny writes me once ever month or so, an sends me pictures of Little Forrest. Last one I got showed him dressed up in a tinymight football suit. They is a girl here that works as a waitress in one of the strip joints an ever once in a wile we get together an ass aroun. Wanda is her name. A lot of times, me an ole Sue an Dan jus cruise aroun the French Quarter an see the sights, an believe me, they is some odd-lookin people there besides us—look like they might be lef over from the Russian Revolution or somethin.

A guy from the local newspaper come by one day an say he want to do a story on me, cause I am the "best one-man band" he ever heard. The feller begun axin me a lot of questions bout my life, an so I begun to tell him the whole story. But even before I got haf thru, he done walked off; say he can't print nothin like that cause nobody would'n ever believe it.

But let me tell you this: sometimes at night, when I look up at the stars, an see the whole sky jus laid out there, don't you think I ain't rememberin it all. I still got dreams like anybody else, an ever so often, I am thinkin about how things might of been. An then, all of a sudden, I'm forty, fifty, sixty years ole, you know?

Well, so what? I may be a idiot, but most of the time, anyway, I tried to do the right thing—an dreams is jus dreams, ain't they? So whatever else has happened, I am figgerin this: I can always look back an say, at least I ain't led no hum-drum life.

You know what I mean?